Dr Kistler,
    I hope that you enjoy
this book. It is very light
but humorous reading. A
college friend of mine wrote
it. This could be any
country boy growing up.
        Merry Christmas
            2001
        Bud Wilkey

ROLLER
A Dirt Road Sport

ROLLER

A Dirt Road Sport

by

Julian Morgan

12/01

Father & Son Publishing
Tallahassee, Florida

ISBN: 0-942407-48-2

02 01 00 99 / 10 9 8 7 6 5 4 3 2 1

Published
by

FATHER & SON
PUBLISHING, INC.

4909 North Monroe Street
Tallahassee, Florida 32303
800-741-2712
http://www.fatherson.com
e-mail lance@fatherson.com

DEDICATION

I am standing upon the seashore. A ship at my side spreads her white sails to the morning breeze and starts for the blue ocean. She is an object of beauty and strength, and I stand and watch her until at length she hangs like a speck of white cloud just where the sea and sky come down to mingle with each other. Then someone at my side says, "There! She's gone!" Gone where? Gone from my sight—that is all. She is just as large in mast and hull and spar as she was when she left my side, and just as able to bear her load of living freight to the place of destination. Her diminished size is in me, not in her, and just at the moment when someone at my side says, "There! She's gone!" there are other eyes watching her coming, and other voices ready to take up the glad shout, "There! She comes!"

Author unknown

In
Loving Memory
of
"Daddy"
Ben Butler Morgan, Sr.
1898 - 1976

ACKNOWLEDGEMENTS

I thank my wife, Linda, my son, Steve, and my daughter, Juli, for their support and their patience during this endeavor.

I also thank my friend, Robert Coram, for his encouragement and advice. His literary talent has been my inspiration.

Thanks, too, to Fred and Barbara Hill.

PROLOGUE

Robert slipped the bail of the coal oil lantern over its hook and allowed the pale yellow light to fill the stall. He spoke softly, "Morning, Luke, you feeling tolerable this morning? I hope so; it's gonna be a cold ride. Least we'll have that north wind to our back till it warms up a spell."

The big strawberry gelding breathed a steamy breath as he exhaled into the cold February air. He shuffled his feet, turned his big frame in the cramped space, and short-stepped up to Robert's waiting hand. Robert rubbed his white blaze face and patted him affectionately on the jaw. "Seems like this trip to St. George gets harder each time, don't it boy?"

Robert slipped the bit into Luke's mouth and pulled the bridle over the horse's ears and buckled the chin strap. "You know what, Luke? They tell me that the railroad will be finished by June. Of course, they said it would be finished years ago, and here it is 1907, and they haven't finished it yet. Know what that means, boy? Well, I'll tell you, that means that they'll start sending the payroll on the train every two weeks and we won't have to go get it." He retrieved the lantern and led Luke into the hallway of the barn.

He covered Luke's back with a tattered wool blanket to break the chill while he harnessed him to the buggy. He continued to encourage him. "Let's see, March, April, May...just six more trips after this one, boy. Won't we be glad?"

Robert finished harnessing Luke and, after retrieving the lantern, led him out into the brisk morning wind and made his way up to the house. He tied Luke to the hand rail at the back steps of the house, out of the wind and convenient to his ride at first light.

Louannie had watched the progress of his lantern through the darkness from the kitchen window and unlatched the back door just as he was about to knock for her. He shivered and made straight for the welcome heat of the wood stove. "Man, that wind will just cut right through you!"

"Robert, why don't you wait 'til it warms up some? You could stay the night in St. George and still be back in plenty of time to pay off tomorrow. Me and the boys will be fine. It's just too cold to make that trip," Louannie pleaded.

"Now Lou, you know that I have to be at the still on Saturday mornings. The gum has to be weighed and tallied and the payroll prepared. I'll be fine. I'll wear the gloves and the sweater you knitted for me, and I've got my duster to break the wind."

He pulled her up to him and hugged her close despite her protruding stomach. "Now don't you worry; you just keep them three little boys warm," he patted her on the swollen belly, "and keep care of little Bobbie there. I'll be fine."

Robert swigged on a cup of dark coffee as he added the sweater to his attire and checked his saddle bags. Louannie had packed his lunch of fried side meat, baked sweet potatoes and cornbread, and a canteen of milk.

"Who's goin' with ya?" she asked.

"I'm supposed to meet L.W. in St. George. He'll be with me for the trip back. I'll be fine, Lou!"

"I know Rob Willie, but I just cringe for you when you're in possession of that payroll. I mean, when they'll steal chickens out of the hen house, they'll do anything."

"Lou, I've made the trips for almost two years now - I'll be all right! Now, you do as I say, and I'll see you 'bout sundown, okay?" He kissed her.

"Okay, Rob Willie, I love you. Please be careful."

"I will," he said, as he squeezed her hand, donned the heavy duster and gloves, and returned to the chilling dawn. After fastening his saddle bags, he climbed aboard the buggy and rode away.

Late that afternoon, on their return to the turpentine still with the bi-monthly cash payroll, he was ambushed by an unknown assailant in the dense smoke of a woods fire. Luke came home about sundown—without his master.

CHAPTER 1
THE WEDDING

Somebody had told him it was a post oak. He couldn't understand that because the tree was so massive—wider at its base than he was tall. His twelve-year-old arms could only reach around a portion of its circumference. It was too big to hug its trunk and get a grip to climb, and the lowest limb was much too high to reach. It stood at the northeast corner of Vilulah Baptist Church cemetery and was his idle-time home on many an afternoon. He thought that a post oak should have something to do with a fence post, and the post that this tree would make would surely require all of the farm hands and all the mules should it be cut and used in some gigantic fence somewhere.

He couldn't think of anyone cutting his tree for a post, though. It was too important. It provided shade for the mules and horses that transported their masters to the store. It provided shade for the Rish family headstones which occupied that corner of the cemetery, and it was his refuge.

Vilulah Baptist Church sat about one hundred yards south of the tree, but across the road. The road from Coleman to Ft. Gaines made a gentle curve to the west just as it passed the tree so that he could look down and across the road, and see right through the front door of the church.

Vilulah, as it was called by almost everyone, had a large and proud congregation. It was a spotless white building, always clean and neat, the churchyard always swept clean with brushbrooms, not a sprig of grass.

At sometime in the past, the members had put a fence around the cemetery. He wasn't sure why the fence was there; maybe it kept the hogs and cows out, for they roamed freely in the wintertime.

1

Farmers had a mark to identify their livestock. Hogs' ears were notched with a tool appropriately called a notcher. Each owner had his own pattern of notches. Many times he had seen the "hands" and Mr. B hold the pigs down and give them their mark, and each time, as he saw the little triangular piece of ear meat fall to the ground, he would reach up and rub his ear. Apparently, the ear of a hog had less feeling in it than his did, less nerves or something! His ears would hurt for hours after the "hog-working," as it was called, but pigs seldom ever squealed.

Of course, hog-working was not simply notching ears. His testicles would hurt for hours, too, after watching Mr. B take a razor-sharp knife and split the skin of the pig's scrotum to pop out the testicles. Mr. B would pull the little oblong balls of meat up and cleanly clip the cords that attached them to the reproductive system of the pig. They would squeal hysterically, but to no avail, and the hands would have pig balls for supper.

The ears and little empty scrotums were then covered with a thick, black liquid to prevent screwworm infestation. Screwworms in the South during the mid-point of the century had devastated the livestock industry. The screwworm was the larvae of a fly that would lay eggs in an open wound of any living thing, and the subsequently developing larvae would feed on the flesh of their host and eventually kill it. This black coal tar was a miracle drug. It repelled the fly until the wound was healed enough to prevent the fly eggs from surviving. Many times after hog-working, Roller would climb the tree and sit on his favorite limb and hold his ear with one hand and his balls with the other.

The fence around the cemetery might have been put there for decoration. It was a woven wire fence with scalloped patterns along the top, and wire thickly woven in places gave the fence a sophisticated look. It had a sacred-looking pattern woven into it as it encircled the many tombstones within its boundaries.

The fence cornered about six feet from the tree, and a wooden brace was nailed from the top of the corner post to the trunk of the tree. Many times he would try to jump up and grab the brace as he had seen the older boys do—grab hold and pull up to do a chin-up—but he was not yet tall enough. He got closer each

2

time he tried, it seemed, and one day soon he would reach it.

For now, though, he would have to hold onto the corner post with both hands, put the toes of his left foot through the holes in the woven wire, and pull up till his right foot reached the top of the wire. He would then balance on top of the wire, holding the top of the post, and swing over onto the brace sitting side-saddle-like. He could then pull one foot up on top of the brace and stand up while leaning down to hold the top of the post for balance. Once balanced, he could stand all the way up and reach the first limb of the tree. Holding on to the flimsy branches of the limb, he could tightrope the brace over to the trunk of the tree. There he could reach several limbs and pull himself up to the sitting place.

The sitting place was an old stump of a main limb that had been cut off many years before. The stump had scarred over on the end and protruded from the tree trunk about eighteen inches—just right to straddle. Above and on each side of the sitting place were two smaller limbs that fit perfectly under each of his armpits. With his back against the tree, he was comfortable.

From the vantage point of the sitting place, he could see the pulpit of Vilulah Church—if the front door was open, of course—and he could see the entire cemetery. To the right of the cemetery, he could see the barns, the livestock lots, and, far around to the right, he could see the store and all its activity. More important to Roller, he could see the road and anyone who traveled it.

The sitting place was concealed by the smaller branches and their foliage just enough so that passers-by would have to look directly at him to see him. But he saw them from the time they rounded the curve from the south and from the time they passed under the limbs of a huge pecan tree that sat in front of the bighouse to the north. The tree stood about halfway between the bighouse and Vilulah.

The store was about the width of the road north of the cemetery fence and sat close to the Coleman to Ft. Gaines Road. It was a big wooden building that was actually part of the old Vilulah community school which previously had sat across the road east of the tree. He had been told how they moved the wing of the school house across the road by rolling it on poles. Eight teams of mules had pulled as all hands from the farm moved the poles up ahead of the building. Each time a pole would roll out from under the rear of the building, the teams were halted and the pole would be carried around in front to be the next carrier of the enormous weight of the heart-pine structure. When it was finally in place and jacked up and blocked, it became what was to be the central site of commerce in the Vilulah Community. A porch was attached to the front of the old school building; this porch was simply a lean-to type roof held up on the front corners by two rounded, solid wood columns. The columns were painted bright red; the rest of the building was painted white. Along the under edge of the porch roof, on all three sides, were signs that read "Drink Coca Cola" on each end with big green letters in the middle that read "Mr. B's General Merchandise." A Prince Albert Smoking Tobacco sign was tacked to each of the columns, and the front and side of the store was covered with small tin signs promoting everything from Sweet Dental Snuff to Hoyts Cologne. His favorite sign, however, was one that read, "Dr. Thatcher's Diarrhea Medicine Sold Here—A Sure Cure for the Green-Apple Quick Steps." The store had a side door on the cemetery side of the building, about midway the building. Each morning except Sunday at 5:00 a.m. the rolling store would back up to the side door to take on its inventory for the day. The rolling store was just that, a store on wheels.

Rural South Georgia during the early fifties had families everywhere. Sharecroppers were predominately colored people who would tend crops on the landowner's fields for a share of the crop proceeds. Usually they had large families with all of the offspring sharing in the duties and requirements of producing a crop of cotton, corn, and peanuts, keeping the household and the yards, and tending livestock.

The rolling store would travel to those who could not travel to the nearest town or country store, and it carried all items that the parent store inventoried. A large metal insulated box held fresh meat and fish with ice to keep them cool during the sixty- to one-hundred-mile journey along the dusty or rain-slick dirt roads of a six-county area. Canned goods, flour, cornmeal, shoes, clothing, candy, and any other practical item could be bought from the front door of the rolling store. It traveled a different route each day of the week, and people along the route knew what day and time to expect Mr. B's Rolling Store.

If the store on wheels had mechanical trouble and was unable to make its appointed rounds, people along its route were "thunderstruck." Menus would have to be changed, cattle would have to wait another week for a salt block, children cried for lack of their weekly treat of Bazooka Bubble Gum, and granny would have to do without her number two sewing thread and Macaboy Snuff. It was a disaster when the rolling store failed to arrive.

It was also a method of communication. Very few telephones were about. Only the paved-road, most well-to-do, and prominent families had telephones, and, other than the mailman who traveled these back roads almost everyday, the rolling store was the only link to local news. People would gather at the rolling store when it stopped, and, after their purchases were made, they would talk to the driver and his helper about everything from politics to how the Yankees were playing. It was a vital, social commerce.

This particular day Roller thought the sitting place would be perfect for awaiting the big event. Mary Ann Rhodes was getting married. The wedding would be at Vilulah at 4:00. It was a typical August Saturday afternoon except that the store was unusually quiet. Normally at this time of the afternoon the store would be packed with colored families from the farms surrounding the community. The white families that traded at Mr. B's would come on Saturday morning. They knew that Saturday afternoons were when all the colored came to trade and the store would be busy and full. Every store clerk would be busy fetching items from the store shelves, tallying bills, and stuffing bag after bag with groceries and dry goods. But this day was so hot that most of the shoppers had decided to wait for the afternoon sun to fade and cool off a bit.

He had not been needed in the store so he had slipped out the side door, turned slightly left, headed for the tree, and made his climb to watch the ceremony through the front door of Vilulah

Church. He was settled in the sitting place but had to keep one arm free of its limb-hold to fan away the gnats. Gnats are an aggravating little insect well known in South Georgia. They buzzed around your mouth and your eyes and just pestered the living daylights out of you. He hated them!

A road from the east intersected the Coleman to Ft. Gaines road directly in front of the store. It was called the Carnegie Road and it was about a mile down Carnegie Road that Cecil and Frank Rhodes farmed. They had but one child, Mary Ann. It had been just recently that Roller had noticed that Mary Ann was so pretty. She was about twenty years old, he guessed, and for some reason he thought about her a lot. He could just picture her as he sat there in the sitting place. He could see her coal black hair curled just above her shoulders. Her dark brown eyes were, for some unknown reason to him, her most beautiful feature. Her thin but perfect face and snow white smile had become an obsession to him. He could just sit and look at her for hours. He often went to Vilulah to church service just to see Mary Ann and to listen to her play the piano.

He could not see around the tree to look down the Carnegie Road, but he knew the sound of Mr. Frank's truck. He would know when they were coming. He sat there looking at the guests as they arrived at Vilulah. Sweat beaded and rolled down his forehead and down the side of his temple, and he thought how hot it must be in those coats and ties and girdles and dresses— and the gnats were everywhere. All the ladies had on their finest clothes. They all had some kind of fan made of bamboo or something. The fans would fold up like an accordion and fit neatly in their purses. But they had the fans going, fanning the heat trying to evaporate sweat to keep cool and fanning the gnats. The men hurried inside to find a Lunsford Funeral Home fan, a simple wooden paddle with a cardboard picture of Jesus knocking on a door on the front and the funeral home ad on the back.

When he heard the train whistle blow at Coleman, he knew it was almost 4:00. Everyday, twice a day, the train went through Coleman at 9:00 in the morning and a little before 4:00 in the afternoon. Each morning the train would travel the twelve miles parallel Cemocheechobee Creek to Ft. Gaines. There it would turn around and come back through Coleman in the afternoon. He couldn't imagine a field big enough to turn that train around. (It would be a long time before he would get to go to Ft. Gaines and watch the train crew turn the engine car around so that it could pull the other cars backward. He saw then that the box-cars did not have a front or a back. They could go either way.)

A truck was coming. He recognized the sound as Mr. Frank's 1949 Ford pickup. It would carry Mr. Frank, Miss Cecil, and Mary Ann.

He leaned on the sitting place as far to his left as possible and waited for the truck to pass the tree. He heard Mr. Frank stop at the intersection, shift into low gear, and accelerate toward Vilulah. He sucked in a breath of air in preparation to yell at Mary Ann when they passed. Then he could see the truck and Mary Ann sitting by the window on the passenger side. He yelled but he made no sound. Mary Ann looked gently to her right toward the cemetery, not knowing that he was just above her line of vision, and again he tried to yell and again he was speechless. She was so pretty she reminded him of Snow White. Her charming prince was waiting for her at Vilulah.

Mr. Frank stopped the truck at the edge of the clean-swept churchyard and went around to Mary Ann's door and helped her out into the hot August sunshine. He and Miss Cecil were very careful of her dress. He watched their every move. She wore what he thought must be a wagonload of white lace and netting and satin. Her dress had long lacy sleeves and was cut low in the front and back with only a lacy strap across her shoulders. He thought, *She must be hot in all that finery but she's lucky— the gnats won't get up her nose. She has her own little net face mask to keep them out.*

He heard the piano music change, and through the front door of Vilulah, he could see the charming prince and Brother Vincent. Brother Vincent was the resident preacher that performed all the weddings and all the funerals and preached loud and long, hellfire-and-damnation sermons.

Miss Cecil looked Mary Ann over one last time and straightened the lace half-covering her breast. With a lace handkerchief she blotted Mary Ann's perspiring forehead, then dried her own tears and turned to lead the way up the steps.

Soon they were all in place and the music faded. Brother Vincent said several lines of the ceremony, and then Mr. B stood up and sang "Always." It was the only time that the fans stopped their ever-waving cadence. It seemed to Roller that even the birds stopped singing. Of course, he knew that birds didn't sing during dog days, but it was quiet except for the piano and Mr. B. When Mr. B was finished with the song, the fans started back their rhythm, people coughed and sniffed, shuffled on those hard pine benches, and the service continued.

He sat there in the sitting place thinking about Mr. B. Mr. B was a farmer. He was owner and operator of Mr. B's General Merchandise store and supervised the rolling store and a grist mill that sat behind the store, and he was a singer. He had a beautiful tenor voice, and he sang all over the country at revivals and homecomings. Someone said that if Mr.B didn't sing at your funeral, you could not go to heaven, and if he didn't sing at your wedding, the marriage would never last.

It seemed to him that Mr. B worked all the time. He was a thin and wiry but dedicated Christian man; he was never still. He had so much to see about that he was always on the go. Mr. B, he thought, was much too busy to be his father, but he was, and both he and Mr. B were proud of it.

He also thought about Mary Ann marrying Prince Charming and moving away. She would be a long way from home. He didn't know how wide Georgia was, but she would be on the other side, for he had heard Muh ask Mr. Frank where they would live and he said, "Waycross Georgia."

As he sat there listening, he scanned over the cemetery and the barnyard for activity. He spotted a rabbit hopping along the back side of the cemetery where it cornered with a little thicket of small tress and honeysuckle vine, and he thought, *One day soon, Mr. Rabbit, I'll come looking for you.*

He liked the sitting place, he could watch the world go by or he could make it still, at least for awhile, anyway.

Finally, his trance was broken...someone was calling his name. He looked down. It was Cooper. "Roller, Roller, don't you hear me calling you? Get down now outa that tree. Lawd, seem like you oughta been a squirrel good as you love to climb. You know Muh done ax me to watch after you while they be at the wedding. Come on now, Roller. Lawd, if you was to fall, I'd jest have to tell Mr. Rish there in the corner of that cemetery to move over, cause here come a dead nigger. Come on, now, we got to feed the hogs. It will be killing time dreckly, and if them hogs ain't fat, we both be in trouble. Seems like half I do is getting you down outa trees."

Cooper was a colored man. (Roller had been taught to call black people colored. That's what they wanted to be called. They would call each other "nigger" or whatever, but they wanted white people to call them colored.) Cooper lived in the third house past the bighouse toward Coleman. Cooper was lean, of medium build, and quite fit for his age. His face, wrinkled but always cleanshaven with dark eyes and white teeth, made it evident that he had been a handsome man in his youth. He was about the same age as Mr. B, and he, too, was always busy— well, almost always. He didn't sharecrop anymore; he tended Mr. B's hogs and cows, cleaned the yards, kept the woodpile, and helped Muh do whatever she needed. His biggest and most important job, however, was keeping Roller out of trouble. He would often say, "Roller, you just too full of mischief for me to handle." But he tried.

In the summer months he and Roller did everything together. If Roller had a chore to do, Cooper would help. If Cooper had a job to do, Roller would help. The only job that they didn't share was when Roller had to work in the store. On Saturdays and other busy days, Roller would help clerk or stock shelves or whatever needed doing, and Cooper would get a much deserved rest. If Roller was confined to the store, Cooper was relieved of his obligation to keep Roller occupied and out of mischief.

When all of the necessary jobs had been done, they would leave the premises and walk the woods. They would pretend to be working fences if Mr. B asked what they had been doing, but in reality they would just leave. They would hike back behind the barns and the paddocks to Mosely Branch. They would fish or hunt or just sit and watch the horny-heads swim in the clear branch water. Roller would often say, "Cooper, we're supposed to be working, but we ain't. You're just too full of mischief for me to handle too."

"How'd you get up there anyways?" Cooper asked. "Come on down now, and be careful." He had taken off his old straw hat and was fanning gnats with it. People were coming out of the church now, still fanning, but talking and standing around. Snow White and Prince Charming were getting ready to leave the church yard, as Roller began his descent from the sitting place. He reversed the process of his climb up, and Cooper said, "Well, I'll be. Roller, ain't nobody's ass could make that climb but you." Cooper would often use the word "ass" in his language, and many times it would be ill-placed.

Roller got to the corner post, grabbed the top of the brace, gave a "Tarzan yodel", swung down to the ground in a half run toward the barn, and yelled, "Cooper let's go feed them hogs. Prince Charming done got my woman anyway!"

Cooper scratched his balding grey head and said, "Huh? Boy, you don't make no sense sometimes."

As they made their way past the side door, past the store, and past the mill house, they both heard the sound of a trickle of water. Roller was thinking about Mary Ann and didn't bother to look for its source, but Cooper did.

"Look-a-there, that Mr. Ollie done stuck his tallywhacker out that knothole taking a pee." Sure enough, Roller looked, and there on the back of the mill house, out of a knothole that he had seen before, urine streamed from a pink and skinny penis. "He oughta be shamed," Cooper declared.

Roller thought in disgust, *One day soon, Mr. Ollie, I'll come looking for you.*

CHAPTER 2
THE HAWK

The summer of 1954 would go down in history as one of the hottest and driest of modern time. It was a devastating drought, and the result was economic ruin for many South Georgia farmers. An agricultural revolution was well underway, and the disastrous drought was very untimely. Mule farming was in its last days, and sharecropping was on a decline. The mechanical mule, the tractor, had transformed the old South, and the simple life, as many perceived Southern agriculture, was losing its simplicity. To replace mules and man labor with equipment was costly but imperative. Modern agriculture was in its infancy and needed the nurturing and kindness of Mother Nature; instead, she gave it a spanking of wrath in the form of drought.

The year began with favorable weather with ample rain and good growing conditions. But after April showers and after a few May sprinkles, the rain ceased. June, July, and August temperatures were above normal, and the rainfall was far below the needs of the peanuts, cotton, and corn on which the farmers were so dependent. The dry earth cracked open, and crops literally burned up under the hot Georgia sun.

Cooper and Roller filled two big cotton baskets with corn still in the shuck and dragged them out to the hog paddock. The hungry pigs came running.

"Roller, Mr. B needs to sell some of them cows. We ain't got nothing to feed them," Cooper explained.

"Well, why don't we turn them in on that corn over there in front of Miss Lucille's?" asked Roller. "They can at least eat the stalks and the fodder; ain't no corn over there noway."

Cooper would often acknowledge a comment by just nodding his head. Now he nodded and thought a minute. "Roller,

11

that shoulda been my idea, ain't that right?"

"Well, if you want it to be, then it was," Roller replied.

"Might make me look good to Mr. B to come up with a good thought now and then, don't you see?"

"Well, okay. Why don't you ask him about it and see what he says?"

Cooper nodded, "He'll be back to the store dreckly."

They finished the feeding and carried the empty baskets back to the barn. They threw ears of corn into the mule trough and stood there a minute watching Kate and Maude and Bob and Nellie crunching the ears, mouthing it until the grain began to shed from the cob and fall back into the trough.

"Don't seem right," Cooper said. "Not long ago we had sixteen mules in this lot. Damn tractors!"

"Cooper, them tractors don't eat when they ain't working," Roller repeated what he had heard the farmers say.

Cooper nodded. He wanted to argue the advantages of mule farming, but he knew it was useless. Something had come to mind that he had been meaning to tell Roller.

"Roller, you know that hawk you been wanting to kill?"

"You mean the one that made me kill my duck?" Roller asked.

"Now, Roller, I done told you, if you hadn't a shot, that hawk woulda flew right on off and eat that duck anyways. He had him in his claws. So you missed the hawk and killed the duck—least he didn't get to eat him."

"Yeah," boasted Roller, "but I can shoot better now. What about the hawk?"

"Roller, ain't many growed folks coulda shot that hawk flying off with that duck with a twenty-two rifle and done more than scare him. You just shot a little low, that's all. You know that bullet gonna drop on a long shot like that," Cooper explained.

"Yeah, yeah, what about the hawk?" Roller insisted.

"Well, I seen him this morning in the pecan grove."

"I'll kill him tomorrow," boasted Roller.

"Morrow's Sunday. You know Muh ain't gonna let you hunt on Sunday."

"Well, Monday then. Monday I'll kill that hawk."

"You better get back to the sto Roller. They will be busy now; beside, I got to go see a man bout a dawg."

Roller knew Cooper was saying that it was late Saturday and time for him to go home. He knew Cooper would be drunk tonight and all day tomorrow but back to work on Monday.

They walked back to the store, and as they reached the front porch, they waited for Muh and Mr. B, who had walked from Vilulah to the bighouse, changed from their Sunday clothes to work clothes, and were making their way back to the store.

Roller asked his mother about the wedding, though he didn't hear her answer. He was listening to Cooper and Mr. B.

"Mr. B, I think we oughta turn them cows in on that corn over in front of Miss Lucille's. It done burnt up anyway."

Mr. B, surprised that he hadn't already thought of that, replied, "Good thinking, Cooper. Have you been around those fences?"

"Oh, yas, Suh."

Mr. B pointed toward the corn field. "Well, go open the gap down in the bottom, and let them have at it. I'll have you a tip when you get back."

Cooper nodded and winked at Roller, who was smiling at the conversation as Cooper walked off in his whistle walk. He had two walking gates—one was his normal slow but determined stride, the other was a peppy, faster pace and he whistled. Roller could tell his mood by his stride. If he whistled, things were going good.

Roller told Muh about the hawk as they went inside, but she reminded, "Tomorrow is first Sunday, Roller. That's preaching day at Wesley Chapel, and tomorrow afternoon they're having a special pray-for-rain service at Vilulah. Besides, you know that you can't hunt on Sunday." He would have to wait until Monday to hunt the hawk.

All of a sudden the store became normal for Saturday afternoon. Colored people filled the store, the porch, and spilled out into the yards. Dozens of children, each begging his or her parents for a nickel or a dime, played around everywhere. They were all bathed and dressed in clean clothes. The girls had their hair greased and platted with strips of brightly colored cloth for bows. The older girls had on lipstick, and Hoyts Cologne filled the air around the store. Families of colored people from all around used the store as their social gathering place on Saturday. They would hug and kiss and fight and sing and laugh and talk as if they had not seen each other for months.

Mothers and fathers of each family would take their turn inside at one of the three counters to buy their needs for the following week. Most of them had large families and would require several large bags of groceries each week. Their menus were simple and economical. They would always buy a slab of Mr. B's bacon, that he had cured and kept in the big walk-in cooler in the back, a bag of flour, ten pounds of Mr. B's corn meal, rice, salt, grits, Jack mackerel salmon, tobacco, and lard.

Roller could almost tell in advance what most of them would need and would assist all three counters. He'd yell out, "Ya'll need rice?" and carry rice to all three counters when he'd go fetch some for the counter he was working. He was quick, both afoot and mentally, and could remember the families that brought a twenty-five pound bag of flour every week and those that bought every two weeks, and he could remember if this was the week they would need flour. Many times he would deliver items to the counter before they called for it. He would know what they would need; he reminded them of things they had forgotten to buy. He was a good clerk! Everybody would be busy. Mr. B would work one counter; Muh would work one counter; and Uncle George, Mr. B's brother-in-law who was a full-time clerk, would work a counter. Roller and Bruh (short for Brother) and Sis would assist all three.

They would all eat supper on Saturday night right there in the store. As they found a few minutes, they would open a can of sardines or potted meat or vienna sausage or cut a slice of bologna and cheese from the hoop and eat on the move. A cold Coca-Cola and Johnny Cake cookie would complete their meal. At 8:00 they would turn on the radio that sat near the front of the store near the electrical service box and was tuned in to the Grand Ole Opry. Usually by then the trading was beginning to slow down, and Hank Williams, Earnest Tubb, and Little Jimmy Dickens would sing to them for the next couple of hours until the rolling store came in and the store was closed.

It seemed to Roller that they spent all week stocking shelves just to empty them on Saturday. But he enjoyed being around people and thrived on the jovial, gregarious Negroes and their never-ending laughter and singing and joking. It amused him that all of the outside activity took place on the front and north side of the store. The cemetery was on the south side, and nobody went near it after sundown.

Occasionally, Roller would slip out the side door, climb the cemetery fence, and wait for one of the shopper families to start walking home down past Vilulah. He'd hide behind a headstone, and as they would pass the cemetery he'd tap on the marble with an empty can and perhaps moan and groan in a low, deep voice and almost laugh out loud as they would run over each other in the dark, screaming and running to get past the cemetery.

They would know all along that it was Roller, but they couldn't help themselves. There was just something awful scary about that white folks cemetery even in the daytime, and at night, with Roller out there tapping those stones, the cemetery was a "hainted" and terrible place for colored people to be and they would not tarry. Tonight, though, he would be preoccupied with thoughts about the hawk, and later, as he tried to find sleep, he dreamed of the hawk.

Roller was what all the old men around Vilulah called a "crack" shot. He had been shooting his .22 caliber rifle several years, and his young keen eyes and steady aim had earned him the reputation of being the best shot around. He could shoot through the hole in a Coke bottle at thirty yards. He could shoot sparrows from the top of the tallest pecan tree. But that hawk had eluded him on several occasions. He had shot at him twice: once when he spotted the hawk perched high up in a pecan tree overlooking the turkey pen, and once when the hawk made the dastardly attempt at attacking and fleeing with his pet duck.

Roller had made no excuse for either miss, yet the first had not bothered him; the hawk had only been looking. But he should have killed him that first time; then there would not have been the heartbreaking second time. The hawk had apparently circled high over the open-topped pen that held a few turkeys, several chickens, and Roller's pet duck that Sis had given him for Easter; had swooped down on an almost vertical dive, drove his razor sharp talons into the duck's back, and lifted itself and the duck back into the air.

Roller had been trying to kill rats near the north end of the mill house, had heard the commotion that the chickens and turkeys had made, and had run toward the pen just in time to see the hawk lifting above the pecan tree that stood behind the smokehouse.

In an instant it all flashed through his mind—that Sis had given him Donald for an Easter gift, that he had watched Donald change from a little yellow ball of fluff into a solid white duckling, that Donald had followed him around the pen quacking as if Roller was his mother, and that Cooper had told him that Donald was really a Daisy. Muh had even promised to get Daisy a mate so that Roller could raise little ducklings.... This hawk was flying away with Donald Daisy!

He took careful aim and squeezed the trigger. He heard the bullet make its contact with the target, and feathers flew as the hawk released the duck and disappeared behind the canopy of the pecan tree. Roller surmised that this was his best shot ever and went to check on his duck. He found the duck—stone dead. He kneeled and picked it up, surprised that the hawk had killed Donald during such a short flight. Then he saw the bullet hole. He had shot his own duck! In the split second of his reaction time, it had not occurred to him that he might miss the hawk and hit the duck. It was utter rage toward the hawk stealing his duck that had placed the rifle against his young shoulder. It was absolute hate and revenge that had drawn a bead on that hawk; that had pulled the sight slightly ahead of the hawk so that the hawk's flight would intercept the bullet's path. It was anger and respite that had squeezed ever so gently the trigger of his faithful .22. His aim had been true, but too true. He had shot his duck. Donald was dead. He cried.

Mr. Ollie had watched the whole episode from the millhouse porch. Cooper had watched from the mule lot. Cooper could see that ole man Ollie was watching, and he knew what Roller would be facing. He knew that not only would Roller have to mourn the death of his duck, but that he would also have to face the teasing and ridicule of all the old men of Vilulah. He knew that Roller had shot against all of them and had beat them all— and that they would savor the knowledge that Roller had shot his own duck.

He went to Roller hoping that Ollie would think that the hawk had killed the duck, and that Roller's shot had made the hawk release his grip. He knew, though, that Ollie had heard the bullet make it's hit, that he had seen, too, the white duck feathers float through the pecan tree, and that the duck had fallen with no sign of life or wounded fluttering. He knew that Ollie knew that Roller had shot the duck.

"Come on now, Roller," said Cooper. "Least that hawk didn't get to eat him."

Roller cried.

"Stop crying now, Roller. Let's go bury him in the white folks cemetery."

Roller took some comfort that his duck would have such a fine final resting place and stood up, half bowed with Donald in his hands. He promised the duck—then looked up and spoke to Cooper, "I'll kill that damn hawk, and I ain't gonna take too kindly to the first person who has something to say about this."

"Now Roller, you know that Mr. Ollie gonna tell everybody bout this, but what you gotta member is if it had been any of them, that hawk, duck ass and all, woulda got way."

Roller dried his eyes, fanned the gnats, stood fully erect and looked at Cooper. He could not speak. Cooper nodded and put his big black hand on Roller's shoulder as they walked up the little hill toward the cemetery.

As they neared the mill house, Ollie stepped down to the first step of the porch steps and sat down. He needed a shave about two weeks ago, had meal dust all over his face, hands, and clothes, and had tobacco juice oozing from the corner of his mouth. He spat and grinned. "Been duck hunting, Roller?"

Roller couldn't think of anything to say. Cooper thought of a lot to say but, he didn't; he just nodded, squeezed Roller's shoulder, and tugged him on toward the cemetery. A shovel was leaning against the pecan tree that stood between the mill house and the store. Cooper picked it up in stride with his left hand as his right hand continued to grasp Roller's shoulder. He could feel Roller's muscles tighten and quiver as they passed Ollie. They both were thinking, *One day soon, Mr. Ollie, I'll come looking for you.*

CHAPTER 3
THE RAIN

It had been another hot, still, and muggy August night, and Sunday began like the previous sixty mornings—dry and hot. Even with a little oscillating fan blowing at him, Roller awoke in a full sweat. His first thought was of the hawk; his next was of his chores. On Sunday it was his task to feed and clean the stall of White Hogan. Cooper would "be seeing a man about a dawg."

White Hogan had been the 1952 Georgia Champion bull at the state fair in Atlanta. He was a registered shorthorn, and he was solid white. He was about fourteen hundred pounds of muscle and bone, but was as gentle as a lamb. He had been around people since he was a few days old because Mr. B had recognized he had prize-winning potential and immediately turned the calf over to Cooper, who had broken him to a halter and to grooming when he was a young calf.

Of all the people that White Hogan knew, he knew Cooper and Roller the best. Together they would bathe him, they would halter and lead him all over the yard, all around the store—even around Vilulah. Cooper would lead, and Roller would ride. Roller had been riding White Hogan since the bull was big enough to sustain his weight. He would scratch White's ears and the back of his neck as they would amble, and White loved it.

Roller carried two buckets full of ground feed, two buckets of water, and a block of hay and was busy shoveling the fresh manure when he noticed that the hog paddock, which was southwest of White's pen, was especially strong smelling this morning. He remembered Cooper saying one time that a morning breeze out of the southwest would bring an afternoon shower. Maybe it would rain today.

White turned away from the feed trough as Minnie, the milk

19

cow, exited the main barn. Bruh had finished milking and had let her back with her calf. Roller smiled as she went by. As White straightened his neck and curled his nose and lips in anticipation of her odor, Roller remembered the day he rode White while White rode Minnie. What a ride!

Cooper had been outraged and said, "It woulda been a cow ass mess if you'd been riding that milk cow!"

He petted White for a while and headed for the bighouse. It would soon be time to get ready for Sunday school and church. He stopped by the mule lot and checked the water, and as he entered the open barnyard, he scanned the sky and the trees for the hawk, but didn't see him anywhere. He was glad because he was hoping not to see him on a day that he couldn't shoot him. Tomorrow was Monday; tomorrow he could shoot.

The first and third Sundays were preaching at Wesley Chapel, the Methodist Church where Roller and his family were regular members. It was about five miles past Vilulah toward Ft. Gaines. Second and fourth Sundays were preaching days at Vilulah. On fifth Sundays neither church had preaching. Roller liked fifth Sundays.

Roller would bathe and dress in his Sunday outfit, and he and Bruh and Sis and Muh and Mr. B would drive to Wesley Chapel. On the way, Muh would find that Roller's ears were not clean. She would wrap her little embroidered handkerchief around her index finger, wet it with her saliva, and scrub his ears inside and out till they were red. This seemed to be a ritual every Sunday morning even though Roller would spend extra time cleaning his ears on Saturday night. They were never clean enough. Sometimes he thought that she mistook his freckles for dirt spots. She just didn't know how sensitive his ears could be!

The conversation on the way to church was the same every Sunday it seemed. Sis and Bruh told who had recently bought a television, and they were still having to walk down to the Blackburn's to watch this new entertainment phenomena. Mr. B would say that the Bible had prophesied the coming of the TV, that it would be the ruin of mankind, and that they couldn't afford one anyway with the drought and all. Muh would say maybe next year.

By the time they got to Wesley Chapel, they would all be pouting. Roller because his ears were red, Sis and Bruh because they wouldn't have a TV for another year, and Muh and Mr. B because they wanted to do more for the children but couldn't and because of the demoralizing effect of the drought and heat. Brother Edenfield would have to work a miracle!

He was the pastor of Wesley Chapel and had initiated a building project during the worst year possible. Wesley Chapel much needed a recreational building, and a special fund had been established for its construction. Now, all of the crops were burning up, and the necessary contributions were doubtful.

Roller didn't understand the Sunday school lesson or the sermon that day. They were both about the power of prayer and that God does answer prayer.

"He may not answer like we want Him to, but He does answer," Brother Edenfield said.

Roller couldn't figure out why God wouldn't answer prayer the way you prayed for it. You might as well pray for something else, he thought, if He was going to answer it the way He wanted to. It was all confusing to Roller.

They announced at Wesley Chapel that there would be a special pray-for-rain service at Vilulah at 4:00 that afternoon. Some special, high Baptist official would be there to conduct the service. Roller decided that he would go in order to see if God would answer a Baptist's prayers any better than He would a Methodist's prayers. He figured that every day that passed without rain was one day closer to God making up his mind and that surely it would rain soon.

After dinner that day, Roller would not go outside; he didn't want to see the hawk. He sat around and played solitaire with Mama. Mama was Muh's mother. She lived in the bighouse and was a great companion to Roller and vice versa. She was a Baptist and a regular member of Vilulah.

At three forty-five, Mama, Roller, and Mr. B walked to Vilulah to pray for rain. As they were leaving the bighouse, Roller picked up an umbrella from the hall tree—there was not a cloud in the sky—and made the walk in the shade of the umbrella. As they reached the clean-swept church yard, there were, as usual, several men of the church standing around outside smoking and talking. They all spoke to Mama first. She was old but spry and tenacious and proud to walk up the steps of Vilulah without any assistance. She wore her black hat, a black-and-white polka dot Sunday dress and white gloves. She always wore gloves to church—even in the summertime. She spoke back to the men, and Mr. B ushered her into the auditorium.

Roller was an obvious target of teasing by all the adult men of the community, especially Uncle Sammy. He was not related to Roller, but everybody called him Uncle. He teased all the young boys, but he loved especially to tease and joke Roller.

He was a little-framed man, younger than Mr. B, but wrinkled and sun-faced. Two days a week he drove the rolling store for a store in Coleman, and occasionally Roller went on the route with him as his helper. He never called anyone by his name, and Roller was not sure, but he thought that Uncle Sammy had given him the name "Roller." He thought that it had something to do with rolling store.

Uncle Sammy laughed at Roller and asked, "You came prepared, didn't you Roller?"

Roller had been teased by all of the men so much that he had learned to anticipate their remarks and was prepared with a comeback line that would reverse the sting of accusation so that whoever delivered the tease would receive more ridicule than he.

Roller popped the umbrella to its closed position, placed it upright against the door frame of the church, and said, "Oh, ye of little faith. Matthew 6:30." (He would often reply to an aspersion with a quote of scripture or a quote from some source of wisdom).

As he went inside, all the men just looked at Uncle Sammy as if to say, "Well, he got you again!"

Everybody teased Roller because of his ability to take teasing. His response to tease remarks were what they wanted to hear. They wouldn't deliberately hurt Roller; they knew he would have the last word. They just wanted to know what his rebuttal would be. Some of them, like Uncle Sammy, would think up things, really concentrate on ways to tease and humiliate him, but Roller was always a step ahead. He would always have a rebuttal, and, like the shooting contest, he always won. That was how he had handled the sarcasm and snide remarks about shooting his duck a few weeks prior; he simply stated, "You know, I learned a valuable lesson from that. Don't ever shoot a thief in the foot, shoot him in the head."

Of course they would argue that he was not trying to shoot that hawk in the foot, so he eventually challenged them to a shooting contest, and again, Roller had the last word.

Every one of the heart-pine pews were filled with hopeful Vilulah citizens as Roller entered the church, and the "pray-for-rain" service began with two hymns: "Showers of Blessings" and "Sweet Hour of Prayer." Mr. B led the congregational singing, then took his seat next to Roller on the front pew.

The visiting speaker was an official with the Southern Baptist Association. He was a powerful Baptist Doctrine preacher. He was short and fat but loud and long-winded—barely visible behind the pulpit, but Roller thought he could have heard him fine if he had stopped at the "sitting place."

His initial scripture was "Ask and ye shall receive...," and he bellowed out a few lines about the power of prayer. But just as the assembly became attentive and involved with his text, he began to promulgate the Baptist doctrine and all the special blessings and benefits of being a Baptist.

In order to emphasize the glory of the Baptist denomination, he asked all the Baptists in the church to stand up and shout "Hallelujah." Everybody in the church stopped the rhythmic motion of the funeral home fans and sprang up and lifted their hands high in the air and shouted "Hallelujah!" Everybody, that is, except Roller and Mr. B—they were Methodists.

The preacher noticed that they had not stood. When everyone had settled down in their seats again, he asked if they would stand up. Mr. B and Roller stood in unison. Roller thought, *If we'd sat in the back, he wouldn't have seen us.*

"Well, gentlemen," spat the preacher, "you didn't stand with all the Baptists."

"No, sir," said Mr. B. "We're not Baptists."

"Well, sir, if you are not Baptists, what are you?"

"We're Methodists."

23

"And why are you Methodists?"

Mr. B and Roller looked at each other and Mr. B answered, "Well, I guess because our fathers before us were Methodists."

After a pause, the preacher breathing heavily out of his nose and looking over the congregation asked, "Well, sir, what would you have been if your fathers before you had been fools?" he smiled.

Mr. B looked down at Roller as Roller tugged on his coat sleeve to prompt him to lean down. They whispered to each other before Mr. B stood erect and said, "Well, sir, I guess in that case, we would have been Baptists."

The congregation erupted with laughter! Even the most devout and staunch Baptist felt that the preacher had quit preaching and gone to meddling; they loved their Methodist neighbors, and they had no pity for the preacher's embarrassment. This was supposed to be a prayer service anyway.

The laughter ended suddenly. What was that noise? Was it thunder? Roller thought about the breeze from the southwest. Yes, it was thunder and more pronounced now. It was getting darker. The westward windows of the church indicated the increasing breeze. There was more thunder, and suddenly it began to rain.

The entire congregation stood and shouted, "Praise God." They clapped and laughed, shook hands with other, hugged each other, and enjoyed the sound of the rain on the tin roof of the church and the smell of the rain on the dry earth. The preacher stood a little taller behind the pulpit.

A short prayer of thanksgiving ended the service, and Roller thought, *God does answer prayers.* Here He had delivered a foot-in-mouth preacher from a point of total embarrassment to a point of total jubilation, and He had delivered the people of Vilulah a much welcomed rain. *Maybe God did answer Baptist prayers the best; He did today.*

Mr. B would wait for the rain to slacken before making the walk to the bighouse, but the entire congregation stood on the porch and in the doorway of Vilulah and watched Mama and Roller, with the only umbrella to be had, walk leisurely out of the church yard and up the road.

24

CHAPTER 4
THE CLAW

Sleep never came easy for Roller. It seemed that the less active his body became, the more active his mind became. He shared a room with Bruh, and most nights he would lay in his feather bed listening to the sounds of Bruh deep in sleep and think about the happenings of the day or anticipate the activities of the coming day.

This night was no exception; he thought of the rain. Though it was much too late to help most crops, it did cool things off, and it offered hope that the awful drought was over. He thought of White Hogan, Mama, Mr. B, and the pray-for-rain service. He wondered what Cooper was doing and if he had a fan to help cool the hot August night; he would ask him. And he thought about the hawk.

As he tossed and turned, his body at rest, but his mind at high speed, he mapped his strategy for the impending hunt. This hawk was smart. He had disappeared for almost two weeks after his attempted heist of Donald Daisy. He would perch high in the tallest pecan tree on the far side of the orchard and await the appropriate time to advance on an unsuspecting prey. He would hold his perch until no one was about the barnyard or the garden or the turkey pen, and when no activity was visible, he would lift from his perch and soar high above the buildings and grounds of Mr. B's farm and homestead in search of a meal.

Roller had seen him dive from high in the sky to catch a tiny mouse. His eyesight was amazing, and Roller would have to conceal himself or the hawk would spot him and be gone again. The hawk also had a sixth sense, or so it seemed to Roller, because several times he had seen him at close range when he was without his trusty .22 rifle; and yet when he was armed and hunting the hawk, the hawk was nowhere to be found or else they would spot each other at the same time and the hawk would vanish before Roller could draw a bead. Roller believed that the hawk knew when he was being hunted and somehow must be deceived. After considering several plans of attack, Roller finally fell asleep.

Just up the road toward Coleman was the homestead of Mr. Lawson Bryan. Mr. Lawson had a big Dominecker rooster that had taken up a resident roost in the pecan orchard just behind the bighouse. Every morning before first light, his crowing would wake up everybody who had slept through noise of the rolling store taking its place at the side door of the store. Roller had dreamed of shooting that rooster on several occasions, and one day he would, providing Mr. Lawson couldn't keep him at home. But on this morning his crowing was welcome, and Roller hopped out of bed at the rooster's first crow.

Roller dressed quietly: blue jeans, no shoes (as usual), an old, unbuttoned khaki work shirt whose sleeves had been removed at the shoulders, and his .22 rifle. He slipped out of the house so as not to disturb anyone.

He made his way in the early morning darkness across the back yard, past the smokehouse, over the orchard fence, and through the corner of the orchard to the hedgerow that separated the pecan orchard from the cattle paddock.

Slipping into in the dew-covered thickness of the hedge, he sat on a field stone that had been thrown out of the orchard. He broke several chinaberry limbs, with their thick, dark green foliage, and arranged them in front of him to form a blind. Thinking that he was perfectly camouflaged, he was satisfied with the early stages of his assault. He waited.

As darkness faded, he picked through his ammunition for his best bullet, finding one with bright brass and whose lead still had its mold markings and was not polished by the abrasion of other bullets in his pocket. He knew that if he was lucky, he would most likely get but one shot; it had to be perfect. He kissed the cartridge and placed it in the chamber. As he sat there waiting and as the light increased, he found an old, dry-cured chinaberry limb about two feet long with a fork on one end. It was just right to place his rifle in the fork while putting the blunt end on the ground to provide a steady prop. He was sure the keen eyesight of the hawk would detect any movement that he made, so he waited there with his rifle shouldered and cocked in the forked prop, motionless for what seemed to be hours.

From his blind, he could hear the activities of the farm begin a new week of work. He heard Punto, Willie, and Walter, tractor hands for Mr. B, crank their model 420 John Deere tractors and head off to the field. The characteristic putt-putt cadence of the two-cylinder engines went out of hearing down the road toward Ft. Gaines.

The ground had been so hard that plowing up peanuts had been impossible. The rain had softened the ground, and they would get started on the sandy land as soon as possible. Most of the Spanish-type peanuts would be bailed into hay. The drought and heat had taken their toll. The peanut vines were dying and had to be harvested, but they had produced but few nuts, not enough to run through the threshing machines to separate them from the vines. Only the cattle would be spared the devastating effects of the drought; they would at least have hay. Maybe the rain would help the later runner-type peanuts.

He heard Doc, Grady, Rupert, and Donnell catching the mules. They, too, would help plow the peanut vines up out of the moist earth. Every advantage of the rain-softened soil had to be taken.

He heard Cooper whistling down the road to begin his feeding chores. Roller thought that "seeing a man about a dog" must have made him happy.

The kitchen light came on, and he knew Muh would be cooking breakfast soon. He was hungry. Sunday night supper was always Sunday dinner leftovers, and he had not eaten much supper. He hoped the hawk would be prompt.

As the sun made its glistening appearance, a blue jay flew overhead suddenly, and Roller snapped to attention; but it was not the hawk. Patiently and motionless he waited and waited and waited....

The hawk was hunting elsewhere, he assumed, but he would stick to his plan. He waited, and finally on the far side of the

27

orchard, down low under the canopy of the trees, he saw a flash of white. It was the hawk! But he had pitched, and Roller could not see him. He had made his perch on a low limb and was hidden in the sagging pecan foliage.

Roller sat there with his eyes strained to spot a flash of white, desperately searching every limb, but he could not find his taloned enemy. He could smell the bacon cooking and knew that Mr. B would be returning from the rolling store routine to the bighouse for breakfast at any moment. He would stick to his plan.

After his initial sighting of the hawk did not afford a clear shot, Roller at last leaned the rifle against the fence inside the hedgerow, climbed the fence, and quietly exited the blind through the opposite side. Never looking back, he crossed the cattle paddock up to the barn, went around the barn and the mill house, and circled back to the bighouse. Breakfast was ready, and so was he.

Muh had fixed some of Mr. B's cured bacon and had made grits, scrambled eggs, coffee and toast. Roller and Mr. B talked as they ate. Mama came in and joined them with her black coffee.

"I was proud of you yesterday, Roller," said Mr. B. "It's times like that, that make it easy to overlook the times when I'm not so proud."

"Yes, sir."

"Boy, that rain really turned a goat into a hero, didn't it? I mean the preacher."

Mama, who hadn't taken Mr. B's comment about the Baptists as being all that funny, interjected, "He was just doing what God had called him to do."

"Yes, ma'am, but he had gone to preaching doctrine instead of praying for rain."

"Well," Mama insisted, "he didn't mean any harm about it, and, besides, it did rain."

"Yes, ma'am." Roller and Mr. B smiled at each other.

As they finished breakfast, Mr. B reminded Roller of his chores, and Mama asked if he could go fishing with her that afternoon. Mama loved to fish, but Muh didn't want her fishing

by herself anymore and insisted that someone be with her. Bruh
and Sis went with her often, but they both had plans that day so
Roller would go with her. He loved to fish, but it irritated him
that Mama could catch more fish than he.

Roller hurried to finish his chores and returned to his plan.
He sneaked on tip toes through the little stretch of back yard
behind the bighouse to the smokehouse and peeped around the
corner to survey the pecan orchard. He stood there with only
the right side of his face and right eye exposed to make his search.
After a long reconnaissance of the orchard, Roller finally spotted
the much-hated thief-with-wings.

The hawk sailed from the far side of the orchard, high above
the tree tops toward the turkey pen, and descended to make a
perch in the top of a tree on the hedgerow side of the orchard.
The plan was working. Roller boldly stepped out into the back
yard and climbed the fence and walked directly toward the
hedgerow. He never looked up and could only assume that the
hawk was still there watching an unarmed boy walk through the
orchard. He hummed "Showers of Blessings," and, with both
arms swinging as if to show the hawk that he carried no weapon
and with blatant determination, he paralleled the fence row. When
he reached the blind, he sprang toward his ready rifle, shouldered it, wheeled around, and dropped to one knee in a single
fluid movement. Instinct directed the barrel tip back toward the
last spot that he had seen the hawk. The hawk was still there
but was lifting rapidly to make his escape. Roller aimed, allowed
for the upward flight of the hawk, compensated for the drop of
the bullet, and squeezed the hair trigger.

Cooper had finished milking and was on course to the
bighouse with a bucket of milk when he heard the crack of the
little .22 rifle, and a second later he heard the thud of its lead
projectile making its mark.

"That damn Roller," he said aloud laughing. "He done killed
that damn ass hawk." He sat the milk at the front door of the
bighouse and almost ran to the orchard. He found Roller kneel-
ing over the dead hawk. They both admired the bullet hole just
below the hawk's left eye, and then they saw another, older
wound. The hawk's left rear talon had been clipped clean about

a quarter of an inch below the cuticle. Roller had hit the hawk in his effort to save Donald Daisy, but the bullet had cut the talon and passed straight through the duck's backbone and through its heart.

They both took comfort that the hawk had not caused the death of the duck without sustaining some damage himself and, more important, that he was finally dead.

Each joyed in the triumphs of the other, and Cooper was proud that Roller had accomplished what he had set out to do. They smiled at each other. Roller and Cooper studied and were amazed at the long curved, needle-sharp talons. It was easy for them to see how small prey would be helpless in their grasp.

Cooper placed his rough, callused hand in Roller's curly, reddish brown hair, sort of shook his hand on his head, and said, "Boy, you won't do."

Roller looked up at Cooper and asked, "Cooper, do you have a fan?"

"A fan? Whatcha talking bout, boy?"

Roller picked up the hawk by the feet, threw him over his shoulder, and stood up. "You know, a fan to blow a breeze on you at night."

"Lawd, boy, what good would a fan do me? Ain't got no lectricity to turn it with."

"You mean you ain't got lights in your house?" Roller asked. He had never even thought about it, and, after thinking a minute, he answered for Cooper, "No, I don't guess you do, do you."

Cooper nodded. They walked back toward the bighouse, and Roller said, "Well we'll just have to get you some electricity won't we."

"Now, Roller," Cooper said, "you go talking bout putting wire in my house, and every nigger on the place be wanting the same ass thing, and that will be expansive."

"We'll see." answered Roller.

Cooper stopped off by the bighouse to be sure Muh had picked up the bucket of milk, and Roller proudly made his way to the store to show off his kill.

Every morning when all the early chores were done and all of the hands were in the field, the adult men of Vilulah would gather at the store to have a Coca-Cola and to chat. Of course, the rain was the topic of conversation this morning. Most of them agreed that the rain was too late to help anything, but it would make it easier to plow up peanuts and maybe help the pastures.

Roller walked in and plopped the hawk on top of the cold, pot-bellied stove that sat in the middle of the floor. The big yellow cat that always lay under the stove smelled the hawk and came out to investigate. He reared on his hind legs and reached for the hawk on top of the stove, and Roller shooed him and kicked at him with his bare foot.

The men stopped their exchange to admire the hawk and the head-shot that Roller had made. There was no teasing this time; the wounded talon was there for all to see, and the doubters of Roller's claim that he was shooting for the hawk's foot could no longer be questioned. They were impressed by Roller's determination and skill, and, like Cooper, they thought that Roller "wouldn't do."

Bruh came in the store and asked, "Did you kill em, Roller?"

"Sure did."

Bruh hurried over to the old stove, admiring the hawk, he suggested to Roller, "You ought to save the feet for a trophy."

"What are you talking about?" asked Roller.

"Come on. Let's go outside, and I'll show you," said Bruh as he hoisted the hawk and exited the store.

He was four years older than Roller and had been Roller's companion until a year or two ago. He had apparently reached the age when he wanted very little to do with a little brother, and sibling companions had become sibling competitors. It was unusual that he would have even been interested in Roller's kill.

They went out on the porch of the store, and Bruh pulled a little Case knife out of his pocket. He showed Roller how to remove the bird's foot at the knee. Bruh held the lower leg in his left hand and cut the skin around the knee joint just below the feather line of the bird's upper leg. Then he popped the knee backwards to loosen the cartilage, after which he cut the ligaments that held the knee in place.

When the leg bones were separated, he pulled the foot hard

31

away from the leg to expose the tendons that controlled the opening and closing of the taloned toes. As he pulled the foot, increasing tension on the tendons, the toes curled to make a tight fist. He exposed as much tendon as possible and then cut the tendons as close to the upper leg bone as possible. The foot snapped free of the upper leg and returned to its open position.

He repeated the process on the other foot and handed them to Roller. He went inside the store for a minute and returned with a short piece of black fishing line. Roller put the foot with the injured talon in his pocket and held the other foot for Bruh so that he could tie the black cord to the end of the exposed tendons. He then placed the palm of the open foot on Roller's arm while holding the lower leg of the foot in one hand and pulled the cord with the other. The toes contracted as if grasping prey, and the sharp talons bit into Roller's arm.

"Hey, Bruh," yelled Roller, "that hurts!"

Bruh relaxed the cord, handed it to Roller, and told him that he would have to flex the foot several times a day for the next few days or else it would dry and the tendons would stick to the inside of the leg and become functionless.

"Thanks, Bruh."

Roller had a new toy. He would later put the injured foot on the wall of his room along with other such trophies: a rattlesnake skin that Bruh had cured, a lizard skin from India that Sidney had given him, a New York Yankees pennant, pictures of White Hogan, and other relics that only he could appreciate. But the prized foot, with its pull-cord, he carried in his pocket. He called it "the claw."

Holding the leg of the claw in his left hand and the pull-cord with his right and in playful flight pretending to be a bald eagle, he would walk along and swoop his arms from above his head, down to the ground, and pick up sticks or whatever lay ahead of him that would fit the open foot.

When he found Cooper and showed it to him, he told him every detail of the hunt. He and Cooper spent the rest of the morning "checking fences."

That afternoon, as on many occasions, they dug fish bait for Mama under the eaves of the tin roof of the barn where the mule lot cornered with the main barn. The earth was always moist there, and the mule manure and urine that leached from the barn enriched the black humus and provided a perfect environment for the little red worms. Cooper called them "little red shit worms." As they turned the rich soil and picked up the worms, Cooper talked about the rain.

"Roller, it rained so hard yesterday that it washed a dog out from under my house that I didn't even know I had."

Roller laughed. "Yeah, and I heard that the water in the swimming hole was so muddy that dust was blowing off of it this morning."

Cooper nodded and grinned, but couldn't respond. They always competed to see who could spin the biggest yarn or exaggeration. He thought a minute and said, "Uh, huh, and Cemocheechobee Creek is running ass forward again this morning."

Confused, Roller asked, "Huh?"

"Yeah, weather's been so dry that the creek done started running backwards."

They laughed and gathered the can of worms and the fork and returned to the bighouse. Cooper whistled as they walked, knowing that Roller would be occupied fishing with Mama that afternoon, and he would be free to "check fences" alone; he needed a nap after his "seeing about a dawg" on Sunday.

Annie Jenny was the cook. She had been at home in the bighouse kitchen for many years, and her loyalty and dedication to the family had gone beyond the normal employee/employer relationship. She had become family. Though not married, she lived with Cooper and walked down to the bighouse every morning about 9:00 to clean the breakfast dishes and prepare a delicious dinner—the noontime meal. After she had cleaned up the dinner dishes, she would sit out in the shady yard of the bighouse in one of several old wooden ladder-back chairs that she, Muh, Mama, and Sis sat in when shelling peas, grating corn, or working other vegetables.

Annie Jenny enjoyed a dip of Sweet Dental snuff as Cooper and Roller approached the yard. Her big buttocks spilled over each edge of the chair seat, and her chubby legs were so short that her fat, bare feet barely touched the ground. She wore an old, faded, cotton smock-dress and an ever-present bandanna turban on her head. Her round, chocolate face framed big brown eyes and a pearly smile; she looked like Aunt Jemima on the grits boxes that stocked the shelves at the store. Mr. B said that one day he would grind grits at the mill and have her picture on the box and call them Annie Jenny Grits.

"You got it gapped open, ain't you Jenny?" grinned Cooper.

Roller was not sure what Cooper was talking about until Annie Jenny closed her legs together, spit, and said, "You hush your mouth nigger, talking like that in front of that boy. Roller, don't pay him no mind."

As she closed her legs, her lap narrowed, and her little tin can of snuff fell to the ground. Roller pulled the claw out of his pocket, dive bombed the can, grasped it with the claw (manipulated by the string), flew it above her lap, and dropped it.

"Lawd God! Roller, what's that?" she asked.

"It's the claw off the hawk that I killed."

"That thing is sharp. Gonna get you in trouble, too, if you ain't careful."

"That reminds me, Cooper," said Roller. "You know that corn cob dart that you made me?"

Cooper nodded, remembering sticking two chicken feathers in the soft core of one end of a corn cob and a sharpened nail with its head ground off in the other. The dart, with its feathered stabilizers and aerodynamics, was accurate but had limited range.

"Well, I want you to help me build a spear, something bigger than the dart. I want to kill that rabbit in the cemetery with it; wouldn't be a challenge to shoot him with the .22, and Muh took my dart away from me when I threw it at Bruh for running through my corn patch on his bicycle."

Roller was referring to two little short rows of corn that he had planted across the road near an old well where Vilulah school used to be. He had pulled water with the rope and bucket out of the well, watered the corn all summer, and, when it neared maturity and was almost ready to eat, Bruh had ridden his bicycle between the two rows, breaking most of it off near the ground at the brace roots. Roller had his dart in his pocket, and with abandonment of judgement or forethought, he had hurled it toward Bruh as he peddled toward his escape. It was nowhere near a hit, but Bruh told Muh, and she had railed Roller. He was punished, and the dart had been taken and destroyed.

"I don't know, "Cooper replied. "I might get in trouble cause you might get in trouble."

"Aw, Cooper, I just want to kill that rabbit. Wouldn't you like to have him for supper?"

"I'll see bout it," said Cooper, meaning he would think it over. "But if I do...." He was interrupted. Mama came out of the bighouse in preparation for their fishing trip. She had on her dungaree jeans covered by a thin, faded skirt, high topped shoes, and a long-sleeved, blue chambray cotton shirt. Her "tackle box" was a homemade bag of mattress ticking material with a shoulder strap that carried extra hooks, line, bottle corks, a cord fish-stringer, lead, and a jar of MacAboy snuff.

"Where we going, Mama? I hear the creek is running forward."

"What do you mean, running forward?" asked Mama.

"Never mind."

"I wish we could go down to Notchaway Creek; them red bellies will be biting, but that's a long way so, I think we'll go to the 'cat-hole.'"

The "cat hole" (populated with catfish, hence the reason for the name) was a beaver pond on Cemocheechobee Creek. The beavers had damned a tributary to the creek, but the high water did not affect the little pond.

When Mama said "cat-hole," a mental revelation took place in Roller's head. *What an idea! Why haven't I already thought of it?* "Cooper, I know how to...." Roller caught himself; he couldn't reveal his sudden inspiration concerning Ollie in front of anyone other than Cooper. "Uh, uh, how to make that spear that I was telling you about."

Uncle George had temporarily closed and locked the big wooden front door of the store and cranked up the old Chevrolet pickup. He drove to the shade of the pecan tree in front of the bighouse and waited for Cooper and Roller to load the poles and bait in the cargo body. They loaded the gear, and Mama and Roller climbed in the cab, Roller in the middle and Mama by the window.

"Afternoon, George."

"Afternoon, Mrs. Lanier," Uncle George replied. Almost all non-family called her by her married name. She was a widow. Her husband had been killed and robbed by a black turpentine worker while she was pregnant with Muh. Roller had heard the old stories how the white men of the turpentine plantations had hanged four black workers to be sure they got the right one.

"Cooper, I'll be back in time to help with the cotton weighing," Roller yelled.

"Okay," replied Cooper.

Uncle George drove them up to where the little woods road ended. They had to walk the rest of the way, about two hundred yards, to the quiet, still-water pond.

"I'll be back about 6:00 and blow the horn for you."

"That's fine, George. Tell them to get the grease hot."

"Okay." He drove away.

Sometimes Roller had ideas that he wished he didn't. They would saturate his mind until he could think of nothing else. They fished, and Mama was pleased with their catch, but Roller was too busy thinking.... *Cat-hole*.

CHAPTER 5
THE ROAD

Roller wheeled his bicycle toward the tree, locked the brakes, and slid sort of sideways up to its huge trunk. He was pretending that he had just committed a most daring heist of a Wells Fargo gold shipment in an old cowboy western and was in escape to the sitting place to hole up awhile for things to cool off. As was typical, he was totally engrossed in the imaginary escapade.

As he quickly dismounted his two-wheeled steed and leaned it against the tree, he hurriedly sought refuge in the limbs and greenery of the old post oak. In an effort to speed his concealment, he jumped for the brace; his hands made the top side of the old wooden two-by-six, and his fingers locked to its surface. He dangled there in total surprise and shock that he had finally made the jump that had previously eluded his many efforts.

He could savor his accomplishment only for a few seconds; his fingers were tiring, and he had to adjust his grip. He had gripped the brace with both hands on the same side. As he snapped his hands to reaffirm his grip, his right hand sustained his weight while instantly his left hand released and came under the brace and back to the top. He could now hand-over-hand walk his hanging torso toward the cemetery corner post.

He swung his feet up to the top of the fence and pulled with his strong young arms, pulled his feet upward, arched his back, and pivoted to stand on top of the fence. Hurriedly, he proceeded with his climb and made the sitting place just as the imaginary sheriff and posse passed beneath the limbs of the tree.

Slowly returning to reality, he rested in the sitting place and savored his achievement of jumping to reach the brace; no longer would he be the only one who could not reach it. It had been more than two weeks since he had claimed temporary residence in the tree. A lot had happened in the past few days, and Roller sat there on the hot mid-August, dog day morning reflecting on things that he had done since he had last visited his herbaceous asylum; more importantly, he thought about things that he had not done.

On Monday before last, he and Mama had gone fishing at the cat-hole and had caught enough fish for lunch on Tuesday. Tuesday morning, however, Roller awoke with a severe case of tonsillitis and had spent the next five days inside, mostly in bed. He had never been so sick! His throat was sore and irritated, and he seemed to hurt all over; he could only eat soup and ice cream. He drank cold tea and Coca-Colas and took medicine and aspirin. Muh took him to Coleman to Dr. Harper. Dr. Harper was a gentle and caring old white-haired man who reluctantly gave shots to children, but penicillin would help and Roller's right butt cheek was still sore from the shot. Mama put a mustard poultice on his neck and took credit for his recovery; she blamed dog days for anything that healed slowly.

It was bad that he felt so terrible, but losing a week of summer vacation, to Roller, was a catastrophe. When he was unable to be outside and a part of the activities of the farm and store, he was unhappy. Cooper had come to see him everyday and had tried to make him feel better by keeping him current on all the chores, the progress of the harvest, and all the news about the Vilulah Negro population. He told Roller that Punto's wife, Minnie Bell, had her baby—a boy. They named him Punto, Jr. He told him about Rupert's daughter, Brenda Joyce (who had been born just a few days after Roller), cutting her foot on a Vienna sausage can. Roller could sympathize with her as he had cut his foot on one of the same kind.

Canned Vienna sausage came with a little metal key attached to the top of the can that, when pried and detached, was used to open it. The can had a little metal tab that, when stuck through the slot in the key and the key twisted around as if winding a clock, would remove a narrow strip of the tin all of the way around the can, exposing the contents in one of two little half-cans created by the process. Both little half-cans had razor sharp edges around the open circumference, and, if tossed aside, they would generally land open end up and await an unaware foot or vehicle tire. They could be very dangerous and produced a painful circular cut that was slow to heal.

Roller's throat hurt, his butt hurt, and then his foot hurt after hearing about Brenda Joy's accident.

Cooper had tried to cheer Roller, but every time he said something that made Roller laugh, it made his throat hurt worse, so they agreed that Cooper would just talk and Roller would listen without response.

Roller did try to tell Cooper how to make the spear that he wanted but was unable to make him understand. He would have to wait until he got well enough to show him what he had in mind. He listened to the radio, played with the claw, and was generally miserable, but after almost a week of convalescence he was well enough to go outside. It was like getting out of school for the summer all over again. He had a lot of catching up to do, and he rejoiced that he was finally free to be a part of things again. Muh and Mama and Annie Jenny also rejoiced that he was able to get out and relieve them of their nursing duties, for he was not a good patient.

As he sat there in the sitting place thinking about the past two weeks, the sight of the rabbit interrupted his thoughts. His spear would be his next weapon, and he would soon make another attempt at bagging the rabbit with a hand-thrown projectile.

Then, just as he began to sink into thought again—about Virginia Hart—he saw from his elevated hide-out a yellow truck atop the hill in front of Mrs. Lucille's. The cows had trampled the corn, and he could see the Ft. Gaines road that ran at its edge.

Two men were walking along the road carrying long sticks painted orange and white in alternating bands. The men walked along, stopping periodically to look back toward the top of the hill. Each took his turn to set one end of the stick on the ground and hold it vertically for a few minutes. After awhile a third man came over the hill carrying what Roller thought was a three-legged telescope. The third man stood his instrument on its three legs, made a few adjustments, and looked through the telescope at the other two men carrying the orange-and-white sticks. He waved his arms, and the stick men walked a little further, stood their sticks on their ends; again, the third man looked at them in the telescope. This process continued down the hill, around the curve, and up toward Vilulah Church.

Roller was completely baffled by the activity of these three strangers on his road. Deliberately and methodically they were making their way toward his tree. Finally, the third man stood his three-legged telescope near the right front corner of the Church, and the two stick-toting men walked toward the tree, stopping randomly to stand the orange-and-white sticks vertically. The lead stick-toter eventually stood directly beneath Roller, holding his stick in front of the tree. He looked back toward the focusing telescope operator and talked aloud to himself.

"This damn tree's gonna be in the way."

"In the way of what?" inquired Roller.

The stick-toter was so startled by Roller's voice that he dropped the stick, wheeled around, and bolted away from the cemetery. He caught himself, stopped, looked up the tree to where the inquiry had originated, and said, "Some-damn-body's in that tree. Who is that? Where are you?"

"It's me," said Roller. "And, I'm right here."

The man spotted Roller. "Boy, you scared the shit outa me! I ain't much on cemeteries noway."

"In the way of what?" Roller insisted.

"What's in the way of what?" asked the man.

"This damn tree is going to be in the way of what?"

"Oh...oh...the tree...uh...is gonna be in the way of the road," stammered the man.

"What road?"

"This road. They're gonna pave it, Son."

The second stick-toter walked up. "What's the matter with you, Jake?"

"This here boy scared the daylights outa me. I thought he was a haint."

"Why is this tree in the way of the road if all they gonna do is pave it?" asked Roller as he made his way down out of the tree.

"Cause, little man," said the second stick-toter, "it's right by the road, and they ain't gonna let a tree stand on the right-of-way of a paved road."

"What's a right-of-way?" asked Roller, swinging down from the brace.

"Well, Son, it's the width of the road plus a little on each side for the ditches," said the first man, trying to explain it in terms Roller would understand.

"Well, ain't no ditch on this side," said Roller.

The men looked at each other in bewilderment. The third man watched the confrontation through his telescope and finally yelled, "Hey, we got work to do."

"I ain't your son, and ya'll better stand your sticks up over that way some," Roller pointed to the far side of the road, "cause this tree ain't been in the right-of-way of nothing for a long time, and it ain't doing nothing no different now than it always did."

"Son, I mean, young man, what is your name?"

"They call me Roller."

"Well, Roller, you'd better talk to that man back there on the transit. He's the engineer on this job."

As the two men shouldered their sticks and walked off up the road toward Coleman, Roller went around the tree, straddled his bike, and peddled toward the third man.

The engineer was busy peeping through the transit and waving signals to the two stick men. Roller coasted up close to him.

"I bet you couldn't do that though, could you, mister?" asked Roller.

"Do what?" chuckled the puzzled man.

"Let me look through that telescope. Could you?"

"Well, I might could," said the man. "They got any cold Coca-Cola's up there at that store?"

"Yes, sir! You got a nickel?"

"Got a dime. You want to go get us one?"

"You mean me and you?"

"Yep," said the man as he pitched Roller the dime.

Roller caught the dime. "Mister, my name is Roller. What's yours?"

"My name is Roy," the man replied. "Glad to meet you,

41

Roller."

"Well, Mr. Roy, could you let me look through your telescope before you move it again; I need to look at something. Glad to meet you too."

Roy moved from behind the instrument and beckoned Roller toward him. "Yeah, come on."

Roller stood on tiptoe and placed his right eye against the peephole. The instrument was aimed straight up the road toward Coleman. The sight path intersected the road bed about midway the little hill, a little south of Mr. Lawson's house.

"I don't see my tree, " Roller said.

Roller pivoted the tip of the scope to his right while keeping his eye glued to the peephole. It seemed to him a long leftward travel of the sight path till he was able to see the tree. "Yeah, there it is. Seems to be plenty of room there without messing with my tree, don't you think?"

"Hum...I don't know," Roy responded.

Roller mounted his bike, stood hard on the right peddle to make the rear wheel spin on the loose gravel of the church yard, and sped off toward the store. "I'll be back with your Coke dreckly."

"That's your tree, huh, Roller?" Roy yelled.

"Yep," Roller answered over his shoulder.

Roller peddled fast to the store, and as he approached the road between the cemetery and the store he met Cooper, who was checking on his whereabouts.

"Where you been, Roller?" Cooper asked.

"I been looking through a telescope; right now, I gotta make a delivery."

"Looking through a what?"

"A telescope. That man down there is engineering paving the road, and I'm gonna make me some money off of him." Roller ran inside the store and got a cold Coca-Cola.

Bottled beverages were kept cool in a drink box that sat just inside and to the right of the front door. Cold water almost completely submerged the upright bottles. Roller noticed that he needed to add more Cokes to the box before he was reminded by Uncle George. He dried the bottle with the towel that hung on

42

the wall above the box and pried off the little metal cap with the opener that was permanently mounted on the wall at the end of the box.

"Give me a nickel change, Uncle George," shouted Roller.

"For what?" George asked softly from behind the main counter.

Roller was irritated at Uncle George for not knowing that he was in a hurry and ran quickly back to the main counter.

"Here's a dime for this Coke," Roller spat. "Give me a nickel change."

Uncle George was a big-framed, kind-hearted old man with a perpetual two-day-old white beard. He loved Roller as the son that he never had, and he respected Roller's accomplishments and maturity beyond his age but was often impatient with Roller and vice versa. Roller considered Uncle George to be too slow, but failed to consider the sixty years difference in their ages. Uncle George considered Roller to be too rambunctious, but also failed to consider that Roller's active age and personality were so far removed from his own. All in all though, they had a good relationship and mutual understanding of each other and respected the needs of each other.

Uncle George peered at Roller through wire-rimmed glasses and pitched a nickel to the counter surface. Roller put the nickel change in his pocket and ran out to make his delivery. Mr. Roy had picked up his three-legged telescope, folded the legs together, shouldered it, and was walking up to the porch of the store as Roller flung open the screen door and let it slam just as Uncle George shouted, "Don't slam that door, Roller!" Too late. It slammed. Softer, he continued, "Please, dammit."

Mr. Roy took the Coke from Roller and leaned his instrument against the gas pump that stood there at the front edge of the porch. His clothes were wet with perspiration, and his face was flushed from the heat. He stood there a moment relishing the shade of the porch and the cool drink.

Cooper stood at the side of the porch, knowing that Roller was up to something and watched as the engineer and Roller exchanged conversation.

"Mr. Roy, this gas pump ain't no farther from the road than

that tree, is it?"

"Hum, I don't know, Roller." He looked at the tree and back at the gas pump. "We'll measure it when I cool off a bit."

"Can me and Cooper measure it with your tape measure?"

"Well, you have to know how to measure it. You measure twenty feet from the center of the road."

"How do you know what the center of the road is?" asked Roller.

"Well, normally you measure from the center of the ditch on one side to the center of the ditch on the other side and divide the distance by two to get the center of the road. But, this ain't normal cause there's not a ditch on this side, and you got that Carnegie Road intersection right here in front of the store. It's gonna take some deciphering."

"Well, you rest a spell, and I'll step it off," Roller said. He backed up to the gas pump with his heels flush against its base. "Now, you tell me when you think I'm at the center of the road."

He stepped those giant steps like when playing "May I?" and counted, "One, two, three, four, five, six, seven...."

"Whoa!" said Mr. Roy. "That's about center."

"Seven steps," Roller said as he ran to the trunk of the tree, backed up to it, placed his heels at its base, and walked again.

"One, two, three, four, five, six...."

"Whoa!" said Mr. Roy. "That's about center."

Roller dropped his head and ambled back to the porch. He looked at Cooper and made a familiar tight-lipped face and in disgust said, "Six steps."

Cooper was not sure what all this measuring was about or what it had to do with making money off of this man, but he knew Roller was busy with something and that it must be important to him.

"Ain't but a step closer. That ain't in the way of nothing, is it Mr. Roy?"

Roy had rested a bit; he stood and sort of scanned the area in thought and finally spoke. "I think I finally got this figured out. You don't want that tree to be in the way of paving this road cause you're afraid that we'll cut it down. Ain't that right?"

Roller nodded.

44

"And you like to climb that tree, and you don't want it bothered."

Again, Roller nodded.

"Well, all I know is our governor, Mr. Herman Talmadge, sent me orders to secure a forty-foot right-of-way for this road, and I'm here today surveying that right-of-way. Now when I get through plotting this road on paper and finish my drawing, I'll tell you about your tree." He handed Roller the empty Coke bottle and continued. "But right now, I got work to do."

"Well, Mr. Roy...." Roller started but paused for fear of irritating him.

"Yeah?"

"Mr. Roy, thanks for the nickel. Uh, you reckon I could get a job when ya'll start on this road?"

Roy liked Roller already. He had a son, too, who liked to climb trees, and he admired Roller for his manners and his ambition.

"A job? You're mighty young to be working on a road, ain't you? What you gone do with the money that you make?"

"Well, I want to buy something, but I can't tell nobody what it is yet." Roller replied.

"Well, I gotta go, Roller. I'll see you in a few days." Roy picked up the three-legged telescope and followed the two stick-toters on up the road.

Roller sat down on an empty drink bottle crate and watched the three men work their way up the hill toward Mr. Lawson's house. He was busy in thought when Cooper, who had put one foot up on the porch floor and had leaned over, propping on his arms that were crossed and resting on his knee, interrupted.

"Roller, you better forget that ass road and your tree, and let's go. Bruh been looking for you. Said me and you and him gotta go down to Mr. Sammy's and get some pears for Muh."

"I ain't studying no pears. I ain't through doing what I was doing." Roller headed for the tree.

"All right, Roller, you gonna get in trouble! You and Bruh gonna get into it again, and you know Muh done said that if she caught ya'll fighting again that she was gonna get in the fight with ya'll."

"Listen, Cooper, you see that brace on that tree?" Roller pointed to the brace. "Well, I jumped up to it this morning, so if Bruh wants to fight, just let him come on; I'm just as big as he is now."

Cooper was referring to the fight that had occurred in the store on Saturday morning. Bruh and Roller had been stocking shelves and preparing the store for the Saturday afternoon shoppers when Bruh, pretending to be Rocky Marciano, the reigning heavyweight champion, started bobbing and weaving and throwing mock punches at Roller. Roller was sweeping the floor. He ignored Bruh and was busy cleaning under and around the old wood heater that sat in the middle of the floor. Bruh bounced up to Roller, crouched, and in a classic boxer's stance—with fists up and ready—threw a left jab at Roller and unintentionally caught him solidly on the left shoulder, sending him falling off balance into the stovepipe that exhausted smoke from the old wood heater. The pipe was jointed in about three-foot sections. They separated at the joints, and the whole tube of joints fell like stacked-up stove wood. A cloud of smoke and soot that lined the pipes enveloped Roller and blackened him all over and a considerable diameter of the floor as well. Uncle George cursed and had a mild stroke as the black cloud of soot settled to the floor.

Roller maintained his footing but blindly stumbled out of the side door of the store just as Mr. Ollie rounded the rear corner and was even with the side door.

Roller was black with soot—only his eyes had been spared. His curly hair was now black. His hands and arms, even his bare feet, were black with soot.

At first Ollie thought that some drunk Negro had stumbled out the door and was coming for him. He dodged the blinded blackfaced figure and almost broke and ran, but caught himself as he recognized Roller's green eyes peeping from his black face.

Ollie thought that Roller was up to one of his tricks and scolded him. "I knew it was you all the time, Roller. You ain't fooled me." Then, as Ollie looked through the door and saw the stovepipe sections and soot all over the floor, he realized what had happened—that Roller had been the victim of an accident or something—and he immediately seized the opportunity to tease Roller. He saw that he had Roller in a situation where he was not likely to have prepared a rebuttal.

Ollie laughed. "Roller, I thought you were that oldest boy of Rupert's."

Roller had one personality when he thought too much, but an entirely different personality when emotion made the thought process impossible. His temper was quick and consumed his controlled actions as though it was fuel for a raging flame. Anger enveloped him like the cloud of soot, and, when the air cleared, he was a wild, belligerent stampede of reckless abandon.

Ripping off his soot-covered, short-sleeve, cotton shirt, he threw it square in Ollie's face and charged back through the side door. Bruh was very familiar with what he saw in Roller's expression. He wanted to continue laughing, but knew all too well that he was about to have his hands full.

Roller knew that Bruh would try to escape his assault via the front door, so he jumped the fallen pipes, cut to his right through the open space behind the wood heater, and tackled Bruh as he darted for the exit.

Together they rolled and wrestled, Bruh on top awhile, then Roller. Finally, Uncle George was able to separate them before a clear decision of the winner could be established. They were both now covered with soot. The store was a total wreck.

Just as Bruh saw an avenue for escape through the front door and just as Uncle George was about to lose his grip on Roller, Muh opened the screen door to come inside. Every muscle in the trio relaxed; silence exploded and time stood staunch still while Muh studied the scene. Finally, after what seemed at least thirty minutes, she calmly spoke.

"My God, how on earth did White Hogan get in this store? Roller, did you ride him in here? Ben, did you? I know somebody brought him in here, cause there's just no way that ya'll could have made this big of a mess without the help of a bull. It sure is sad that White Hogan can't clean up behind himself, so I suggest ya'll do it for him, and I also suggest that you do it right this very minute. And, by the way, the next time there's a fight,

I'm gonna be the referee. Do you hear me?"

In unison all three tried to explain, "Muh, I can tell you...."
Muh was walking out the door, and everyone knew that she
wanted no explanation. She wanted action!

Roller looked at Bruh as if to say with his eyes, "This ain't
the end of this." Bruh knew what his eyes were saying. They
both looked around at the mess and caught a subtle grin on Uncle
George's face. He laughed softly and said, "Boys, we got to get
to work." Then he burst out in laughter as Bruh began to laugh
and finally Roller joined in the humor of the whole episode and
laughed uncontrollably. When Ollie saw that it was okay to
laugh, he, too, joined in, and they all cleaned up the store.

"Now, Cooper, I'm fixing to climb back up in that tree for a
little while cause those road-paving men came along and dis-
turbed me. If Bruh comes looking for me, you tell him that I
said that them pears ain't going nowhere for a little while, and I
ain't either."

Cooper nodded and said nothing. He knew when not to argue with Roller. He knew that if left alone a while, Roller would
come around and do his share of any job. That if he was allowed
to take a task in his own time and at his own pace, he would
usually do it better and quicker than even some adults.

Roller didn't feel like jumping for the brace. He climbed
the tree in his conventional manner and returned to the sitting
place. His thoughts immediately returned to the potential problem of the road right-of-way and where his tree stood both in
reality and in the plans for a road. Why would Governor
Talmadge do this to him? Mr. B had campaigned for him vigor-
ously, and he planned to support Mr. Talmadge in his bid for
election to the U.S. Senate. Surely Mr. Roy would help him and
move the road over at least one step.

Roller's hideaway was being threatened by progress, by
change, by modernization. Maybe Cooper was right when he
said, "Peoples getting too use to having too much." Maybe one
day we will be spoiled by convenience and not know how to provide for ourselves. Maybe mules are better than tractors. Maybe
people are crazy nowadays cause they cook and eat outside and

take a dump inside.

Roller was confused by all the talk of things to come; he understood the past and the present and didn't like to think of the future. Everytime he thought of the future, he thought of starting back to school and being in Miss E. Holley's fifth grade class. Everybody hated and feared Miss E.; she was so strict. Bruh and Sis and every other person that had been in her class had told Roller about how she demanded perfection.

He would not think of that now. He would think about Virginia Hart. Would he ever see her again? When would she return from Atlanta to visit her Aunt Charlotte again? How old was she? Eighteen? No, at least twenty. Did she like him? Did she have a boy friend?

Something caught Roller's attention as he sat there in thought. Doc had hitched Maude and Nellie to a wagon loaded tall with cotton and was leaving for the gin. The gin was about two miles down past Vilulah and was a fascinating place to spend the normal two to three hours' time that it took to wait your turn at the suck pipe to have your load of cotton ginned. Doc talked to the team as he drove them up the little hill between the store and the cemetery. They passed close to the trunk of the tree, and Roller again acted without thinking. He stood on the sitting place, climbed out to his left, and jumped onto the wagon as it passed beneath him. Doc urged the mules along from the front of the wagon unaware that Roller had joined him. Roller snuggled down in the white fluffy cotton and continued his thoughts about Virginia Hart.

CHAPTER 6
THE STROKE

Sidney Saunders visited the store almost every day. He was a jack-of-all-trades, and people who needed a plumbing repair, a small carpenter job, or an electrical repair would leave a message for him at the store. He didn't tease Roller like the other men of Vilulah. In fact, he taught Roller how to shoot and how to think. He always told Roller that the Lord gave everybody the ability to think, and that a God-given talent left unused was a sin. He taught Roller how to think a job before doing a job, showed him how to minimize manual labor by maximizing mental labor, and constantly reminded Roller that trouble found those who didn't think. Roller considered him a very intelligent man. He knew, it seemed, a little bit about everything.

Sidney had one major problem—he was an alcoholic and spent more drunk days than he did sober days. He was a veteran of World War II, and had several very bad war experiences. If he ever mentioned to Roller something that had happened to him or one of his buddies during the war, a three- or four-day drunk would ensue.

Roller loved to hear all the stories about Normandy Beach, about Versailles, and about Sidney's fighting in the vineyard valleys of Italy, but he soon realized that reliving those experiences made Sidney seek refuge and solace in alcohol of any source. Roller made it a point not to let him get started on one of his war stories because Mr. B had given strict orders not to sell Sidney anything with even the slightest alcohol content—Vitalis hair tonic, Old Spice After Shave, shoe polish, Hadacol Tonic, vanilla flavoring, Cheracol Cough Syrup, or any other concoction with an alcohol base. When no one would sell it to him, he would try to catch a busy clerk looking the other way and steal the forbidden liquid. Finally, all products with any alcohol content were hidden out of view behind and down under the main counter.

Sidney came in the store that morning complaining about the heat and the summer cold he had caught. He wanted some Cheracol Cough Syrup to cut the phlegm out of his throat—knowing, of course, that no one would sell him any and that it wasn't stocked on the shelves anymore, but he asked for it anyway.

Roller was busy filling the drink box and had placed all of cold drinks at one end of the box so that they would not be mixed with the hot ones. Sidney got a cold Coke out of the box and spoke to Roller.

"Roller, I hear you got in big trouble for going to the gin without telling anybody."

"Yes, sir."

"I done told you about doing things without thinking about the consequences, haven't I?"

"Yes, sir."

"Well, what kind of punishment did you get?"

"I've got to work in the store, help with cotton weighing everyday, including Saturday, help sharpen the mill rocks when they pull them up tomorrow, and I can't go fishing or hunting or swimming until after school starts."

"Dawg, Roller," exclaimed Sidney. "I bet you'll think next time won't you?"

"Well, I'll tell you, Sidney," Roller said quietly so no one else would hear. "I'da had to do all that work anyway, and the fish don't bite during dog days, and hunting season ain't in yet, so all I'm really gonna miss is swimming. Course, if Virginia Hart comes back to Miss Charlotte's, I might just have to slip off again."

Sidney had done some work for Miss Charlotte and had seen Virginia a time or two. "She's strong as new rope, ain't she Roller?"

"I don't know how strong she is, but she sure is easy to look at," said Roller. "Say, you mind stepping out here on the porch with me a minute?"

"Naw, what is it?" They walked outside to find privacy

51

from Uncle George and Mr. Lawson, who were having their own conversation at the main counter about the road paving.

"Sidney, I ain't never seen nothing to beat it."

"What you talking bout, Roller?"

"Well," Roller looked around to be sure they were alone, "you won't tell nobody will you?"

"Now, Roller, you know that I don't tell our secrets."

"Well, I ain't been able to think of nothing else since it happened."

"Roller, what in hell are you talking about?" asked Sidney impatiently.

"Virginia Hart.... I saw her without no clothes on!" Roller declared.

Then Sidney looked around to be sure they were alone and quieted his voice. "Roller, you don't mean it.... How? You been looking through the peep hole at Miss Charlotte's bath house ain't you?"

"No, sir, she uh...." Ollie walked around the corner, and Roller cut his sentence at mid-syllable.

"Morning," Ollie nodded.

"Morning, Ollie," said Sidney.

"Morning," said Roller.

"Roller, you kinda got in trouble, didn't you? You sho had everybody looking' for you the other day. What made you want to leave without telling nobody?"

"I don't know. I just wasn't thinking I guess," answered Roller.

"Well, I understand you gonna help us sharpen the rocks tomorrow."

"Yes, sir."

"It's gonna be a hot one," declared Ollie.

"Yes, sir. Ya'll got the rocks up yet?"

"We're working on it," said Ollie. "We'll be ready."

"So will I."

Ollie went into the store, and Roller waited for the big yellow tom cat to come running out. Cats hated Ollie and vice versa, and every time Ollie went in the store, Tom went out. He either went out the side door or ran into the front screen door to bump it open for escape. As he ran to the front door, Roller opened it for him, and he continued his escape around to the rear of the store. He would return when Ollie went back to the mill.

Mr. Lawson had a very unique and unmistakable laugh. It was a long, high-pitched cackle that not only was laughter but produced laughter. When he laughed, everyone laughed, and he laughed at almost anything—especially when that cat skiddaddled in fear of Ollie. His laugh pierced the air, and everyone within hearing also chuckled.

Roller and Sidney looked around so as to continue the conversation about Virginia, but Mr. B had topped the hill down the Bethel Road, and was bringing the old 1949 Dodge pickup to a stop at the intersection.

"I'll have to tell you about it some other time, Sidney. Don't tell anybody what I told you."

"I won't."

Mr. B jumped out of the old truck, and as usual he was in a hurry. The terrible drought and the resulting poor crop were taking their toll on him. The ground had gotten hard again, and plowing up peanuts was next to impossible. They were barely worth the trouble of harvest.

"Roller, I need for you to find Cooper and two pitch forks. I've got something that I need for ya'll to do. Morning, Sidney."

"Morning, Mr. Ben."

"Yes, sir," responded Roller, running from the porch toward the barn. He knew that Cooper would be there somewhere. As he ran by the mill house—and even though he knew Ollie was in the store—his eyes were drawn to the knot hole, as always.

Mr. B and Sidney stood there on the porch talking. "Sidney, that boy.... I just don't know."

"Oh, he's a dirt road sport, sure enough, but he'll be all right. He'll make you real proud one of these days."

"Oh, he makes me proud a lot now. He just gets into so much mischief and does things without thinking sometimes. Then at other times, he does things with too much thinking." They both laughed.

"Yeah," Sidney agreed. "But he's got a good head on his shoulders, and he'll do anything to help anybody who needs help.

He gets that after you, Ben. He's a chip off the ole block in a lot of respects."

Mr. B went inside to get a cold drink, and as he entered the door he turned back to Sidney and said, "I guess I'm getting too old, but it sure does seem like we got a long row to hoe with Roller."

"He'll do fine. Just remember he ain't but twelve years old." Sidney followed Mr. B inside. "I won't ever forget the day he was born. That July 4, I had just come home from the war all shot-up and bandaged from head to toe when I heard about it, and I thought to myself, 'I bet that's gonna be a firecracker boy.' And sho nuff, he is."

Roller found Cooper at the little blacksmith room at the barn working religiously on something that he recognized as the spear that he had described to Cooper.

"What you doing Cooper?" asked Roller.

"I'm working on your confound spear that I ain't got no business doing," Cooper answered.

"Well, that'll have to wait. Daddy wants me and you to come go with him and bring two pitchforks."

"I need to talk to him anyway bout that litter of Duroc pigs. Let's go." Cooper responded.

They found two hay forks and made a fast pace around to the front to wait for Mr. B to come out. Cooper loaded the forks in the body of the truck and took a seat on the tailgate that was let down and suspended by a chain on each side. Roller climbed in the cab with Mr. B, and he drove them to the peanut field to gather the scattered peanut vines at the ends of the rows, vines that would be missed by the thrashing machine if not picked up with forks and made a part of the main windrows.

Roller talked as they rode. "Daddy, you reckon Governor Talmadge would do us a favor?"

"Like what, Son?"

"Well, those surveying men told me that my tree was in the way of them paving the road, and I think we ought to talk to him about it."

"Roller, I got too much to think about right now, but we'll see about it later."

"Yes, sir."

When they reached the field and Mr. B had given them their instructions, Cooper asked, "Mr. B, can I talk to you a minute bout that litter of Duroc pigs?"

"Yeah, Cooper. What is it?"

"Well, suh, they bout ready to cut, and I just wanted to remind you, but you know they ain't but two boar pigs in that litter, and I think either one would make a fine stock hog; maybe we ought to let'm grow some more, and see how they turn out."

"That's fine, Cooper. I want you to pay special attention to them cause I'm real busy right now. I sure do want that biggest one for breeding stock; he really looks good to me."

"Yas, suh."

Mr. B left the field, again in a hurry. Punto and Willie were plowing up the should-be crop of peanuts. Nuts were so sparse on the vines that it made Roller feel guilty if he stooped down to pick a few to eat. It reminded him of the story going around about a neighboring farmer who was thrashing peanuts.

The threshing machine stripped the peanuts from the vines, separated them from the dirt and trash, and a pneumatic system blew them into burlap bags. The bagging mechanism was simply a double spout valve on which a burlap bag was hung on each spout. When one bag was filled, a directional valve was manually tripped to direct the nuts into the awaiting other empty bag. Another empty bag would replace the full one and await the filling of the other bag. The bagging apparatus and the operator were located on a little platform that was a part of the moving machinery. In good peanuts, one man would have to work constantly and strenuously to keep up with the flow of peanuts.

The story going around was that one of Mr. Fendley's Negro laborers that rode the bagging platform of the thresher had gone to sleep between bags and, when confronted by Mr. Fendley concerning his lackadaisical performance, had responded, "Yas, suh, Mr. Fendley." He acted busy and pointed to the bags. "I'm watching 'em .... Yas, suh, here come one right now!"

The story, for area farmers, had been a source of laughter in an otherwise dismal time. Smiles were as scarce as the rain.

Roller wanted to tell Cooper about Virginia and what he had seen, but telling a colored man about a naked white woman was something that even a youthful, naive Roller would never do. He did make conversation as they worked, however.

"Cooper, you ever seen a naked woman?"

"Boy, you ax too many questions. What you wanta know for?"

"I don't know. I was just asking."

Cooper nodded, and after a while, wiping his sweaty brow, he responded. "I mighta seen one a two."

"Did you like what you saw?"

"Well...yeah...but some I liked better than others."

Roller had been intrigued by this topic for several days, and now that he was talking about it with somebody he was increasingly inquisitive and curious. "Which ones did you like the best?" He stood propped on the fork, looking toward the horizon.

Cooper was relaxing a bit. "Well, I seen a girl name Cora in a tub of water one time a bathing, and she stood up to dry off, and she didn't ass know I had my eyes on her, and she just stood there and dried herself off, and I'll tell you, the drier she got the wetter I got. She was so black that lighting bugs followed her around in the daytime, but that was a pretty hammerknocker! She was tall and thin, and you coulda set a cup a coffee on her high ass, and her tits looked like two black peaches, and.... Lawd, listen at me going on. What I telling you all this for?"

They worked in silence awhile. Neither spoke, but both thought—Cooper about Cora and Roller about Virginia. After several minutes Cooper said with a sigh, "I shore wish I hada knowed then what I know now."

"What do you know now?" Roller quizzed.

"Nothing," Cooper responded promptly.

Again they worked in silence, and finally Cooper repeated, "That was a pretty hammerknocker."

"She sure was!" Roller replied. "I mean...she was?"

Annie Jenny and Mama had prepared a typical delicious lunch: pork roast and gravy, rice, fried sweet potato slices sprinkled with sugar, butter beans, fresh sliced tomatoes, and fried lace corn bread. They were all seated (which was becoming a rare occurrence), and after the blessing, Mr. B, Bruh, and

Roller talked of the progressing harvest, things to be done that afternoon, and the rock sharpening to take place tomorrow. Muh, Mama, and Sis talked about the wedding.

Sis had been engaged since June and was planning a December wedding at Wesley Chapel. She was marrying a city boy who was away in the Navy and would be home on leave around Christmas.

Mr. B tried not to listen to the wedding plans. He didn't need the expense of the wedding in a year that produced the worst crop that he had ever made. He knew that money would be short and that Christmas spending would have to be cut.

"We'll work something out," he said when told of the plans.

That afternoon, Roller and Cooper returned to the peanut field. They talked about everything except Virginia. They worked at a slow steady pace. The heat prohibited a fast pace, and the shade of chinaberry trees on the field borders were most welcome and regularly visited. Punto and Willie were almost through plowing up the field, and their little John Deere tractors putt-putted a steady rhythm.

Roller and Cooper fought the heat and the gnats in hopes of finishing their jobs in concert with the tractors. Roller was a few steps ahead of Cooper and had picked up the work pace.

"Cooper, did you ever help sharpen the mill rocks?"

Cooper didn't answer, which was nothing unusual. Roller assumed that he had nodded as he often did.

"Well, is it as bad as Mr. Ollie says it is?" Roller gathered a fork full of vines and tossed them toward the fresh windrow.

Cooper still said nothing.

"Cooper, are you gonna answer?" Roller looked, and Cooper was on the ground face down in the fetal position; his bald forehead was touching the dry earth, and his hat lay upside down a foot or so from his head. His fork was standing vertical with its tines stuck in the hard ground.

"Cooper! What's the matter with you?" yelled Roller, running to him. He kneeled down, calling Cooper's name and pulling at his sweat soaked shirt as he rolled him over on his side.

"Cooper, Cooper! Are you all right?"

Cooper managed to answer in a slurred monotone voice.

"Yeah, you all right?"

As Cooper rolled to his side, his body went straight and rigid and continued to roll till he was face up. His body jerked and trembled.

"Cooper, Cooper, what is it!" Roller yelled.

Cooper's eyes were wide, but his pupils had dilated independently and unequally. His mouth was taunt, his teeth clenched, and his jaw muscle bulged from the side of his face. He said nothing and saliva drooled from the corner of his lips. His skin was hot and dry.

Roller knew but refused to believe that something was critically wrong with Cooper. Louder now, he pleaded with Cooper to talk to him, to snap out of it, to be all right again, but Cooper seemed unaware of his efforts.

Punto was headed toward them, plowing two of the remaining few rows of the field. Roller jumped up waving both arms in a crisscross panic motion. Punto saw him, saw that Cooper was down, and immediately lifted the plow, shifted into a higher gear, and came full throttle down the unplowed rows toward them. As he shifted the gear to neutral, he jumped from the still rolling-tractor with his water jug in his hand.

Roller took his shirt off, wadded it to form a pillow, and gently placed it under Cooper's head. For some reason, today he had also worn a T-shirt; he stripped it off, too, and Punto poured the cool water on it and began to wipe Cooper's face. They both talked, begged, and coaxed Cooper to respond. Roller was crying.

Suddenly, Cooper's cramped, rigid body relaxed and became still and limp; his eyes closed, his jaw slackened, and his mouth opened slightly. Foamy saliva oozed from his open lips. *He's dead*, Roller thought.

Willie, seeing the commotion, raced his tractor to the scene. Before he could come to a full stop, Roller, half crying, yelled to him, "Go get help! Find Daddy or Bruh or somebody!"

Willie yanked the throttle down and sped away. He had barely made it to the Carnegie Road when Cooper opened his eyes.

Again, in a slurred speech he asked, "Roller, you all right?"

Cooper propped up on his elbows. "I musta got too ass hot." His speech was better now. Roller and Punto helped him sit up, and he took the wet T-shirt and wiped his face and around his mouth.

"Hell, I'm okay. Ya'll better get back to work."

They helped him to stand, but held to him a minute as he wiped the dirt from his forehead and the back of his head. He took a few small swallows of Punto's water and put on his hat that Punto had handed to him.

"Cooper you need to go to the doctor. You went out like a light." Roller sniffed. He dried his cheeks with the top of his gritty hand.

"Naw, I'm all right, just let me cool off a bit." He took a few steps and gathered his equilibrium. "I'm all right, I tell you."

"Well, you gonna go to the doctor whether you all right or not." Roller declared.

Punto added, "Yeah, Mr. Cooper, you better let Dr. Harper check you out. A heat stroke can hurt you."

Uncle George came tearing down the road in the old Chevrolet truck, wheeled up close to them, and asked, "You all right, Cooper?"

"Yas, suh, Mr. George," Cooper nodded.

"Well, you better come on and let me take you up to Dr. Harper's, and let him check you."

"Naw, suh, I'll be okay. Just care me to the house and let me get shed of this headache."

They all helped him into the cab of the pickup. Roller jumped in the back, and Uncle George drove back to the store. When they reached the intersection, Uncle George yelled back to Roller. "Roller, go in there and get Cooper a B.C. powder."

Roller did as he was told, and when he returned Uncle George told him to watch the store while he carried Cooper home. As he drove away, Roller yelled to Cooper, "I'll be up there to check on you in a few minutes."

Uncle George told Cooper as he climbed out of the truck, "Cooper, if that headache don't go away, you let me know, and I'll take you to the doctor."

"Yas, suh. I will."

When Uncle George returned to the store, Roller was no-where to be found. He called for him inside; no answer, he went outside and called. Roller answered from the sitting place. "I'm up here. I'll be down in a few minutes."

Roller had never used the sitting place as a place to cry, but today he was overwhelmed. He had been so frightened that Cooper was gone to never return that the experience had made him conscious of several things that made him increasingly emotional.

First, it had been obvious to Roller that even in semicon-sciousness that he had been Cooper's primary concern. Cooper had not thought of his own condition but had thought of Roller. Now, Roller knew that Cooper not only felt a responsibility for him, but had a genuine and parental love for him.

The experience also made Roller aware that practically all of the people who were closest to him were old, and he feared that the death of those people would become, at some time in his near future, a common occurrence. Mr. B would be sixty years old in just four short years, and Cooper was probably older than that. Muh was just eight years younger than Mr. B, and Mama was her mother! God, she must be seventy-five! Uncle George was old, and Annie Jenny was no spring chicken; all of his aunts and uncles were elderly, and some of his relatives and other citizens of Vilulah had already died. They had just buried Mr. Clarence Bigbie back in the spring, and his widow, Cousin Grady, was at least seventy. He had only been to a few funerals in his short life, and Mr. Clarence was the first dead person that he had ever seen, but if God granted him a long life, there would be plenty of both.

The rabbit hopped along the far edge of the cemetery and was a welcome distraction to Roller's somber line of thought. Cooper had been, as time would permit, putting the finishing touches on his spear. He would try it out as soon as he could go hunting again. He gradually began to think of other things.

Governor Talmadge had been in Ft. Gaines on Veteran's Day along with a lot of other politicians. If he had just known, Roller thought, about this road paving, he could have talked to him then about the tree. Tic Forrester had been there, and he and Mr. B were real close friends. Maybe he could help.

Veteran's Day. Boy, that had been a big day for Ft. Gaines! Thousands of people had crowded the little town to hear politicians of all descriptions, to eat barbecue, and to celebrate. The veterans of the surrounding area had cooked 3,000 pounds of pork, had made several hundred gallons of Brunswick stew, and had fed more than 700 people. Mr. Jim Woodruff of the Tri-Rivers Association had announced that Ft. Gaines would be the home of a huge dam and hydroelectric plant and that the swift and treacherous Chattahoochee River would become a tranquil, beautiful, and bountiful 48,000-acre lake. Ft. Gaines would become a boomtown and an economic opportunity for all citizens of the area. Construction would begin next March.

As Roller thought back on it, he remembered some of the words that Mr. Woodruff had spoken, words that were exciting and stimulating at the time but were less appealing to him now. Words like progress, change, growth, development, opportunity, and commercialization.

One thing was certain to him as he sat there and surveyed his favorite place: no longer would time stand still for him. Change was on its way, and he must learn to accept it, be prepared for it, and make the best of it.

CHAPTER 7
THE CAT

The day began as it would remain—hot, humid and sunless. A dog-day, August fog covered the sun and produced a smothering, smokey haze under the cloud cover. The air was thick and still; even the slightest breeze was absent. The dawn temperature varied little from the noon temperature, and the humidity worsened as the day progressed. The threat of rain lingered all day but never came. Dawn lasted until sunset.

Since the rock sharpening was to begin at first light, Roller was awakened earlier than normal. After gobbling down his corn flakes and toast, he hurried out to his bike. He had to go check on Cooper before the work at the mill started. The evening before, when he had checked on him, Cooper had been asleep.

He peddled hard up the left rut of the dusty dirt road. The fog was thick but failed to settle the dust, and visibility was difficult. Just as he began to pull the hill at Mr. Lawson's, he met Cooper whistling down the road.

"Morning, Roller. How's your hammer hanging?"

"Morning, Cooper. How's your headache?"

"Well, it's better, but I woke up with the backache. I think I might get Mr. George to care me up to Dr. Harper's on up in the day."

Roller turned his bike around and coasted down one rut as Cooper walked the other. They talked as they made their way to the work of the day.

"Roller, you know that big ole ass oak tree down there at the upper swimming hole?"

There were two swimming holes on Mosley Branch. The upper hole was the origin of the spring fed stream. A beautiful, clear spring boiled out of a clay bank and filled a little pool with

sparkling, clear blue and icy cold water. Trees shaded the little
pool, and even the hottest days of August seemed like springtime. A huge, white oak tree leaned its massive crown over the
pool, and Roller and Cooper, with their backs to the trunk of the
tree and legs outstretched, spent many hours there "checking
fences." It was one of the most peaceful and pleasing places
that Roller had ever seen.

"Yeah. What about it?"

"Well, I dreamed bout it last night. Dreamed me and my
paw was sitting there talking bout old times."

"Your paw? You never talked bout your paw before. Tell
me bout em."

"Ain't much to tell; white folks hanged em dead when I was
a little boy."

"Hanged 'em!" A chill went up Roller's spine.

"Yep, we lived down there in Charlton County on a turpentine farm. Somebody kilt the straw boss and stole the payroll,
and them white folks with them ass white suits and pointed hats
come and hanged foe niggers 'acause of it."

Roller felt his face flush as Cooper talked; he had heard this
before but from Mama. He was speechless and addled. His
thought processes refused to cooperate; he must change the subject and think about this later.

"Cooper, how you coming with my spear?"

"All I like is to sharpen it up some more and put the feathers
on it. You need to find me two or three good feathers in the
turkey yard, and I can prolly finish it."

They passed by the bighouse just as Mr. B came out. Bruh
had loaded the rolling store so that Mr. B could enjoy his breakfast before coming out to start the day of activity. He instructed
them as they walked toward the store.

"Cooper, I want you to feed up and meet me back at the
store at nine. I'm gonna take you up to Dr. Harper's and let him
check you before you do anything too strenuous."

"Yas, suh," Cooper nodded.

"Roller, I want you to stay on top of that rock sharpening.
We need to finish it today if possible. You know that everyday
that it's down it cost us money, and with these peanuts like they

are, we'll need every dime we can get our hands on."

"Yes, sir. Is Bruh going to help too?"

"Yeah, everybody that's not working with the peanuts is going to help."

"Yes, sir."

Roller had seen the mill rock-sharpening process but had never helped with it. He was excited about being a part of any operation, but he was especially excited about this one. He knew that the work would be hard, but it would also be a learning experience. He had always marveled at the way corn fell into the top center of the turning limestone rock and came out a warm, toasted-smelling coarse powder called meal. He also knew that there would be several people working there, including some of the colored boys of the farm that were about his age, and more important, he thought he might get a chance to teach Ollie a lesson about peeing through the knot hole. He had a plan.

The day before, Bruh had helped Ollie and a couple of the older boys ready the mill for the stone-sharpening ordeal. The wooden cowling that encased the upper millstone, the corn hopper, and the feed mechanism that sat on top of the cowling had been lifted away. The upper stone had to be lifted and turned over to expose its working surface.

A heavy, wooden pivoting derrick had been installed when the mill had been built. The derrick was swung out above the upper stone, and a big steel wishbone-shaped clamp was used to grasp the stone. The wishbone clamp had a coarsely threaded turnscrew that went through a hole in the derrick beam, and a threaded wheel on top of the beam was turned to literally screw-lift the stone away from its mate.

Once it was lifted clear of the lower stone, the derrick was swung around so as to make clearance for the flipping of the upper stone.

The wishbone clamp had a protruding horizontal metal peg on the end of each leg. The pegs pointed inward and were inserted into holes that had been chipped out of the side of the stone. The holes were only slightly larger than the pegs and were exactly opposite each other, so that when the stone was clear of any obstruction it could be flipped over inside the wishbone clamp. An arrangement of wooden blocks and beams was placed under the stone, and the turnscrew reversed to lower the stone onto its temporary foundation. The wishbone clamp and derrick were then swung back to their original out-the-way position, leaving both stones face-up and ready to be sharpened.

Each of the stones was about eighteen inches thick, approximately forty-eight inches in diameter, and weighed about 2,000 pounds, and each had a hole through the center. The donut-shaped stones had a pattern of grooves chiseled into them that carried, by centrifugal force, the ground corn meal out to the edge of the stone to the cowling that covered and surrounded it. A hole cut in the cowling allowed the meal to escape the grinding process and fall into a holding bin.

The grooves had to be chiseled deeper, and the worn-smooth grinding surface between the grooves, called bays, had to be chipped to produce a pitted, rough, and coarse-textured finish. Little hand-held hammers were used to reshape the surface of the grinding stones. Chisel-shaped hammers, called groovers, deepened and shaped the grooves, and hammers with multi-pointed heads, called peckers, were used to resurface the stone grinding face.

Roller arrived at the mill just as the rest of the crew was selecting sitting places around the stones. Bruh would be late; he was eating breakfast after loading the rolling store.

Ollie, three colored boys from the farm (Willie Joe, Grady, Jr., and Hun), and Roller awaited instructions on the pecking process that would last all day and into the night.

"Roller, you want a groover or a pecker?" Ollie asked.

"It don't matter to me," replied Roller.

"Well, you want a right-handed pecker or a left-handed pecker?" asked Ollie, smiling.

They all looked the same to Roller, but he fell for Ollie's gag.

"A right-handed, I guess. I'm right handed."

"So," said Ollie, "you work your pecker with your right hand, huh?"

Roller did not reply.

Ollie laughed and continued his tease.

"Which hand do you wipe your ass with, Roller?"

Roller must not have been thinking clearly. He fell again. "My right hand," he said, still thinking that his dexterity had something to do with his ability to sharpen the rock.

Again, Ollie laughed. "Well, I use toilet paper myself," Ollie quipped, and everybody laughed.

"Well, you better give all us one of those groovers then," Roller demanded, as he began to think more clearly, "cause one pecker like you is enough!"

Ollie knew when to hush; he passed out goggles to everyone, instructed them about how the stone should be sharpened, and the work began. Ollie worked on the grooves as everyone else pecked the bays.

Bruh came in after awhile, bringing the oscillating fan from their bedroom. He situated it so as to provide everyone an intermittent breeze. For a couple of hours, Roller enjoyed the work. He talked to Bruh and the colored boys and used the time to think, but as the heat of the day increased and his hands and arms tired, he enjoyed it less and less. The only thing that kept him going was his plan to stop the knothole-pissing once and for all.

Roller lifted his head to stretch and to rest his neck and arms and glanced through the mill house door just as the yellow truck pulled up to the store.

It's Mr. Roy, Roller thought. *I gotta talk to him.*

"Pee time for me. I'll be right back," he informed the others. He dropped his hammer and ran to the store. Mr. Roy saw him coming and waited at the front of the truck, listening to the hammers.

"All right, how you, Mr. Roy."

"Hi, Roller, I'm doing fine. What's all that noise out there?"

"We're sharpening the mill stones. Did you get the road plotted, Mr. Roy?"

"Well, yes, I did," Roy answered as he looked down to the ground.

"Well, what about my tree?" Roller knew by Mr. Roy's expression what his answer would be.

"Roller, I'll tell you, that tree figured four and a half feet on the right of way, so I moved the road over to the east as far as I could, over two feet, but there's still over half of that tree that's gonna be in the way."

Roller had a funny feeling; a lump formed in his throat, and his face flushed. It was the same kind of feeling that he had when he saw Cooper lying face down on the ground the day before. This strange emotion had also come over him earlier this morning when Cooper had told him about his paw. It was like his mind was full of thoughts, but none of them connected so that he could respond; no single thought prevailed over the others, and he was momentarily confused. It was like he was watching something dreadful happening but could do nothing about it. He felt helpless, and his stomach felt weak and almost nauseated. He never remembered having this feeling before, and yet he had felt it three times in the last two days. He was puzzled, but he was finally able to speak.

"What about the gas pump?" He asked softly and despondently.

"Roller, when I moved the road over those two feet, the gas pump is almost three feet off of the right-of-way. It's going to be okay. But there is another problem too. That pecan tree there in front of that house," he pointed toward the bighouse. "Is that where ya'll live? Well, it's about three and a half feet over the cut line. I mean it's in the way too."

Roller suddenly felt relieved. If his tree belonged to anybody it belonged to him, and if that pecan tree in front of the bighouse belonged to anybody it belonged to Muh, and Roller was confident that nobody would cut Muh's tree down. Why hadn't he thought of it before? It was obvious that the pecan tree was closer to the road than his mighty oak, and it was now obvious that he should have talked to Muh about this sooner. Muh had a way of getting what she wanted, and Roller was sure if Muh wanted her tree to be spared, then it would certainly be spared, and if her tree was spared, then certainly he had an argument that his tree be spared. After all, his tree was farther from the road than her's. All that he had to do was figure out a way to tell her that the road people were going to cut her tree down—in a way that would get her head-strong and determined that nobody would take her tree. He felt much better, and the feeling that had just a minute ago filled his mind, body, and soul was suddenly and completely reversed.

"Well, Mr. Roy, you just told me something that me and my tree are glad to know, and I'm much obliged to you for doing all you did to help me. But tell me one more thing. When will the work begin on the road?"

Roy was puzzled; it was obvious to him that Roller was no longer worried about his tree. What had he told Roller that had so distinctly provided relief for him? What could Roller have planned to save his tree? He rubbed his chin and thought a minute.

"Roller, as soon as I get the deeds signed by all of the land-owners along the road, we'll get started with the grade work and clearing of the right-of-way.... I'd say about two weeks. In fact, they will probably start on the new bridge up on the creek this week."

"Yes, sir. Well, thank you, sir." Roller was not looking at him anymore; he was looking at the pecan tree. "I'll see you." He stood there looking and thinking, unaware that Mr. Roy was still talking to him.

"I'll get me a Coke and get back to work. I'll see you, Roller."

Roller did not respond.

Roy went inside the store, and when he returned Roller was gone.

The stone-sharpening crew took a break about mid-morning and had cold Royal Crown Colas from the store. Again as they entered the store, Tom sensed the presence of Ollie and, with ears laid back and hair standing, made his immediate exit out of the side door.

Roller remarked, "Mr. Ollie, one of these days, that cat ain't gonna run from you."

As they were returning to the mill, Mr. B and Cooper came back from Dr. Harper's. Mr. B parked the old pick-up in front of the store, and Cooper joined the crew as they proceeded toward the mill.

"What did Dr. Harper say about you?" asked Roller.

"Ahh, he said that I'm older than I've ever been...said I was okay."

All the crew were genuinely interested in Cooper's well-being and listened as he repeated the prognosis that he said Dr. Harper had made.

"He gave me two bottles of pills, told me to take one pill in the morning and the other pill at night, said the morning pill will keep my back from petering out...said the night pill will keep my peter from backing out...."

The crew laughed wildly and realized that Cooper was up to his foolishness, but also realized that he must be all right. He continued, "I'll tell you, though. I done already took one of them night pills; my peter needs more help than my back...but I'll tell you, I musta swallowed it too ass slow, cause my neck done got so ass stiff I can't hardly turn my head. I shore hope it works that good all the way down!"

Again everyone laughed and proceeded back to the stone. Cooper became part of the crew, and conversation increased as they worked except, for Roller; he had very little interest.

The job became more and more monotonous and boring. The steady peck-peck-ping of the hammers and the hot humid day became irritating.

Roller pecked the stone the balance of the day with very little to say, but with a lot to think. He thought about the road paving, his tree, and Virginia Hart, but he refused to think about school, about all the old people in his life, or about Cooper's paw. He also continued to think about his plan for Ollie.

About thirty minutes after the break, Ollie laid down his groover tool and stepped away from the stone. Roller was busy in thought and failed to notice that Ollie had vacated his spot. When he did notice, he leaned over the stone to look through the storage room door, and Ollie was pulling away from the knot-hole and was zipping his fly.

Dawg, I missed my opportunity. I better watch him more closely.

He had to have a way of knowing when Ollie intended to visit the knothole. The only way his plan would work was to know exactly when Ollie's penis would appear through the back

69

side of the mill house. How would he know this? The Royal
Crown Cola! Sure, it had been about a half hour since break and
since the RC Cola. After lunch, about mid-afternoon, he would
see to it that Ollie had all the RC that he wanted. He'd watch
him very carefully.

Annie Jenny had another delicious dinner, and afterwards
Roller lay under the big pecan tree in its shade and closed his
eyes in thought, but his thoughts turned to dreams as the morning work and early awakening called for rest.

His dream was a replay of the conversation that had taken
place at the dinner table. Mr. B had given his accounting of Dr.
Harper's prognosis of Cooper. Cooper had suffered a mild stroke;
a blood vessel in his brain had ruptured, and though there seemed
to be no permanent damage or loss of function, he could probably have another one or more. It could happen any time or it
could be years or it could never happen, but his work should
remain non-strenuous, and he should avoid getting too hot. Dr.
Harper told him to quit drinking that rot-gut whiskey and to start
using his time away from the job as a time to rest and not as a
time to "take drunk."

Then his dream became a replay of Cooper's stroke, and the
scene of Cooper lying there curled in the fetal position, face down
in the dirt, played over and over until Bruh woke him.

"Come on Roller," Bruh shook his shoulders. "It's time to
go back to work. Come on, wake up."

Roller tried to wake up, tried to gather his senses and become coherent. At first he was relieved in his semiconscious-
ness; it had all been a dream, and he was glad to be awake, but
then, as his senses returned, he realized that it had only partially
been a dream, and he wanted to return to sleep, hopefully to another dream. The hammers were already pecking as he made his
way in the midday heat back to the mill house. As he entered
the door, Bruh tossed him his hammer, and he was forced to catch
it right in front of his face, just short of a bloody nose.

"Bruh, I ain't up to none of your mess, so don't start anything," Roller demanded as he stared straight into Bruh's brown
eyes. Bruh acknowledged and recognized the stare, but paid it
little attention.

"You're just mad because you can't go camping with the Vilulah Boys," Bruh countered.

The Vilulah Boys were a group of boys from the surrounding farms that were all Bruh's age. There were seven of them, and they had a little clubhouse down on Mosley Branch that they had built out of sweet gum poles and pine boughs. They had an age minimum, set by their own accord, that eliminated boys Roller's age, and they had to pass certain tasks to become members. They had their own camping trips and wiener roasts, and the club had long been a source of friction between Bruh and Roller. Naturally, Roller wanted to be part of it; he could outshoot any of them, he could outwork most of them, and he could do almost anything they could do and do it better than most. As a means of eliminating all of their younger brothers, the seven members had deliberately set the age requirement so that Roller and the boys his age could not join. They had a camping trip planned for the last weekend before school started, and Roller had asked Muh to make Bruh let him go with them, but Bruh had won his case and Roller was refused. Roller had become reconciled with the matter.

"I don't care about the Vilulah Boys or ya'll's camping trip, but I do care about you throwing stuff at me, and I'm telling you that my ass is just like turnip greens...anytime you want a mess, just come on."

"You better watch your mouth. You know what kind of trouble you'll be in if I tell Muh that you been cussing."

Muh did not tolerate cursing. She knew that Bruh and Roller were exposed to all kinds of language being around the hands and the older men that came to the store, and she couldn't help what they heard, but she certainly could help what they said. A curse word to her was a sin and was absolutely unacceptable from anybody.

Once she had walked all the way across the pecan orchard to the field that bellied in behind it and across half of the field to tell Doc to stop cussing the mules. It was one of those days when sound traveled too good, and she could hear Doc talking to the mules from the back yard.

There were a lot of things about being "all boy" that she

tolerated and overlooked as far as Roller was concerned, but cursing was not one of them.

"Yeah, and you know what kind of trouble you'll be in if you tell her, too," Roller spat.

Ollie interceded, "All right boys, Mr. B told me that if I had any trouble with ya'll to let him know; now ya'll cut out the lollygagging, and let's go; we got a long way to go before we finish these stones."

Yeah, Mr. Ollie, Roller thought. *If you wag your weenie out that knothole again, you'll be lollygagging or zigzagging or something.* He smiled as he composed a poem to himself.

Roller was lollygagging,
Ollie was weenie wagging,
Now Ollie is zigzagging,
His weenie is sore and sagging,
But Roller isn't bragging!

He hummed the poem to a tune as he pecked the stone and almost laughed aloud. He was not sure why Ollie relieved his bladder through the knothole. Was he just too lazy to go to the barn like everybody else, or did he have a control problem? Whatever the reason, Roller didn't like it, and corn bread had not tasted as good to him since he had seen the yellow stream the first time.

Roller's mind was occupied, and time passed quickly. Grady, Jr., quizzed Roller. "Roller, why don't you go get us all one of them sixteen-ounce Lotta Cola's and a Baby Ruth out the sto."

That sounded good to Roller; surely that sixteen-ounce Lotta Cola would send Ollie to the knothole.

"Yeah, that's a good suggestion. I'll be right back."

He went to the store and got seven of the big colas and seven five-cent Baby Ruth bars. Everyone was waiting in the shade of the pecan tree when he returned, and everyone was appreciative except Ollie, who apparently had not heard Grady, Jr.

"Baby Ruth!" he exclaimed. "I don't eat nothing that looks like the dawg mighta dropped it."

"Well, Mr. Ollie, you don't have to. I love Baby Ruths, and I can eat two of them, and I can drink two of the Lotta Colas too if you don't want it," Roller replied.

"No!" Ollie responded. "I love Lotta Colas, I think I could drink two of them myself right now, but you can have that Baby Ruth. Looks too much like a turd to me."

Maybe Ollie had some redeeming traits, but Roller had not found them.

Surely he has some morals. He certainly hadn't used up many of them. Surely there was good there somewhere, but where? He did help clean up the soot when Bruh tried to challenge Ezzard Charles for the world heavyweight boxing title. But, for the most part, Ollie irritated Roller, and each time he made some smart or vulgar remark, Roller became more determined to carry out his plan.

"I've got to go to the barn a minute." Roller winked at Cooper, and Cooper knew that the wink meant for him to come too.

"Yeah, me too," Cooper replied.

They walked around behind the mill house toward the barn, and Roller explained his plan. "Now, Cooper, the only way that this will work is for you to help me. Now, Mr. Ollie is gonna go to the knothole in about thirty minutes."

"How you know that?"

"Never mind how I know. This is what I need you to do. You know me and you are sitting side by side with our backs to the door."

Cooper nodded.

"And Bruh and the others are sitting side by side with their backs to us."

Again, Cooper nodded.

"And Ollie is sitting facing us. Now when he lays down his hammer, he'll be headed for the knothole. Now, the knothole is just inside of the storage room. I want you to take my hammer and chip with both hands for a few minutes. I don't want anybody to notice a change in the noise and turn around to look and see me gone. Now, Willie Joe and Hun are gonna see me leave, so I want you to give them the 'keep quiet' signal, and, when you can talk to them, tell them not to tell anything to anybody. Okay?"

"Roller, what you gonna do? Now don't you ass go hurt that

man's tallywhacker!"

"I'm not going to hurt him. I'm not going to do anything...the cat is."

"Huh, the cat? How the hell is the cat gonna ass...."

Roller cut him off. "Just do as I say. Okay?"

Cooper nodded. "I reckon."

They went back to the mill and took their places along with everyone else and pecked the stone. The day was getting longer and longer. The unyielding heat was stifling; the gnats were horrendous, and the humidity was sweltering. What Roller thought was interesting at daybreak was now uninteresting and miserable. His hands had blisters, his arms and shoulders were tight and aching, and his clothes were wet with sweat. The steady clang of the hammers was hypnotizing and grew louder and louder with each minute that passed. The stones seemed to grow larger and larger, and the flying grit from the hammer impacts filled his hair and clothes. Just to think about cornbread made him sick.

It had to be the longest day that Roller had ever experienced. He needed a distraction, a revitalization of his body and spirit. He needed physical and mental relief. He needed for Ollie to take a leak!

Suddenly and without announcement, Ollie laid down his hammer, stood and stretched his back and arms, wiped his brow on his shirt sleeve, and dried the sweat from his goggles.

Roller watched from the corner of his eye but never missed a beat with the seemingly forty-pound hammer. Ollie just stood there motionless as if in deep concentration, finally put his goggles back on, and picked up his hammer to resume pecking.

Roller's heart was pounding with anticipation, and when Ollie sat back down without a visit to the knothole it was almost unbearable. A feeling of faint came over him as his right arm cramped, and the hammer fell from his hand. He quickly recovered the hammer with his left hand and continued.

"Dawg, is he ever gonna drain his lizard?" Roller thought aloud but inaudibly above the noise of the hammer.

Again boredom took over. Only alternating thoughts of Virginia Hart and the knothole kept him going. By this time everyone was tiring. No one spoke, and only the occasional sweat wiping broke the rhythm of the eight hammers.

Finally, two hours after the Lotta Colas, Ollie laid down his hammer and made a fast pace to the storage room. He almost caught Roller off guard, so he would have to hurry to reach the knothole with the necessary perfect timing that the plan mandated.

He tapped Cooper on the arm and handed him his hammer as he crept down from his seat at the stone. He watched everyone to be certain that his exit was not noticed as he backstepped on his tiptoes out the door and onto the porch. Only the farm boys had seen him as he jumped off the porch and ran around the north end of the mill. When he rounded the back corner, he saw the pink head of Ollie's penis push through the knothole.

He quickly tiptoed along the edge of the wooden structure, and, stopping just short of the protruding organ, he suddenly faced a decision that he had not anticipated. His plan, just as the plan of attack to kill the hawk, had been carefully prepared in his mind. His plan included what to do and how to do it. But now, precisely when to do it was a dilemma.

Ollie's manhood jutted motionless from the knothole, but no urine emitted from it. Roller abruptly had several questions: *Should I make my move now? Should I wait till midstream, or should I wait until Ollie is through peeing? Is Ollie having trouble making water? Why is he taking so long?*

Suddenly the question of waiting was answered as urine made its appearance and formed a low-pressure, yellow-liquid arch. Roller decided to wait until he was through; he didn't want to chance urine spewing around and splashing on him.

Roller was somewhat perplexed because he had been forced to make a midcourse adjustment to this maneuver. His heart raced with excitement and fear of being caught. He breathed rapidly, and sweat poured from every pore on his body, especially his hands. The stream of urine began to lessen, and time and timing grew increasingly important. In Roller's bewilderment he had forgotten the most strategic component of the plan. He had forgotten to ready his weapon. Hurriedly he dried his hands on his jeans, reached into his right pants pocket, and retrieved "the claw."

CHAPTER 8
THE SPEAR

Sunrise the next morning hinted the slightest promise of autumn. The dog day haze was gone, and a clear golden glow filled the eastern sky as the sun made its prompt and predictable conquest of darkness that had enveloped Roller's remote world.

He was awakened early by the crowing of Mr. Lawson's boisterous and early-rising rooster and immediately noticed the northerly breeze that entered his bedroom window. He lumbered his sore, aching young body out of bed and to the window to see if he could find the rooster in the darkness, and as he scanned the back yard and orchard he vowed to kill that loudmouth on the next full moon; he would have enough light then to spot and draw a bead on him. He had warned Mr. Lawson for the last time that he should keep the rooster at home; soon he would offer him the primary ingredient for rooster pie.

Roller's arms and wrists wreaked with pain. The chip hammer had demanded the use of muscles that were unaccustomed to such strenuous and taxing exercise. He wondered if that Sloan's Liniment at the store would help ease the pain; he would give it a try later.

As his mental faculties begin to awaken, he thought of the previous day and wondered if Cooper had overworked himself. He had a very uncomfortable feeling that his asking Cooper to work the stone with two hammers for that few minutes had been too much for him. He became anxious to see him and to know his condition. As he walked to the bathroom, which had a door that opened onto the screened porch, he heard Cooper whistling down the road. He noticed, as on prior mornings, that Cooper stopped whistling as he got even with the bighouse, and he knew that Cooper was listening for activity inside the house—and, more precisely, that he was listening for Roller.

Roller walked to the edge of the front porch still in his underwear and spoke. "How's your hammer hanging?"

"Well, it's hanging," Cooper chuckled. "My medicine didn't work good as I hoped it would, but I be fine. How you be?"

"Man, my hands and arms hurt like the devil. I'm glad we finished those stones last night; I don't think I could go again today."

"Well," Cooper responded, "sore muscles come back a little ass stronger; the way you growing and filling out, work like that will make a man outa you." He paused and cocked his head. "I hear White bellowing out yonder. I better go feed up. I think Miss Lucille is gonna lead her milk cow over here this morning for White to tend to. He got a good ass life don't he Roller?" Nodding, "Yeah, all he got to do is eat and...," he caught himself, paused, and continued, "uh, tend to them freshening cows and heifers."

"Yeah, I guess," Roller replied.

"I better go; I'll be out to the barn when you get ready."

"Ready for what?" Roller quizzed.

"Hey, we gotta go check them fences down to the upper swimming hole!" He pointed westward and winked at Roller. "You done forgot bout that?"

Roller caught on. "Oh, yeah, I'll be on in a little while."

Muh came out of her bedroom, which also joined the front porch. She heard Roller's reply to Cooper and interrupted.

"Cooper, I want you and Roller to get the brush brooms and sweep the yards this morning. I've got the missionary society coming here today for our monthly meeting, and it's so hot I think we'll put chairs out there under the pecan tree and meet out there in the shade. Ya'll will need to get the chairs out of the store and help me move some kitchen chairs out there and set them up in a circle. They'll be here at 10:00, so ya'll need to get right to work as soon as you feed up."

"Yes, ma'am," Cooper nodded.

Roller suddenly became fully awake. His eyes widened as he smiled inadvertently. He had a plan.

"Roller, go get your clothes on! I've told you and told you

about running around here in your drawers. Now, git!"

"Yes, ma'am!" Roller ran to the bathroom, suddenly realizing that he was about to wet his pants. The door was locked. Sis had laid claim to it, and Roller knew that she would be there for a spell. He ran back through Muh's bedroom into his and Bruh's room and climbed through the window onto the back porch, yanking down his briefs just in time. Peeing off the back porch was forbidden, but Roller had no other choice. Besides, he sort of enjoyed peeing there. It was a high porch, and he liked watching his urine stream out into the open air and fall its distance to the ground.

He thought about Ollie as his bladder found relief. There he was peeing off the back porch, and to him it was all right. Was he feeling guilty about what he had done to Ollie? He would be in big trouble if anyone found out! Well, Ollie was a grown man, and he was just a boy. But Ollie was grinding meal that would be consumed by people. No, he wasn't feeling guilty!

He thought about the devotional that Mr. B had read the night before from the *Upper Room*, the Methodist devotional book that Mr. B read to the family almost every night. Each lesson began with a scripture verse and was followed by a brief mini sermon. The scripture that night was from James 2:8: "If you fulfill the law according to the scripture, Thou shalt love thy neighbor as thyself, and thy shall do well." The lesson had explained, as Roller perceived it, that you should not do anything to anyone that you wouldn't do to yourself. Surely he would not pull the claw cord on his own penis!

He quickly pulled up his briefs, let the elastic pop against his flat, hard belly, and cupped his genitalia in his hand as if protecting them from the razor sharp talons of "the claw."

The sudden flapping of Mr. Lawson's rooster as it flew from the roost in the big pecan tree frightened Roller and broke his momentary trance.

"Damn you!" he said aloud and then looked around for fear someone had heard him.

"Roller, I heard that!" shouted Sis from the bathroom.

"Well, I heard you tooting in there, too," Roller replied loudly, "but, we ain't gonna tell anybody are we?"

Sis remained silent a moment and then mumbled something inaudible to Roller as he climbed back through the window into his room. He pulled on a pair of denim shorts and a striped T-shirt and hurried to the kitchen. Mama had made coffee. She heard Roller coming and poured him a half cup of the dark brew. Roller put in two teaspoons of sugar, filled the cup with milk, and sat down at the table for his corn flakes and toast.

He waited for Muh to leave the kitchen before he quizzed Mama. "Mama, you never told me that Cooper's paw was one of the colored men that they hanged when Grandpa was killed."

Mama looked at him with an expression that seemed to say, "Well, I knew you would find out about it sooner or later." She sat down by him, staring at nothing across the room, and said, "Roller, I've always felt so bad about it that I just couldn't tell you."

"Can you tell me now?"

"You see, Cooper was about your age when it happened, and his mother had seven children to look after. I was expecting your mother, and I had your Uncles Hugh, Leslie, and your name-sake, Jessie, to look after, so we moved up to Elmodel to my sister and brother-in-law's farm. You know—Aunt Nancy."

"Yes, ma'am."

"Do you remember Uncle Charles?"

"Yes, ma'am."

"He was a good man. Well, we lived on their farm for several years. But not long after we moved there, Charles sent down to Charlton county and moved Cooper and his family up there on the farm with us. When Cooper got grown, he moved down to Florida for a while, and when he came back we had moved up here. Your mother had married Ben, and they wanted me to come live with them. When Cooper found out where we were, he walked all the way up here and has been here ever since. Did he tell you about his paw?"

"Yes, ma'am. Well, he tried, but I made him talk about something else."

"Huh. To my knowledge he has never mentioned his paw to anybody. I had hoped he had forgot it; it was a terrible thing."

"Mama, do you think his paw killed Grandpa?"

"Roller, it doesn't matter. Cooper can't help what his paw might have done."

"I know but...."

"They never found the payroll that your grandpa was carrying; the real killer might have escaped."

"You mean they hanged four people to be sure they hanged the right one, and they still might not have hanged the right one?"

"That's right, but things were a lot different back then."

"I'll help you say!" he spat. "Cooper said something about men in white suits and pointed hats."

"Yes," Mama responded, "that was the Klan."

"The Klan?"

"The Klan was the law back then."

"Sounds like to me they broke the law. Who were they?"

"They were white people that dressed up in white hoods and robes so that they couldn't be recognized. They were evil but...I think they were a necessary evil."

"Necessary?"

"Well, I'm not condoning the things they did, and I'm certainly not saying that they were right, but after the Civil War and all the slaves were freed, a lot of colored people thought that white people owed them something for their bondage all that time, and they would do anything. They stole everything they could—cows, hogs, crops, chickens, anything they could get their hands on. They didn't want to work for a living; they wanted the white people to give them a living, and a lot of them got out of hand with their vengeance for the whites. There wasn't much law enforcement, not nearly enough, so some of the white men would band together to keep things in order. Each county had a Klan, and they kinda took the law in their own hands sometimes, but they kept both colored and white troublemakers in accord. They still do in some places."

"You mean they still hang colored people?"

"No, Roller, they don't hang people anymore. The law enforcement is much better now, but they're still active in some places, but not around here anywhere."

"How much money did Grandpa have on him when he was killed?"

"I don't know for sure, but I think it was about three hundred dollars, and that was a lot of money back then."

"Three hundred dollars!"

"You see, your grandpa was the strawboss for a big turpentine still down in Charlton county, and they had about fifty workers that they paid off in cash every two weeks."

"If he'd had my rifle with him, he could've protected himself!"

"Oh, he normally had an armed guard with him every time he picked up the payroll, but this time he was alone. The killer, they thought, started a woods fire along the road that he was traveling, and somehow, in the smoke and confusion, your grandpa was shot and the saddle bags with the payroll disappeared. After the fire died down, they found an old double-barrel shotgun that they said was used in the killing. They said it belonged to one of the colored men, but it was all burned and charred. I think they were guessing."

"Well, I don't believe Cooper's paw did it."

"I never did either," Mama replied.

Muh came back into the kitchen and reminded Roller about the yard sweeping. He hurriedly finished his breakfast, ran to the edge of the front porch, jumped straddled-legged onto the saddle of his awaiting imaginary horse, and galloped around the house to the smokehouse. He "whoaed" his trusty steed to a stop at the corner of the old weathered wood structure and pretended to dismount and tie him to one of the lap boards.

During the summer, when it was not used for smoking meat, the smokehouse was used for storage. The yard brooms, tightly bound bunches of dogwood saplings that he and Cooper had cut, bundled together, and wrapped with wire, were stored in the smokehouse. He found them and carried them to the front yard where he began sweeping the gravelly yard in hopes that Cooper would join him soon.

His mind raced. This would be the perfect time to carry out his newest plan. He and Cooper would have to wait till they finished the yards to go check the fences. Bruh would be through helping with the rolling store soon; he could help sweep too. Was Ollie late for work today? How many days till school started? Dang! just seven more days of freedom. Did Cooper tell Willie Joe and the others what he had done? Had he told them to keep quiet about it. These gnats ought to go somewhere and fly around a mule's butt! What was Virginia Hart doing? Why had her swim in the nude excited him so? Why couldn't he stop thinking about her? Why did she have so much hair down there? Why couldn't he go camping with the Vilulah Boys? After all, before they changed the age requirement and were still allowing members according to ability to pass all those tests, he could meet all the criteria to become a member. He could jump across the little gully at the upper end of the spring; he could climb any tree that they could climb—and faster than most of them; he could swing on the vine above Mosely Branch further than any of them; he could throw a knife or hatchet as accurately as any of them; and he could certainly out shoot any of them. Sure, they had to change the requirements to keep him out!

"Roller, Roller," Cooper pleaded. Louder. "Roller! Boy, don't you hear me talking to you? Dang if you don't think too ass hard sometimes. I been trying to tell you something."

Roller snapped around to see that Cooper had already joined him and had swept a little portion of the yard. "I didn't hear you come up."

"Yeah, you's thinking bout that naked ass woman again, won't cha? I been trying to tell you that the knothole done been plugged with something." He looked toward the mill.

"What?"

"Somebody, I reckon Mr. Ollie, done plugged ass up the knothole with rags or something."

"Yeah, well yesterday when he was begging the cat to turn his tallywhacker loose, he declared that he wouldn't never stick it in another hole that didn't have hair round it."

Cooper bent over laughing wildly. Roller, realizing now that he had successfully stopped the knothole peeing—and feeling secure that he would probably not be found out—started to laugh uncontrollably. He dropped down on his knees and laughed till his stomach cramped. Cooper laughed and coughed and spit and half laughing said, "Boy, you won't do!"

"What's he done now?" Bruh interrupted as he passed on the way to the bighouse.

"Nothing!" Roller laughed and then ordered strongly, "You come on and help us sweep this yard. Muh's having the Missionary Society meeting out here at 10:00."

"Looks like to me ya'll will be through in plenty of time. I've got other things to do."

Roller could see their sibling feud building again, and he knew that it wouldn't be long before some cutting remark or some frivolous act would set off a violent reaction by one or the other, or both, of them and that another "world heavyweight title" bout would be instigated. This time he would win.

Muh had warned them, though, about fighting, and they both knew that Muh meant business. They would hold back any temptation, any animosity, any skirmish until that final eruption of anger when war would be declared.

As they continued to sweep and talk, Cooper asked Roller for every detail of the knothole episode again and again, and each time Roller dramatized the story a little more.

They finished sweeping and arranged the chairs in the shade of the big pecan tree, and before Muh could give them anymore instructions they carried the brush brooms back to the smokehouse and skirted around the turkey pen toward the barn. As they passed the pen, Roller climbed the fence to gather several of the wing feathers that had been shed and hurried to catch up with Cooper.

"Are these the kind of feathers that you need to finish my spear?" Roller asked.

Cooper studied them a moment. "Yeah, they be just fine. Come on, let's go fix it now afore we go check them fences."

They went into the old blacksmith shop, and Cooper retrieved the spear from behind an old wooden barrel where he had stashed it. "Now, Roller, you better keep this thang hid out here somewhere, cause I'll get in big trouble if anybody finds out I made this thang."

"Yeah, okay, let me see it."

Cooper held up the spear, and Roller gasped. "Man, that thing is really something. How did you make it like that? What kind of metal is that? Where did you get it?"

"Hold on a minute, will you. I ain't even through with it yet! You know them flowers they put up on them three-legged stands around a burying spot when they bury somebody?" He nodded toward the cemetery.

"Yeah."

"Well, them little stands is made out of this metal rod that I used for the shaft. I found some that they had throwed away down there in that little thicket at the back of the cemetery. What I did was I took the back leg of the stand, cause it was the longest leg, and took it apart from the other two. Then I hammer the one end of it out flat so I could sharpen it off to a point. Then I file it off ass sharp and file them notches in it like a real Indian arrowhead. Then I cored out this corncob and slid it longways down on the shaft to make a throwing handle." He fanned the gnats and continued. "Then, I takes another corncob and sticks it on the end up here longways like this. Then I takes them feathers and sticks the quill down in the soft core of the cob, like this, and there your spear is all finished. Cept we may have to adjust them feathers if it don't throw straight."

Roller took the spear from Cooper, held it by the corn cob throwing handle, and drew it back to feel the balance. He rocked his arm back and forth in a slow motion, throwing-action while looking at it from end to end.

"Dang, Cooper, this thing will kill a rabbit or anything if I can learn to throw it right."

"Yeah, well, you gonna have to practice with it. You need to get you a bale of hay to practice on so as you don't dull the point on it."

"What did you mean, we might have to adjust the feathers?" He pretended to throw it.

"The feathers will keep it straight from side to side when you throw it. If they are justed right, they will keep the back-end straight behind the front-end. Now, if the front-end falls down or if the back-end drops down when you throw it, we'll have to slide the throwing handle one way or nother to make the balance just right."

"I see."

"Now, you hide that thang behind that barrel," he motioned toward the corner where the barrel stood, "till you can practice with it. I'll get you a bale of hay out where you can throw at it. Come on, let's go feed them boar pigs. Man, they getting ass bigger ever day. Won't be long they will be riding ever gilt in sight. They nutsack way yonder ass bigger than mine already."

Roller obeyed and followed several steps behind Cooper with head down, watching where he put his feet. He lifted his eyes to see a convoy of yellow trucks coming over the hill at Miss Lucille's. A bellowing cloud of red dust filled the air around and above the road. They were becoming a more common occurrence. He thought about the dust and what it might do the missionary society meeting. Maybe they would all be passed by that time. His plan might work better, though, if about a dozen of them came barrelling through about 10:30. He couldn't be that lucky.

"Cooper, I've got to be back to the house by about 10:00. I've got to attend to some business."

"Yeah, what kinda business you got now?"

"I'm gonna save my tree this morning."

"Huh? How you gonna do that?"

"You'll see!"

They carried a basket of corn over to the hog pasture and called the pigs. The pigs had already heard Cooper and Roller talking and had started to walk toward the feeding area, but when Cooper called to them they broke into a run. Their stampede kicked up a dust as they squealed and grunted and snorted toward the ears of corn that were tossed to them. The big boar pig was always the last one to reach the feeding area, but it didn't matter. He would simply throw his snout into the side of one of the smaller pigs and shove him away. His superior size and strength allowed him to bully the other pigs. Roller hated bullies, and, even though the boar pig was considered a prize by Mr. B and Cooper, his hostile personality had caused Roller to dislike him.

Roller threw an ear of corn at him, hitting him on the flank, and yelled, "You leave that pig alone. There's plenty of corn here! You don't have to hurt anybody; you big bully! Cooper, I don't like that scoundrel; he's mean."

"That hog just like a lot of peoples I know."

"What do you mean?"

"Well, the fat gets fatter. Always been that way—always will."

Roller thought a minute. He knew what Cooper was referring to. He had heard other people say "The rich get richer, and the poor get poorer."

"You see Roller, them that's got—gets. That pig got the size to get all the corn he want. Now you put him over yonder in the pen with them big boys, and he'll lose out cause they got the size to get the corn. Same ass way with some of these big-shots round here."

"Who you talking about?"

"You take the Reverend Major Page.... He done shouted and hollered round here at all them churches and got them women folk all crazy over him and done passed the plate round enough to buy him that car, and now he eat fried chicken two or three times a week."

Roller had heard other people, both colored and white, talk about the Reverend Major Page and how he had preached his way to considerable wealth. He did drive a 1950 Buick, usually loaded with women, that he carried to Coleman or Fort Gaines or wherever, and charged them a fare. Some people called him the taxi preacher.

"Now you take that Buick away from him, and he ain't nothing but a dressed up ass nigger. But he done got fat, so he gonna get fatter. Takes money to make money," Cooper continued.

Roller laughed out loud as he thought about the day that the Reverend Page had pulled up to the store to get gas.

****

The shiny black Buick had slowed to a stop at the gas pump, and Roller hurried out to service the reverend's car. The car was spotless and carried the Reverend and five older colored ladies all dressed for their Saturday trip into town.

After the dust settled, the Reverend rolled down his window, took his cigar from his lips, turned to Roller, and said, "Yes suh, Mr. Roller, let me have ten gallons of gas, please suh."

"Yes, sir, Reverend."

Roller went to the gas pump and pumped the handle back and forth until the light orange liquid filled the glass cylinder on top of the pump up to the ten-gallon mark. He stuck the nozzle into the fill port of the Buick and allowed the gas to drain from the reservoir. He replaced the fuel cap and hung the nozzle back in its place and returned to the window.

"That'll be two dollars, Reverend. Can I check the hood for you?"

"Naw, son, it's all right, but I think the ladies want a cold drink."

"Yes, sir, what can I get for ya'll?"

Roller looked into the spacious Roadmaster and immediately recognized all of its passengers. Prudie Dixon and her sister Mattie Spann and Minnie Dockins sat in the back seat, and Boots Daniels sat by the passenger window while her seductive daughter-in-law Rethel Daniels sat by the Reverend.

A buzz of conversation among the ladies erupted when the Reverend announced that he would buy them a cold soda. "All right, Rethel," the Reverend asked, "what you want?"

"Do you have a strawberry soda?"

"Yes, ma'am," Roller answered.

"I want a strawberry then," she requested.

"Okay," said the Reverend. "How bout you, Miss Boots? What you want?"

Boots managed to speak in spite of the big dip of snuff in her lip, "Ax the man if he got a Lotta Cola."

"Do you got a Lotta Cola?" asked the Reverend.

"Yes, sir," Roller responded.

"Yeah, he got a Lotta Cola, Miss Boots," the Reverend returned.

"Well, that's what I wants—a Lotta Cola."

"Now, Miss Prudie, what you want?" quizzed the Reverend.

"Ax the young man if he got a Royal Crown Cola."

Roller heard her request and answered to the Reverend,

"Yes, sir, we've got RCs."

"Yeah, they got Royal Crowns, Miss Prudie."

"Well, that's what I wants. A Royal Crown."

"Now let me see here now," the Reverend went on. "That's a strawberry and a Lotta Cola and a Royal Crown, and I wants a Orange soda. All right, Miss Minnie, what do you wants?"

"See if they got a NuGrape," she replied.

"No, sir, we don't have a NuGrape, but we do have a NeHi grape soda."

"He don't have a NuGrape, Miss Minnie, but he do got a NeHi grape."

Miss Minnie was hard-of-hearing, so she turned to Miss Mattie and asked what the Reverend had said.

Miss Mattie spoke loud to her. "He say he don't have no NuGrape, but he got a NeHi grape soda, Miss Minnie."

"Naw, I don't want no NeHi grape. Ax him do he got a NeHi peach," Miss Minnie insisted.

"Do you got a NeHi peach?" the Reverend asked impatiently.

"Yes, sir, I've got a NeHi peach."

"Yes, ma'am, he got a NeHi peach, Miss Minnie."

"What did he say?" Miss Minnie asked Miss Mattie.

Loudly, she replied, "Yes, ma'am, he do."

"Well, that's what I wants—a NeHi peach soda."

"Now, let me see here...," said Reverend Page with uncertainty, "that's one strawberry, one Lotta Cola, one Royal Crown, and I wants a orange and one NeHi grape—naw, I mean a NeHi peach. Now, Miss Mattie, what do you want?"

"See if he got a Seven-Up."

"Do you got a Seven-Up?" asked the Reverend.

"No, sir, but I do have an Upper 10."

"He don't have no Seven-Up, but he do got a Upper 10," the Reverend relayed to Miss Mattie.

"Naw, suh, I don't want no Upper 10; how bout a Dr. Pepper?"

"Does you have a Dr. Pepper, Mr. Roller?"

"Yes, sir, we have a Dr. Pepper," Roller nodded affirmatively.

Everyone stared at Miss Mattie as she paused several seconds.

"Well, that's what I wants—a Dr. Pepper."

"Well, thank Gawd Almighty!" said the Reverend with relief. "Now, let me see here again—that's one strawberry soda," he counted on his fingers looking at each person, "one Lotta Cola, one Royal Crown, and I wants a orange, and one NeHi grape for Miss Minnie, and one...."

"Naaaw...," Miss Prudie and Miss Boots interrupted simultaneously, "Minnie want a NeHi peach!"

"Yeah, yeah, a NeHi peach for Miss Minnie, and a Seven-Up for Miss Mattie."

"Naw, I don't want no Seven-Up," cried Miss Mattie. I wants a Dr...."

"Aw, hell!" shouted the Reverend Major Page. "I'm buying these damn sodas. Mr. Roller bring me six Coca-Colas, and hurry up, please, suh. I won't never get to Coleman at this rate!"

****

"What you laughing at now, Roller?" Cooper demanded.

"Oh, I was just thinking about something," he said as his attention abruptly returned to their conversation and chore of feeding the pigs.

"So, what you're saying is that you can use what you do have to help you get something that you don't have. Is that right?"

"That's right, but be careful not to hurt the little fellow."

"Yeah, okay."

They were interrupted by the loud non-stop bellowing of White Hogan and the tinkling of a cow bell. They looked across the hog pasture and saw Miss Lucille leading her milk cow along the road. White had many visitors, and he had learned that the tingling of a bell coming from any direction were usually chimes of impending pleasure.

His normal docile and lackadaisical attitude would change immediately. He became a rowdy and uncontrollable danger. Everyone had learned to stay clear of him when the smell of a willing visitor filled his nostrils.

He trotted to the edge of his little paddock, stretched his thick muscular neck above the wide board that restrained him, bellowed, and smelled the air. Recognizing the smell and the appearance of Miss Lucille's jersey milk cow, who annually made her nuptial stroll to his paddock, White went into an earth-pawing, nose-blowing, anticipatory rage.

"Roller, we gonna have to wait awhile afore we go check them fences. I gotta take care of this pregnating. Now you know you gonna have to go somewhere else; Mr. B ain't gonna allow for you to watch no cow riding."

"Yeah, well I got to go get ready to save my tree anyway."

Roller went back to the store and pretended to be busy until all of the ladies arrived at the bighouse for the missionary society meeting.

Muh had everything arranged to perfection. A card table set up with punch and pound cake for refreshments was adjacent to the circle of chairs. She had used her finest Sunday dessert dishes, a borrowed cut-glass punch bowl and cups, and linen napkins. A small vase of day lilies and iris that she had picked from her flower garden further beautified her table.

As the ladies arrived, they were served their refreshments by Annie Jenny, who loyally tended the table and fanned the gnats and flies as she awaited each arrival, graciously serving each of them.

When they were all served and had taken their seats in the circle of chairs, Annie Jenny covered the refreshments with a white table cloth and returned to the kitchen to prepare lunch.

Roller periodically opened the screen door of the store and leaned out to check the progress of the meeting. He had watched these meetings before, and he knew that Miss Mable Ingram would read a selection of scripture, and the ladies would all hold hands for a prayer by Miss Grady Bigbie. Then Miss Mable would give a short devotional concerning the scripture and how it related to modern-day life. After the program the ladies would sit around the circle and talk about coming events at the church or some social function or generally gossip about whatever came up.

Roller was about to make his appearance at the missionary meeting when, as luck would have it, Mr. Roy pulled up in his yellow truck.

"Hi, Mr. Roy."

"Hello, Roller."

"I see ya'll are getting real busy with the road, Mr. Roy."

"Yep, we're working on the bridge up there at Cemocheechobee and putting in culverts where we need to. By the way, we'll be putting in a culvert under the road down there in the bottom," he pointed toward Mr. Lawson's house, "and down there in that bottom," he turned and pointed towards Miss Lucille's house, "and if you want that job you were talking about, I'll pay you twenty-five cents a day to light the flambeaus every night and put them out every morning."

"Yes, sir!" Roller answered excitedly.

"Well, its a very important job, Roller. The flambeaus are danger indicators, and they must be lit every night, rain or shine."

"Yes, sir, I can do it, Mr. Roy," Roller begged.

"Okay, I'll show you all about it this afternoon, and tomorrow will be your first day."

"Yes, sir!" He reached out to shake hands with Mr. Roy as he had seen adults consummate deals.

"Thank you, Mr. Roy. I'll do you a good job."

Roller was elated about his employment and his perspective wealth. He had definite plans for the money that he would earn. He also had definite plans about saving his tree, and in his excitement while talking to Mr. Roy he almost forgot the importance of timing his entrance into the circle of Methodists ladies that were enjoying the shade of Muh's pecan tree.

Mr. Roy stood there in bewilderment as Roller's expression changed from an excited smile and sparkling green eyes to a broken-hearted frown and his eyes filled with tears—a look of total depression and remorse. Roy couldn't believe his eyes, nor could he understand, why Roller had made such a drastic reversal of appearance and personality. As he stood there scratching his head and calling Roller by name, Roller turned away and made a slow, deliberate, head-hung march toward the ladies.

CHAPTER 9
THE KILL

The sun barely peeped over the hill up the Carnegie Road as Roller made his way up to the sitting place. It had been several weeks since he had found time to make the climb. The autumn chill required long pants, shoes, a long-sleeved, shirt and a jacket; thus the ritual ascent to his favorite hideaway was more difficult than usual.

The old oak had started to shed some of its dull greenish brown leaves, a result of the hot, dry summer and the early fall chill. The sparsely green countryside had turned completely to a dull tan; only the pines scattered in the woods and along the hedgerows retained the emerald hue that had welcomed the summer months.

The harvest, such as it was, was almost completed. The meager yield of peanuts had been harvested; most of the slightly better cotton had been picked; and only the early-planted corn, which had enough of the spring rains to produce, remained unharvested. A one-row, tractor-drawn harvester called a snapper would soon begin the final stage of the harvest of 1954.

Coral spider lilies laced the borders of the Rish family cemetery plot; and Roller, as always, read the Lizzie Rish headstone. The unequaled height and the magnificence of her stone demanded his immediate attention each time he settled himself in the sitting place. He always wondered why her headstone was so much more prominent and elaborate than all the others. He had called her Queen Lizzie. She must have been a special lady to have such a fine and prominent granite marker towering over her remains. It read:

Lizzie B. Rish
July 2, 1845
December 20, 1922
Our loss will be her gain
With Christ she's gone to reign

Roller reconnoitered the thicket at the rear of the cemetery for the challenging rabbit. He had hunted it with his spear on several occasions but to no avail. He vowed to continue his quest to spear him. Maybe when the weather got really cold, he could find it bedded up in hiding. He would not abandon his assault; he would alter his tactics.

A thousand summer memories filled his mind. Overall it had been a good summer, and the agony of the fifth grade now made it all the better. Even the bad times—the drought, the threat of losing his tree, the camping trip that he couldn't attend, even those strange feelings that he had experienced—now seemed trivial compared to the dread and torture of Miss E Holley, his teacher, his tyrant. Only Cooper's stroke loomed as terrible as having to go to school.

He thought how easy it would be to just sit there in his sitting place and allow the bus to pass, then to climb down when it returned in pretense that he had gone to school. Bruh, of course, would not allow such a deceit. He, too, had spent his term in the fifth grade jail, and he thought it only fitting that Roller suffer through his sentence now just as he had.

Roller tried to think of more pleasant things. Mr. Roy had been so nice to him as to allow him to maintain the flambeaus. He had earned almost eight dollars and had stashed it behind a rock in the chimney and was saving it for Christmas.

The road construction was making considerable progress. Most of the culverts were placed, and much of the grade work was near completion, but Mr. Roy had explained that the onset of cooler weather would delay the paving until next spring. The wider, contoured, and better-scraped road had allowed an increase in traffic speed, and Cooper, Bruh, and Roller had worked on a new pen for the chickens; too many of them had become victims of progress.

The pen was Muh's mandate. Roller and Bruh, on a few occasions, had secretly herded the flock of chickens toward the road and flushed them into the path of an oncoming car so that they could have fried chicken for dinner. But the demise of the flock population, in her opinion, caused need for a new pen.

The plan to get Muh involved in saving the trees has worked

perfectly. She had been outraged when Roller so mournfully announced to the missionary society the reason for his tearful sadness. The circle of church ladies had moaned with sympathy when Roller told them that the mean old highway man was going to push down Muh's beautiful pecan tree and the tree at the cemetery corner.

Muh had comforted Roller, told him not to worry, and had assured him and the assembly of ladies in no uncertain terms that nobody was going to push anything—especially her or her tree.

She immediately began a campaign to have the trees spared. She wrote letters, made phone calls, and had even put a sign on her tree that read:

> To whom it may Concern,
> Do not harm this tree!
> Signed: Mrs. B. B. Hogan

Roller made a sign for his tree that read:

> THIS ONE EITHER!
> Signed: Roller

The signs and the rest of Muh's campaign had created quiet a stir of conversation around Vilulah, especially with the gossipy old men at the store. The letter to U.S. Congressman, The Honorable E. L. (Tic) Forrester, had been the winning blow in her fight.

Mr. B had actively campaigned for Tic Forrester in his election to the congress, and the entire family had become very close to him and he to them. A mutual love and respect grew out of their relationship, and Mr. Forrester would do anything he could to help the Hogan family—whatever the need.

He had called Muh on the phone and explained that he had no authority over state roads, but that he would be happy to make a few phone calls for her. The calls had brought results.

Mr. Roy had informed all the construction crew and Roller that he had been instructed, even though the trees encroached on the right of way, to disregard them temporarily.

Roller smiled as he remembered Virginia Hart's swim in the nude. It was his favorite recollection of the summer. Each time he thought about her and how she looked, his emotions swirled in a hundred directions. He felt ashamed that he had stood there in hiding and watched her swim in the complete comfort that she was alone. He had invaded her privacy. He had been a Peeping Tom, yet he had made his presence known to her. He had back peddled up the path and whistled a tune loudly to forewarn her that somebody was approaching, and still she made no attempt to clothe herself; she just kept swimming. So she knew he was coming down the path; did she also know that he had been watching her for some time? Why had she allowed him to see her? It was as if she enjoyed it, too.

It excited him to think about her, and a strange stirring filled his loins, and some kind of unexplained energy filled his spirit. Inwardly, for some unknown reason, he thought about White Hogan with Miss Lucille's milk cow as he replayed Virginia's nakedness in his mind; her tanned skin, her long blond hair, her full pointed breasts, and the brown patch between her legs.

Many times he had seen White mount a waiting cow, and he knew enough about what White was doing to want to know more. Somehow there was a connection to White's many cow rides, and why he thought about him when he relived Virginia's naked swim.

The rabbit hopped out and bounced along the thicket edge. The periphery motion caught Roller's attention and broke his chain of thought just as the roar of the school bus broke the morning silence. He vowed to hunt the rabbit today after school.

Roller hated the sound of the bus. It signaled the start of another long day of torture. The fifth grade was contrary to all that Roller thought was right and good. Miss E was a fanatic for perfection. A misspelled word, a forgotten decimal or dollar sign, or other errant work would cause a red check on the top of the page. The recipient of the red check had to stay in the classroom at recess until the error was found and corrected to Miss E's satisfaction.

The school term was now several weeks old, and Roller had not enjoyed a recess yet. It seemed that the harder he tried for perfection, the more mistakes he made. The more mistakes he made, the more time it took to find and correct them, thus the less time outside the confines of the classroom. His blue jeans were always clean when he returned home in the afternoon.

All work and no play had certainly made Roller a dull boy. His normal jovial personality had turned sour. His tolerance of jokes and teasing by Uncle Sammy or anyone else had been extinguished. His temper was even more explosive, and his relationship with Bruh and the rest of his family had deteriorated—especially with Bruh.

Bruh was enjoying the ninth grade. He was playing B-team basketball and was a sure bet to make the varsity track team. He had his learner's driver's license and was allowed to drive the family to church every Sunday. He would be sixteen years old in January and would then be able to get the car and drive unaccompanied. He had a girlfriend, lots of high school friends, and he made good grades. He had very little time for Roller. Roller was jealous and envied Bruh's freedom.

Roller climbed down from the sitting place and swung down on the brace just as the school bus came to a stop. He retrieved his books from beside the tree trunk and hurried to beat Bruh onto the bus.

The ride into Fort Gaines had, in his years past, been a fun-filled preamble to a fun-filled day of learning and playing. Now, though, it seemed to Roller to be a bus ride to hell. He was oblivious to all the laughing and joking of the other students. He sat in quiet study and solitude and tried to think of things other than school and homework. His thoughts, however, always returned to the dread of the day: the impending imprisonment, the long day of boredom. His only relief came in thought of the bus ride home and a temporary escape from the shackles of Miss E and her authority. Even then, after school, he could not escape her completely. She always gave homework—and lots of it—and her demands for perfection required several hours of study each day. Muh monitored the completion of the homework with strict enforcement of two rules—no playing or climbing trees until all homework was finished, and no radio playing on nights when unsatisfactory grades were received.

Roller had very little recreational time, and listening to the radio had become another summer memory. The Ezzard Charles and Rocky Marciano heavyweight bout on September 17 had been Muh's only relaxation of the radio rule.

The bus made its predictable arrival at the Clay County School and deposited its load of energetic passengers—except for Roller.

Roller sat back near the rear of the bus staring out of the window. Somehow he just could not bring himself to stand and walk off the bus. He just sat there.

The bus driver, Mr. Marcine Brooks, checking in his coach mirror to be sure all of the students had exited the bus, spotted Roller sitting there. He called to him, "Roller. Roller, are you going to get off the bus?"

"No, sir." Roller answered, as he looked toward the mirror and made eye contact with Mr. Marcine.

"You're not?"

"No, sir."

"Why not?" Mr. Marcine swung his feet around from under the steering wheel, stood up and walked back to Roller.

"I just don't feel like going to school today."

"Are you sick?"

"Yes, sir. That's it, I'm sick."

"Well, you come on, and let's go see Mr. White. He'll take you to the doctor."

"No, sir, I don't need to see no doctor."

"Well, Roller, you can't stay on this bus; now, you'll have to see Mr. White, and he'll take you back home if he thinks you ought to go."

"Why don't you take me home? You brought me down here?"

"I can't do that Roller. Come on, now, and let's go see Mr. White."

Roller knew that Mr. White was the new school principal and that the only time people went to see the principal was when they were in big trouble. He didn't want to be in trouble; he just didn't want to go back in that classroom today. He knew that his work would have mistakes and what those mistakes would cost in time of confinement.

Mr. White always watched the unloading of the buses from

his office window, and he knew by the delay of Mr. Marcine's bus that there must be a problem. He walked out to the bus and stepped inside just as Roller was about to refuse again to leave the bus.

"What's the problem, Mr. Brooks?"

"Well, sir, Roller here don't want to go to school today."

"I see," said Mr. White as he walked back to them. "Good morning, Roller," he continued.

Roller had seen Mr. White only twice before this, once when he came around to all of the classes on the first day of school, and again one day at the lunchroom. He seemed like a nice man.

"Good morning, sir." Roller responded.

"Are you sick, Roller?"

"Well, actually, Mr. White, I think it's my heart."

Mr. White looked at Mr. Brooks and grinned, "Your heart, huh?"

"Yes, sir."

"Um, you better come on with me then, Roller, and let's see if we can find something that will make you feel better, okay?"

Roller looked back from his stare out the window and took hold of Mr. White's outstretched hand. "Yes, sir."

Mr. White winked at Mr. Brooks and led Roller from the bus. They talked as they walked toward the big front door of the school building.

"What grade are you in Roller, the fifth?"

"Yes, sir." Roller answered solemnly.

"Uh huh, is that why your heart is giving you problems?"

"Must be."

"Well, you come on and wait in my office. I'll be right back."

Mr. White escorted Roller into his office and instructed him to wait there for a few minutes. He left the office and stayed gone for what seemed like an eternity.

Roller began to think. *Am I in big trouble? Is Mr. White going to tell Miss E that I didn't want to go to her classroom? That will make her even worse. Is he going to send home a note to Muh and Daddy? If I am in trouble, what will be my punishment?*

Finally, Mr. White finished the early morning chore of getting the school day started and returned to his office. He seemed predisposed and to have forgotten about Roller as he took his seat at his large neat desk, but suddenly devoted his attention to Roller and asked, "Does your heart feel better now, Roller?"

"I guess so, yes, sir."

Mr. White was of medium build, neat, and well-dressed. His face was smooth and strongly chiseled, square-jawed and friendly. His nose was keen, and his eyes squinted with concern and concentration. His eyes and lips were expressive, and his mood readily became his demeanor.

"Roller."

"Yes, sir?"

"That is your nickname isn't it?"

"Yes, sir."

"What is your real name?"

"Jessie."

"Had you rather that I call you Roller?"

"Yes, sir."

"Okay. Well, Roller, what is the real reason that you don't want to go to school today?"

"Sir, it's not just today; I don't ever want to go to school, but I've been trying real hard to make the best of it."

Mr. White, trying to hide a little grin, continued, "What do you dislike about it?"

"Miss E," Roller quipped.

"Miss E?"

"Yes, sir."

"Do you mean you like everything about school except Miss E?"

"Just about. Yes, sir."

"What is it about Miss E that you dislike?"

"Well, she doesn't like me, so I don't like her."

"What makes you think that she doesn't like you?" Mr. White propped his chin on his folded hands.

"If she liked me, it looks to me like she would help me find my mistakes and let me go out for recess once in a while."

"Uh huh, tell me more about that."

"You see, if you make a mistake on a paper, she just puts a red check at the top, and you have to stay in the classroom during recess until you find it. She won't help you find your mistake, so I look so hard for the mistake that I'll correct things that were correct to start with, then I've got more mistakes.... I haven't had a recess all year. Just look at this paper." Roller pulled a piece of notebook paper out of his arithmetic book and handed it to Mr. White. "You see. I've corrected this paper so much that I've erased holes in it, and I still don't know what's wrong with it."

Mr. White took the paper and studied it for a few minutes. "Hum. I don't see anything wrong with it either; let me look again." He studied it again. Again, he didn't see a mistake. With a puzzled look on his face he turned the paper over and looked at the backside.

"Well, I'm sure if Miss E says there is an error on this paper, that there must be one here somewhere." He placed the paper flat on his desk and seriously searched each problem, checking them for errors.

Roller talked as Mr. White studied the paper. "I think she ought to go back to Missouri."

"Missouri?" Mr. White looked up from the paper in puzzlement.

"Yes, sir. She's always saying that she is from Missouri, the 'Show Me State,' and when she says that, you know that you've got trouble ahead trying to find some mistake or another and that there won't be a recess again."

Mr. White, grinning, returned to the paper. "Roller, have you ever thought that Miss E is hard like that because she does like you?"

"No, sir!"

"Don't you think that she is trying to teach you all these things that you'll need to know before you go to the sixth grade, and that if she didn't like you or if she didn't care about you that she wouldn't be so intent on your getting things right? You know, if she didn't like you, she wouldn't care if you passed to the sixth grade or not."

Roller sat up in his chair. "Yes, sir, I guess that's right, but

I sure would like to go outside and play sometimes."

Suddenly Roller thought about what Cooper had said about using what you have to gain something you don't have. He decided that all he had in this case was an audience with Mr. White and maybe a sympathetic ear. He also decided that he had very little to lose and a lot to gain and that playing on Mr. White's sympathy couldn't hurt. He started to cry.

"Now, Roller, you're too big to cry about this," assured Mr. White. "You just calm down now, and I'll check into this. Did you say that you haven't been out for recess all year long?" as he studied the paper again.

Roller sniffed and replied, "That's right; the only time I get to go outside is when we walk to the lunchroom at lunch."

Mr. White grunted under his breath and studied the paper. They were quiet for several minutes.

"I think I've found your mistake here, Roller. Come here and look at this word problem."

Roller stood up and approached Mr. White's left side behind his big desk.

"This problem says if Bob shared equally a box of twenty-five apples with three other boys and has one remaining, what do each of the boys have?"

"Yes, sir."

"And you answered six."

"Yes, sir. Well four goes into twenty-five six times with one remaining. I put six first, and then I tried eight thinking three boys, but it says shared with three other boys, so that means four in all, so then I put six again."

"Well, she must want you to write six apples, because there is nothing else wrong here."

"Yes, sir, that sounds like something she would want. That must be it."

"Why don't you write apples here behind your number six and take it to her? I want you to come back by my office, and let me know if that was the mistake. Okay?"

"Yes, sir. I will. Uh...uh...Mr. White, don't you think you could tell Miss E without her knowing that I asked you, to let us have recess now and then?"

"Roller, Miss E has been teaching here a long time, and I haven't been here but a couple of months. Now, I can't tell her how to do her teaching. I'll tell you what though," Mr. White stood up from his desk, put his hand on Roller's shoulder, and looked down at him. "You try real hard to do better, and remember that Miss E just wants you to learn things that you'll need to know later, and you'll see that things will get better. Okay?"

"Yes, sir, I'll try. Thank you, sir."

"Now, you take this tardy excuse, and run along to your classroom. I'll look for you to let me know about your paper."

"Yes, sir." Roller felt much better. Mr. White was a kind man. He acted like he understood that school should be a little bit fun. Roller wanted to please him, to show him that he was a good student. He wanted Mr. White to like him.

Gathering his books, he walked listlessly through the huge auditorium to his fifth grade class. As he opened the classroom door, every student, as well as Miss E, turned to witness his late arrival.

Miss E was a large bulb of a woman; her face and arms sagged with fat. She wore little wire-framed glasses that magnified her grey mysterious eyes. She wore her greying black hair in a bun on the back of her head. Instead of turning her head, she scanned her subjects by darting her eyes from side to side. An infrequent smile exonerated her irregular yellow teeth, and she periodically sucked the saliva from the corner of her mouth with an inhaling hiss. Roller, like most of the boys, called her "Big Bertha."

"Roller, do you have a tardy excuse?" demanded Miss E.

"Yes, ma'am," he said, walking to the desk and handing her the note.

She read it and acknowledged, "Well, take your seat. We're on page one hundred one in your geography book."

Roller did as he was told, taking his seat behind Billy Chitwood. Billy grinned at him as he passed by. Billy had been one of the best things about the fifth grade.

The construction on the new dam and hydroelectric plant at Fort Gaines was set to begin in about six months, and several survey engineers had already moved there to begin the mapping and elevation studies for the project.

Billy's father was one of those engineers that had moved his family there during the summer from Tennessee. He and Roller had become good friends. He had to stay in at recess too, and likewise he hated Miss E. At every opportunity Roller and Billy jokingly fantasized about ways to kill Miss E, or to maim her so that she couldn't teach. They would cut imaginary holes in the floor for her to step in. When she would step on one of the make-believe-spots as she lumbered around the room, Roller would tap Billy on the back and make a little muffled sound like a bomb exploding. After class, or whenever possible, they would replay the booby trap episode and laugh and joke about it.

Later that day during the afternoon recess, Roller presented the paper that Mr. White had examined to Miss E along with several others. It was correct, but two of the others were incorrect.

Roller worked for most of the recess period but finally found his mistakes and was allowed a few minutes to go outside. Instead of playing or talking to Billy as he would ordinarily do, he ran around the big brick building to the front door and inside to see Mr. White.

Mr. White sat at his big desk and peered over his glasses as Roller appeared in front of the open door. "Come in Roller."

"I just wanted to tell you, sir, that six apples was the correct answer."

"Well good, I'm pleased to hear that. Now, what did you learn from that, Roller?"

Roller thought a minute and answered, "I guess I learned that somebody from Missouri is a very hard person to please. I've got to go now. Bye, Mr. White."

Mr. White leaned back in his chair and chuckled out loud as Roller exited the front door and ran around the building.

Later, when the school day was over and they had boarded the bus for the return home, Bruh came back to Roller and with a smirk on his face, in front of all the other children, quizzed him about having to go to the office.

"You got in trouble didn't you? You had to go to Mr. White's office didn't you?"

"How did you know about it?" Roller responded. "It ain't none of your business anyway."

"I bet it'll be Muh's business when she finds out."

"Muh don't need to know about it. It was nothing. I did not get in trouble, and you'd better keep your lip zipped about it," Roller demanded.

"You know she's gonna find out about it," Bruh insisted. "You better tell her about it before she finds out from somebody else."

"Well, if she finds out about it from somebody else, that's fine, but if she finds out about it from you....your ass is grass, and I'm the lawnmower!" shouted Roller.

"You better watch your mouth. You'll be in big trouble sure enough."

"Well, you just shut yours before I shut it for you, Mr. Highschool!"

Roller stared out the window and ignored him and all of the other busy conversation. *Dang, I have enough to think about, enough to dread, without having to worry about Muh. If Bruh squeals on me, I am going to bust him..... Then, of course, I will be in big trouble for fighting....so be it.* He was tired of Bruh bullying him around. He hated bullies. He was going to settle the score one of these days. Maybe he should tell Muh before she heard about it. That way, she would hear his side of the story first. What the heck, he hadn't done anything wrong—had he?

The bus ride home always seemed longer that the ride to school, and days were getting shorter. He'd only have an hour or so of daylight to hunt the rabbit, to do his chores, and that cursed homework. Thankfully, he didn't have much homework today.

The bus slowed to a stop in front of the store, and as Roller and Bruh made their departure, Roller noticed that the car was not under the pecan tree where it was normally parked—a good indication that Muh was not at home. This might be his opportunity to hunt the rabbit. He dropped his books on the porch and ran through the store in search of a snack. He got a cold RC out of the box, dried the water with the towel, cut a thin slice of hoop cheese, and grabbed a handful of Johnny cookies out of the big display jar. Sandwiching the cheese midway the stack of cookies, he informed Uncle George, who had been napping in one of the old rockers until the screen door slammed, what he had.

"Uncle George, I've got an RC, six Johnny cookies and a nickel's worth of cheese. Charge it, please, sir." He ran to retrieve his books before Uncle George could hardly respond.

Gathering up his books and snacks, he hurried to the bighouse hoping Muh was gone. She was, but Mama was there to insist on the homework ritual.

"Yes, ma'am, I know, but I've got to check on something first. I won't be long, and I'll get right on it. I don't have much anyway."

Mama was a lot more tolerant and understanding of Roller's need for time away from the drudgery of homework.

"Roller, you know that you are supposed to do your homework before you do anything else. Now you come right on back."

"Yes, ma'am, I will," he said, still munching on the cheese and cookies in one hand and the RC in the other. By the time he got to the blacksmith shop where his spear was stashed, he had finished his snack. He put the RC bottle on the wooden barrel so that he could deliver it back to the store when he returned to hide the spear after his hunt. Uncle George was very demanding about bringing bottles back to the store; there was a two-cent deposit on them.

He pulled the spear from its hiding place and again felt its perfect balance in an overhead back and forth motion. Since he had practiced throwing, he had become quite good at it. He had twice hit the bull's-eye of an empty Lucky Strike cigarette pack at ten paces. The spear was true and his aim was good, but the true test would be launching it toward his prey under the pressure of knowing that he would only get one chance.

He crossed the barnyard and entered the cemetery. He didn't take time to study the tombstones as he normally would—he was preoccupied with his plan of attack, and he instinctively assumed a crouched, stalking profile as he crept up to the edge of the thicket.

The thicket sat in the southwest corner of the cemetery. Its boundaries were the hog paddock fence on the south and west and the open graveyard on the third side of its triangular shape. It had few trees of any height—mostly scrub oaks and privet hedge. Honeysuckle vine carpeted its floor and covered a few old gravestones that had been abandoned. The rabbit had a million hiding places.

Cooper had taught him how to bed a rabbit by slowly and quietly searching the tangles of vines with an ever sharp eye for the slight color difference or twitching ears of a crouched rabbit.

To find a rabbit in the bed took time, patience, good eyes, and careful study of the undergrowth. A step too close would flush the wary prey who might run for some distance before bedding again.

Roller lifted the spear and held it in the ready position. He stalked the little trails in the viney cover very slowly and deliberately. His eyes shifted and pierced the dense mat of vines and brambles in search of the almost perfectly camouflaged rabbit. He barely noticed the rust breasted robins that flirted in the scrubby trees. He paid no attention to the field rats as they scurried beneath the vines. The squawking jays and crows were disregarded; the sparrows and thrashers were neglected. His only thought was the rabbit!

He pretended, as he stealthily pursued his quarry, to be a young Indian brave in search of a meal for his family. He talked to himself in some unknown Indian dialect, encouraging himself to press on, to let nothing distract him, to seek and destroy the hidden enemy.

His arm was tiring from being held in the constantly drawn, ready position. Tension mounted as he slowly but surely reduced the area that concealed the rabbit. Weaving in and out around each patch of cover, crisscrossing the width of the thicket, he had only a small corner left unhunted. Surely this able brave had not overlooked his prey, and surely it crouched in hiding somewhere in the little triangle of thicket that lay ahead.

He crept even more slowly when he paced west, taking extra time to compensate for the glare of the sun that was settling toward the horizon.

Just as he neared the fence that separated the thicket from the hog paddock, a flicker of movement caught his eye, and his heart raced in anticipation of a clear shot at the wary rabbit. His eyes strained against the glare to identify his target. He coaxed himself in that imaginary Indian tongue. Suddenly, right near the base of the fence, a clear silhouette of the rabbit became apparent!

It happened so quickly! The rabbit had warily maneuvered just ahead of Roller's stalk, and, as his available cover was reduced, he sought a path alongside the fence in order to sneak by Roller's assault and to take cover in the territory already searched.

The big bully pig, Mr. B's prize breeding stock, smelled, then spotted the tipping rabbit, and charged it just as Roller fully drew the spear to its throwing status. Roller, unaware of the charging pig, heaved the spear toward the rabbit's profile and shouted in that Indian gobbledygook, "Humbagowa!" as the spear sought its mark. The rabbit sprang in escape as the spear made a solid thunking noise. An immediate blood-curdling squeal filled the air. Roller rushed toward the fence in time to see Mr. B's most prized boar pig stumbling and falling backwards with the spear stuck directly and deeply between its eyes.

CHAPTER 10
THE SALE

An occasional leaf fell to the surface of the upper swimming hole as Roller sat there staring at its peaceful beauty. The autumn chill was obvious—the woods had changed into several shades of tan and brown. The sky was thick with grey clouds.

His mood matched the dull, lackluster of his surroundings. Even the chattering squirrels were of no interest to him. He wished to be one of the little minnows that swam so carefree and effortlessly in the clear glassy pool. They seemed to have such a peaceful, worry-free life. He assumed that they had no concerns, no guilt or shame.

Cooper had developed a very noticeable limp, and slightly drug his left foot when he walked. Roller was glad to hear him shuffling and whistling down the leaf-covered path to the swimming hole, for he was not particularly enjoying his solitude. Maybe Cooper's company would lessen his guilt.

The big boar pig had died, and Cooper had burned the carcass before Mr. B had a chance to examine it. The cause of death to everyone other than Cooper and Roller was unknown. After quizzing Cooper, Mr. B had reprimanded him for destroying the carcass. Roller had overheard the conversation. "Well, Cooper, did the hog have any marks on him, or was he bloated or anything? Did he have bloody-diarrhea or a lot of slobber at his mouth? Was there anything that would tell us what happened to him?"

Cooper nodded, even though he had a negative response. "I tell you what, Mr. B, that hog was so greedy that he prolly choked to deaf. He always push them other pigs out the way and gobble up feed like that suck-pipe be sucking cotton at the gin. And I believe he suck a roasting ear down his throat and choke to deaf

108

on it, sho nuff."

"I have never heard of a hog choking to death! I just hope it wasn't that cholera. That stuff can wipe out a whole pasture of hogs in no time."

Cooper remembered burning hog carcasses that died with cholera. "Naw, suh, his skin wasn't red at all. He'da had blistered-looking skin if it was cholera. Naw, suh."

"Yeah, well okay, just let me look at them before you burn them from now on."

"Yas, suh." Cooper nodded.

Cooper settled down by the base of the old oak beside Roller and rolled a cigarette. Neither of them spoke for a long time. Finally Roller asked, "What did you do with my spear?"

Cooper exhaled little clouds of smoke and watched the breeze blow it away. "Boy, you must have one powerful throwing arm. I liked to never ass pull that spear outa that nincompoop's head.... I put it up like I shoulda done long time ago. Naw, I shoulda never made the damn thang anyhow. I knowed it was gonna be trouble. I don't know what I was thinking bout."

Now Cooper was feeling guilty too, so Roller tried to change the subject. "I thought Dr. Harper told you to quit smoking that Prince Albert tobacco."

"He did." Cooper responded. "Man, I sho nuff did want to dress that big ole pig. He sho woulda been some good ass eating."

"Yeah, well, I feel bad enough about it. Seems like the harder I try to stay out of trouble, the more trouble I get into."

"We would both been in trouble if I hadn't burnt that hog when I did, but as it is, we ain't in trouble, we just feels bad about it. Thang is, I didn't have no business turning you loose with the dang thang. Well, maybe we both learned a lesson."

"Yeah." Roller continued to stare at the pool.

"Roller, I sho wish you'd kill me a mess of them squirrels. Hey, you better get back to the sto. I saw Walter and his chillen coming down the road while ago. All the Saturday crowd gonna be there dreckly."

"Yeah," Roller halfheartedly replied. He thought a minute about what Cooper had said, and then asked, "Cooper, why don't you shoot your own squirrels?"

"Naw, man, I ain't shot a gun since I was a little boy."

Roller suddenly remembered that he had never seen Cooper shoot a gun, that he wouldn't shoot the hogs at killing time, but that he had taught him a lot about hunting.

"Well, how is it that you know so much about hunting and bedding rabbits and shooting and all?"

"My paw taught me all that stuff." Cooper tossed his cigarette onto the silver surface of the swimming hole, and they watched the minnows dart up to investigate it. Roller waited in anticipation for Cooper to continue. "Taught me how to tan hides, skin squirrels, and all that stuff; had me shooting a shotgun when I was nine years old."

For the first time Roller looked away from the hypnotizing shimmer of the little pool of spring water. He looked straight at Cooper's aging dark eyes and stared. Mama's account of his granddaddy's murder suddenly exploded in his mind. She had said that a shotgun was the murder weapon and that a burned shotgun was found after the woods fire had been extinguished.

Roller didn't really want to ask the question, but he had to, and somehow he already knew the answer. "What kind of shotgun did he teach you how to shoot?"

"It was one of them double-barrel, rabbit ear, twelve gauges. Man, that thang like to kick me down one time. Bruised my shoulder to the bone, and I ain't shot a gun since that day."

Roller stared back at the swimming hole as one of those strange feelings came over him. His skin tingled as if being pricked with a million tiny pins. He heard nothing, and he seemed to be lightheaded and faint. It took several minutes before he could think again. Cooper continued to talk, but Roller didn't hear a word that he said.

Dang, maybe Cooper's paw did kill grandpa. Oh, well, if he did, then he was punished for it. But what if he didn't. Then he was punished unjustly. How could he find out for sure? Why did he care? It was such a long time ago, and certainly knowing all about it would be of no real value. He couldn't change things, and it wouldn't change his relationship with Cooper.

Cooper, apparently, knew very little about the murder. If he had known that a double-barrel shotgun was the murder weapon, surely he would not have ever mentioned it. He might not even know that it was Roller's granddaddy who was killed, resulting in the hanging of his paw.

He wanted to ask Cooper more questions, but he didn't want to make him think that he was suspicious of his paw. He'd have to wait to know more. He'd have to find another way to get his questions answered. He needed a plan.

Finally he became aware of Cooper's conversation again. He didn't know what he had missed. Cooper was rattling on about the hog killing that would start next week if it turned a little cooler, and the turkey killing that would start the week before Thanksgiving regardless of the weather.

"You better get back to the sto now! Don't you be in trouble sho nuff," Cooper insisted as he stood up and brushed off the seat of his denim coveralls.

"Yeah."

"Roller, afore we go...." He leaned against the trunk of the old oak and rubbed back and forth scratching his back.

"Yeah?"

"Tell me again bout a grabbing Ollie's ding-dong with that claw."

"Aw, Cooper, I done told you about it umpteen times. What you want to hear it again for?"

Cooper laughed aloud. "I just like to hear you tell it. Come on, tell me bout it, then we'll go."

Roller sort of settled himself against the trunk of the tree and recounted the episode. He always found a way to embellish the story each time he told it. "You see, just about the time I got to the knothole, Ollie's ole tallywhacker stuck his head out as if it was looking around to see if anybody was looking at him. Seemed like after it looked around a minute, it stuck on out a little further and started to pee. I kinda got scared and almost forgot to get the claw out of my pocket. So I reached in my pocket and pulled on the leg, and the claws caught on the lining of my pocket. I pulled harder, and one of the claws dug into my leg and I almost hollered out loud. I had to pull my pocket inside out and unhook the claws."

Cooper stared up into the thick sky beyond the shedding forest and savored every word of Roller's tale.

"Just about the time I got it untangled, his stream started to slow up, so I held the claw in my left hand and held the string good and tight with my right hand. I waited till he was just about through peeing, and I grabbed it real quick. When I pulled the string, the toes curled around that joker, and the claws bit into it. Ollie squealed out like a pig getting his balls cut out and tried to pull his tallywhacker back through the knothole. But the harder he pulled, the tighter the claws bit in. I guess he realized that trying to pull back wasn't going to work, so he pushed it all the way out, and I could hear the boards on the mill house squeak as he leaned all his weight against the inside wall. He began to call real soft-like `Kit-ty, kit-ty.'"

Cooper laughed wildly!

"It was like he was begging that old cat to turn him loose. He pitched his voice up real high and pleaded again, 'kit-ty, kit-ty.' I heard him say, 'Now what the hell am I gonna do? I ought to know better than to stick my pecker in any hole that ain't got no hair round it. Gol dang cat! I mean kit-ty, kit-ty. Shit, if somebody was to see me like this, I wouldn't never live it down. Please, Mr. Kitty Cat, I won't never bother you no more.'

"I knew that I could release my grip on the claw, and it would slowly relax and slacken its hold. So I dropped it and ran back around the millhouse and back to my seat at the stone sharpening. As I rounded the corner, I heard Ollie banging on the wall, yelling 'Scat! Scat! You som-a-bitch!'"

Cooper laughed hysterically.

"When we got through that day, I went back and picked up the claw off the ground. Say, You know what I saw the other day?"

Cooper nodded and asked, "What?"

"I saw that cat rubbing up against old Ollie's leg just like he does everybody else's."

"The hell you say!"

"Beat anything I ever saw. Reckon why that cat all of a sudden likes Ollie?"

"Dang if I know. Maybe he can sense something ass different about Ollie. You know a cat is magic anyhow."

"Magic?" quizzed Roller.

"Yeah, man. They got nine lives."

Roller stood up and followed Cooper up the trail. "Nine lives. What does that mean?" Roller quizzed.

"Means that a cat can dodge deaf nine ass times. They can't dodge castor oil though."

"Castor oil?"

"That's right. I give a cat some castor oil one time, and he shit hisself slam away."

Roller knew Cooper was up to one of his jokes, but he went along. "He did what?"

"Yeah, that cat dug so many holes to shit in that he wasted away to nothing. Last time I saw him, he farted and disappeared right in front of my eyes."

They both laughed, but Cooper laughed for several minutes. When he finally stopped, Roller said, "Cooper you won't do!"

Cooper fondly rubbed his rough hand in Roller's curly hair. "You the one what won't do."

They crossed the fence and walked across the paddock toward the rear of the barn. Cooper fixed his eyes on the barn. "Roller, you don't remember when the barn burned, do you?"

"Naw. I remember hearing tell about it. What made you think about that?"

"I don't know. It sho was a mess. Thirteen mules burned to deaf; two sows with eighteen pigs and the milk cow. That was the only time I ever saw your daddy cry. Happened at night; the farm bell woke everybody up. I think Bruh was the one what woke up and saw the fire out his window."

"Yeah."

"Everybody on the farm come running, but it was too far gone. We did manage to let a bull and a horse out. Everything else burned to deaf. Next morning, bout sunup, me and Mr. B sat down side by side watching the smoking remains of that fine barn and them fine animals, and cried like two little younguns. They said lightning struck it, but I always will believe that fire was sot."

"Sot? You mean you think somebody started the fire on

purpose?"

"Sho do, and I think I know who done it."

"Who?"

"Well, I ain't saying." He paused. "That must be a awful way to die—burning up like that. Man, them mules and all done some pitiful screaming that night. That sho was a bad ass thang to have to listen to."

"Who set the fire, Cooper?" Roller spat.

"I ain't gonna say cause I can't prove it, but there was one nigger—the name Cooper used for colored people that he didn't like—what showed up at the fire that night with all his fine clothes on. Rest of us just grabbed a shirt and some overalls and come running to the bell. Some of us just had on some overalls—no shirt, no shoes. That one, though, was fully dressed, and he got there bout the same time the rest of us did. One thang for sho, a man that will set one fire will set another. He gonna slip up one a these days. Then I'll tell you."

As they rounded the barn and millhouse, Cooper looked at the cloth-stuffed knothole and chuckled. "Boy, you won't do! Dang, here it is time for me to go see a man about a dog. See you."

Annie Jenny had finished cleaning the kitchen from dinner and was sitting in her regular place in the shade of the big pecan tree. Cooper spotting her, cut left at the rear of the store, and headed toward her. Roller continued along the south side of the store. He yelled back at Cooper, "Hey, don't you overdo it."

"I ain't," nodded Cooper.

Just as Roller reached the little stoop at the back door and was about to step up into the store, an airborne dishpan full of water met him full in the face. Bruh had been cleaning the meat-cutting knives and cleavers and had innocently swashed Roller as he emptied the cleaning water.

Roller was drenched and, of course, thought Bruh had deliberately thrown the water at him. Slinging his arms and hands and wiping his eyes on his soaked shirt sleeve, he attacked. Half-blinded with the dirty dishwater and with his notorious, reckless abandon, he charged inside the store in search of Bruh, who was retreating with equal ferocity.

The store was practically full of shoppers. Both counters were piled high with groceries, and everybody was busy. This was no place for a skirmish, but Roller's wild temper had been triggered, his fuse had been lit, and to defuse his rages was no easy task.

Bruh had seen Roller's fury many times and sought his escape behind the meat showcase, and, as he reached the main counter, he ducked down below its level in hopes of reaching the front door without Roller seeing him.

Uncle George, Muh, and Mr. B were all busy behind the counter, and Bruh's half crawl, half duck-walk had many obstacles.

Roller bolted behind the meat counter before he saw that Bruh had apparently taken the isle behind the main counter as his escape route. He knew that Bruh would have a slow pace because the isle was full. He also knew that the front door would be Bruh's destination. He reversed his course, ran for the back door, and launched himself off the stoop at full speed around the outside of the store to the front porch. Bruh, however, had managed a peep through the glass candy showcase and saw Roller as he went out the back door. He knew that Roller would be headed for the front door to intercept him, so he rounded the end of the main counter and headed for the back door. Just as Roller threw open the front screen door, Bruh launched himself off the stoop at full speed around the rear of the store to safety.

Roller knew that Bruh had not made the front door, but he had not seen him exit the back door. He thought that Bruh was hiding somewhere behind the main counter, so he vaulted the end of the counter and landed square in front of—and in the grasp of—Muh, who all the while had been trying to get her hands on somebody, for her shouted command to 'stop this foolishness' had flown past unhearing ears, unheeded and unobeyed.

"Whoa, what's going on here? Where have you been, and how did you get so wet?"

Muh was normally the gentle and gracious lady that her charming but unconscious beauty exemplified. When she lost her temper, though, it was easy to see that Roller was truly a product of her genetic composition. Her lips tightened, her eyes

115

squinted, and her voice strengthened. She shook him by his wet shoulder. "I am sick and tired of this mess between you and Ben, and I'm going to stop it. Do you hear me?"

Roller never understood why she always asked, "Do you hear me?" She was face to face with him. How could he help but hear her?

"Yes, ma'am."

She shook him again. "Now you go put on a dry shirt and get back in here to help with the trade. Do you hear me?"

"Yes, ma'am."

"Now get! Do you hear me?" She turned him around by twisting his shoulders, faced him toward the front door, and popped him on the buttocks with her bare hand.

"Yes, ma'am!" Roller hurried out. It seemed to him that a thousand dark eyes were watching the altercation as all of the colored people in and out of the store had stopped their shopping or their gabbing to witness the outcome of this event. He was wet, he was mad, he was embarrassed, and, worst of all, he was irritated that the revenge he sought had been interrupted by one of the few people who could.

He trotted to the bighouse past Annie Jenny who asked, "Boy how you get so wet?"

"Bruh did it."

Mama was sitting in her rocking chair on the front porch, and she too, quizzed Roller about how he got wet.

"Mama, Bruh did this to me, and I'm gonna kick his you-know-what."

"Now, Roller...."

He knew he was about to receive a little mini-sermon about "turning the other cheek" or "do unto others" or "the meek shall inherit the earth." "Mama, I'm under strict orders to hurry back to the store. I gotta go."

He wrestled off the wet shirt as he entered the bathroom, took a reddish orange bar of Lifebuoy soap from the soap dish, and washed his face and neck. The dishwater had left a smell of old meat all over him. He washed his hair and rewashed his face, all the while trying to think of the worst curse word that he knew to punctuate what he was thinking of Bruh.

He found a clean shirt and retraced his steps to the store. Muh had asked Punto, who was waiting his turn to shop, to find Bruh and return him to the store. Muh had stationed Bruh behind the meat counter and instructed Roller to work the drink box and gas pumps, thereby keeping a considerable distance between the feuding brothers. She instructed both of them that she would not tolerate any more of their foolishness and that they would apologize to each other before the day was over. Roller insisted that he didn't owe Bruh any apology.

"Muh, Bruh started this. He threw the water on me. I don't have anything to apologize about. The only thing I'm sorry of is that I couldn't get my hands on him."

"Now you hush that kind of talk. Do you hear? Bruh says that it was an accident, that he didn't know you were there."

"He had to know that I was there. I had just yelled out to Cooper. He had to have heard me."

"Well, I've told him and I'm telling you, the next time ya'll fight.... Do you hear me? I'm going to put something on you that Spic-n-Span won't take off. Do you hear me?"

"Yes, ma'am." Roller knew when to hush. He kept his place and worked his area and avoided Bruh for the rest of the day.

It was almost sundown when a shiny black Cadillac pulled up to the gas pump. Very few Cadillacs came to the Vilulah community. Naturally, Roller hurried out to investigate the needs of this new customer. He studied, in awe, the beautiful Eldorado Cadillac with its shiny chrome and continental kit. The man that climbed out of the big car was equally impressive. He was tall and robust and wore a Stetson cowboy hat, a western cut suit with a string tie, a big silver belt buckle, and the shiniest pair of cowboy boots that Roller had ever seen. He reminded Roller of Gene Autry and appeared to be about the same age.

Roller, and the crowd of colored people as well, was overcome with wondrous admiration of the big cigar-smoking cowboy and his big black ride. After stretching his large frame by the side of the car for a second or two, he finally spoke to Roller. "Young man."

Roller snapped out of his trance. "Yes, sir, you need some gas?"

"Well, not really, young man, but this ole horse will eat a bag of oats most anytime you give her one. Might as well put in about ten gallons. Say, you got a cold beer in there?" He nodded toward the store.

"No, sir, we don't sell beer, but we got some cold Coca-Colas."

The big cowboy leaned down and looked into the Cadillac and asked, "Do you want a drink, Darling?"

Roller had been so impressed with Gene Autry that he had failed to see Dale Evans. She was a beautiful blonde lady who also wore a Western-cut suit and cowgirl boots. She held a little white fluffy dog in her lap, and even though the afternoon light was dimming she seemed to shine and illuminate the big car. Without question, she was the prettiest woman that he had ever seen! He thought about Virginia Hart.

"Yes, that sounds good," she answered with a clear, high-pitched Southern drawl, "and get Fifi some cookies, okay." She rubbed the little dog's fluffy head.

The big cowboy pulled at the waist of his pants and shifted his cigar to one side and spoke out of the open side of his mouth. "I'm looking for Mr. B.B. Hogan."

"Yes, sir, he's right there inside the store. You want me to get him?"

"Naw, young man. I'm going in to get a Coke. Are you gonna pump the gas?"

"Oh, yes, sir!" Roller reached the open air for the pump handle with his right hand as he watched the big man walk inside. His hand found the handle, and he turned his attention to filling the globe up to the ten-gallon mark.

He noticed as he pulled the nozzle hose to the other side of the car that it had a Georgia tag—that the first digit in the tag number was three. He remembered that the first digit of any Georgia tag number indicated what county the car was from.

Let's see, one is Fulton, two is Dekalb, and three is Chatham. Dang! What is the cowboy from Chatham County doing here, and what does he want with Daddy? Where is Chatham County, anyway? Gene Autry must be some kind of politician or something. He had to find out.

He drained the gasoline from the globe, replaced the cap and hung the nozzle back in its place, and proceeded to clean that part of the windshield that he could reach. He couldn't help but stare at Dale Evans through the glass. The little dog barked at him as he approached the passenger side. The pretty cowgirl talked to Fifi, but Roller couldn't understand her baby talk.

When he finished the windshield, he came back to the open driver side door and peeped in. "What kind of little dog is that, ma'am?"

The little dog growled at him. "Oh, she's a miniature French poodle. Her name is Fifi. Isn't that right Fifi? And what's your name young man?"

"My name is Roller. I don't think I've ever seen such a fancy little dog before. What makes her hair grow like that?"

"Well, she's a French Poodle—isn't that right, Fifi? Would you like to pet her, Roller? Her hair is cut like that."

"Yes, ma'am. What did you say your name is, ma'am?"

"I didn't say, but my name is Marilyn."

That's it, Roller thought. *She must be Marilyn Monroe.* He had seen a picture of Marilyn Monroe with a little white dog. *What is Marilyn Monroe doing here?*

"Are you Marilyn Monroe?"

Marilyn laughed. "Oh, no. I wish. No, my name is Marilyn Newton."

"Do you mind, Miss Marilyn, if I sit down in your car?"

"No, Roller. Come on and sit down."

The big cowboy had the seat so far back that Roller could barely reach the steering wheel and could not see above it at all. He pretended to drive the big car as he talked to Marilyn.

"I see ya'll are from Chatham County. What town is that?" He reached over to pet Fifi's head.

"We're from Savannah. Oh, Fifi!" Marilyn hurriedly rolled down her window. A dreadful odor filled the car.

Roller tried to ignore it, and continued to admire the luxurious upholstery and dashboard of the Eldorado. "Ya'll are a long way from home."

"Yes, we left home about dinner time."

Mr. B and Gene Autry came out of the store. The big cowboy brought Marilyn a Coke and Fifi two Johnny cookies.

"Roller, get out of that man's car and leave Mrs. Newton alone," Mr. B demanded.

"Aw, he's all right, Mr. Hogan. Leave him be. Marilyn needs somebody to talk to. Here, young man, would you hand Marilyn her Coke, and here's two cookies for that damn dog."

"Yes, sir." Roller passed the Coke and cookies to her as Mr. B and the big cowboy walked away talking.

After a minute or two of silence, Roller asked, "Is Mr. Newton a politician?"

Marilyn giggled. "No, what makes you think that? Oh, Fifi, you've done it again!" Again the horrendous odor filled the car, and again, Roller tried to ignore it.

"Oh, I don't know, he just sorta looks like a politician."

"No, Roller. He's a real cowboy. We have a cattle ranch over near Savannah."

"Really?"

"Yes, we both ride horses almost everyday. Seems like we're always working cattle or checking fences or something."

"Yeah, I know about checking fences too. Me and Cooper do it all the time," Roller responded with a smile.

"Who's Cooper?"

"He's a colored man friend of mine that works for my daddy. He just works mostly with the livestock now though."

Again a putrid invisible cloud filled the car. Marilyn rolled down her window again, but otherwise tried to ignore this one; it was much worse than the others. After a minute or two, Roller quipped. "Now I know why you call that little dog a pootle!"

"Why is that, Roller?"

"Cause she poots all the time." He fanned the air in front of his face.

Marilyn laughed out! Several of the colored ladies that were sitting on the store porch had been very quiet and listening to Roller's exchange with the pretty cowgirl. They waited to see what Marilyn's response would be before they joined her laughter.

Mr. B and Mr. Newton stepped up onto the store porch from the south side of the store just as the laughter erupted. As it

subsided, Roller continued. "I bet you're glad she's a miniature. If she was full grown, she'd be dangerous!"

Again Marilyn and the colored ladies laughed hysterically.

The big cowboy startled Roller as he walked up to the car.
"Young man, sounds like you've been keeping good company
with my wife there, but we've got to hit the trail."

"Oh, yes, sir," exclaimed Roller as he scampered out. "Sure
is a nice car, Mr. Autry, I mean Mr. Newton." He stepped back
away from the car. "Nice talking to you, ma'am."

"You, too," chuckled Marilyn.

Mr. Newton turned and shook Mr. B's hand. "Well, it's a
pleasure doing business with you, Mr. Hogan. I'll have a truck
over here Monday morning to pick him up." He climbed into
the car.

"Same here, Mr. Newton, this'll sure come in handy." Mr.
B patted his shirt pocket. "You know we had such a dry year
here that it's kinda rake and scrape for us."

Roller suddenly dropped his head in meditation. *What was
going on here? A truck to pick up who? What will come in
handy?* What had Mr. B and the big man been talking about.
His heart began to sink; somehow he knew what this was all
about. No, he wouldn't think about it. It can't be. Another of
those strange feelings came over him as the cowboy tipped his
Stetson and drove away. Marilyn waved to Roller, but he was
too indulged with fear of the real reason for her visit to respond.

Mr. B knew that Roller would be upset by what he had just
done. As he placed his gentle hand in Roller's curly hair, he
tried to comfort him in advance of what he was about to tell him.
"Come on, Son, walk around here with me." He coaxed Roller
off the north side of the porch and around the side of the store.
"You know, Son, sometimes we have to do things that we
don't...." Roller drifted into thought, and it was several minutes
before he became aware of what his daddy was saying. Somehow he knew what had taken place, and he understood all of the
reasons why. He understood the joys and the discomforts of farm
life. He understood the cycles of life that he had been taught.
He understood that there was a "time to sow and a time to reap,
a time to build up and a time to tear down, a time to work and a

time to rest, a time to laugh and a time to cry."

He understood more than anything else that change was inevitable, and that he had to tolerate and accept it, but he didn't have to like it. He knew that this was surely a time to cry. Tears trickled down his cheek and mixed with the beaded sweat on his trembling lip. His throat knotted, and his stomach cramped as Mr. B continued his effort to explain. "Normally, I wouldn't have taken a pretty for him, but after the bad crop and all and with what Mr. Newton agreed to pay, I just felt like it was best that we sell White Hogan...."

Roller didn't hear the rest of his explanation.

CHAPTER 11
THE TOSS

After a long, steady rain during the night, the day dawned with an icy-cold north wind. Roller's ascent to the sitting place was slippery, and his heavy clothing and gloves made his climb cumbersome. The view and solitude of his observatory were again worth the effort.

A heavy frost sparkled the familiar features of the Vilulah landscape. The green rosettes of the spider lily, which added color to the otherwise grey cemetery, were laced with frosty pinafores. A thin fringe of ice embellished the numerous puddles of muddy water, and brilliant rays of the rising sun glistened on a million tiny specks of hoarfrost. Everything that breathed did so with a steamy breath. Old Man Winter had definitely blown his first blast of warning that the seasons had changed.

Everybody on the farm awoke with excitement to the cold chill knowing what the day would bring. Everything had been ready for several days; the knives were sharp, the scalding vat was in place, and firewood was cut and piled high. The only thing that had been lacking for hog killing was cold weather. Today it was cold.

All the farm hands stood around a large fire in the open yard between the millhouse and the barn. Another fire heated water in the scalding vat.

Roller watched the hands as they laughed and joked around the fire awaiting Mr. B to bring the .22 rifle to fire the first shot that would signal the start of a long day of activity. There was Cooper dragging his left foot but ready to get started.

He sank in thought. It didn't seem right that he was not able to see White Hogan standing out there somewhere. He could picture him and almost hear him bellowing. Mr. Newton had been real nice. He had come back to get White himself and had taken a Kodak picture of Roller and Bruh standing by the big white bull. Several days later he sent the picture with a letter saying how happy White was to be with so many cows, and that he was fine. He also invited any of the family to come to his ranch anytime to visit with White.

Roller cursed under his breath. It never seemed fair to him that he and his family had things—or didn't have things—according to how the rain fell, that long hours of work, day after day, went unrewarded if the clouds failed to form. He remembered a sermon that Brother Edenfield had preached about the rain falling on the just and the unjust. He wondered why God forgot to send rain during the summer, or did He forget or just deliberately not send rain. Did God control the clouds?

A movement to his left caught his attention, and he knew before his eyes could adjust that it was the rabbit at the thicket edge. He silently cursed the elusive rascal as he thought back on the hunt that had resulted in the death of Mr. B's prize boar pig. He still felt so bad about it. Things had been bad enough with the terrible drought. The family had tightened every belt and pinched every penny in order to survive financially until things got better. Mama, Muh, and Sis had canned corn, snap beans, and any other vegetable that could be gathered. Clothes were darned, altered, and handed down. Everybody had contributed in some way to help the family through these hard times, yet he had, in one swift flip of his wrist, killed a pig that could have helped not only the family, but also the whole farm operation. "I'll get you Mr. Rabbit," Roller whispered.

He felt terrible about the pig, but he felt worse that he hadn't been able to admit his guilt to Mr. B. Several times he had tried to confess the terrible incident, but he just couldn't bring himself to do it. It weighed heavily on his mind, so he would try again.

A movement to his right caught his eye. The leaves of Muh's pecan tree had shed, and he could plainly see Mr. Lawson walking down the road. Mr. Lawson always helped Uncle George make sausage. He, too, knew what would be happening today. Roller had not seen him since he had delivered him his deceased rooster the day before. He had feared that Mr. Lawson would be mad about it, but instead he had acted proud to get him.

It had been Thanksgiving morning, and Roller had planned to sleep late. The rooster, however, had no intentions of sleeping late or letting anyone else enjoy the holiday. He had crowed loudly from his roost in the big pecan tree long before daylight and woke Roller. For what seemed like hours, he would crow again just as Roller would drift back to sleep.

Finally, in angry disgust, Roller crawled out of his warm nest, found his .22 rifle, and quietly raised the window. Even with most of the leaves gone from the tree, the rooster was hard to spot. Roller pinpointed his position by zeroing in on his crowing, but the wily bird was roosted in a fork in one of the main limbs of the tree where he was protected from Roller's assault.

When the rooster crowed again, Roller spotted his head stretch out into the open, but was unable to take aim before the rooster pulled his head back behind cover. Roller held his aim on the spot where the bird's head appeared and waited for the next crow.

After a long wait and just before giving up his aim, the rooster's last crow was cut in half as Roller's bullet blew away the back side of his feathery head just behind the eye. The big bird wedged in the fork with his bleeding head dangling in the air.

Assured that nothing would bother the bird lodged there in the tree, Roller went back to bed. The rest of the household grinned a secret, thankful grin and buried a little deeper in their respective autumn-cool feather beds.

Later in the morning after breakfast, Roller climbed the tree, retrieved the rooster, and took him to Mr. Lawson. He was met at the back door by Mr. Lawson, who took the bird and told him that the rooster would be Thanksgiving dinner. The timely use of the bird made Roller feel better about killing it.

Again, Roller drifted into thought. *Two days of no school! What a relief!* Then back for three weeks, then two whole weeks for Christmas holidays. He could hardly wait! The fifth grade was still hell on earth. Miss E had not relaxed her iron grip one iota. Roller still sat through every recess correcting mistakes

that he couldn't find. So far, if Mr. White had tried to change
her dictatorship, he had failed. Some of the older students had
said that she would get better after Christmas; Roller prayed that
they were right. *I wonder,* he thought, *what I can get her for
Christmas that would make her like me. Hum.... Maybe I could
poot in a jug and plug it up real quick and tell her it was pot-
pourri.* He laughed to himself.

His train of thought changed as he saw Cooper limp over to
the scalding vat to throw a few pieces of wood onto the fire. He
began to recount what he knew about his grandfather's death.
Mama had said that he was shot to death and robbed by a black
man and that four black men were hanged by the Klan to be sure
that the guilty man was punished. She said that Cooper's paw
was one of the four that was hanged and that they found a charred,
double-barrelled shotgun in the ashes of the woods fire that was
apparently set by the murderer as a diversion in order to perfect
the ambush.

Cooper said that his paw taught him how to shoot a double-
barrelled shotgun and that he had not shot a gun since the shotgun recoil bruised his shoulder. Could it be that he had not shot
a gun since then because the gun burned in the fire and not because it bruised his shoulder? Could it be that the shotgun that
Cooper learned to shoot was the same shotgun that killed his
grandpa? What did it matter? He didn't know why he was so
curious about something that had happened fifty years ago; there
was nothing that could be done about it; but it was always there
in the back of his mind. It seemed so unfair that three, possibly
four, innocent men were unjustly put to their deaths. Somehow
he must find out more about the truth of his grandpa's death.

He watched Bruh walk up to the gang of colored men and
warm his hands toward the heat of the fire. He and Bruh had
tolerated each other and had avoided any kind of altercation.
They had, in fact, gotten along pretty good.

Bruh had come home from school one day with a basketball
hoop and net, and he and Roller had made a backboard out of
some old boards that they found out in the barn. They had gone
to the woods together to cut a pole to support the backboard.
Cooper had harnessed one of the mules and pulled the pole out

of the woods and across the road from the sitting place. They dug a hole and erected the pole and backboard in place. They had shared the project. They had worked together toward a common goal and had done so without argument or disagreement. Maybe, he thought, he and Bruh had learned to live together.

Back to what he could get Miss E for Christmas.... Maybe he could get Annie Jenny to make her some Ex-Lax cookies. He laughed out again. "No," he said aloud, "I know the perfect gift for her." He had some money saved up and hidden in the chimney. It would be enough to get Cooper's gift and Muh's and the others, and he would surely get this special gift for her.

His reverie subsided as Mr. B arrived at the fire with the rifle, and Roller could tell that he was saying something like, "All right, men, ya'll ready to get started? I want to kill at least three today, three tomorrow, and two or three a day next week—as long as this weather holds." Roller knew that with good weather they would average about ten kills per week.

Hog killing was an exciting occasion, and news of it would travel fast. People from all around would come to the store to buy fresh pork sausage, pork chops, and tenderloin. The smokehouse would weep its hickory smoke for most of the winter and would be full of hanging bacon sides, shoulders, hams, and link sausage. Mama would make liver hash, Roller's favorite dish. Annie Jenny would make hogshead Brunswick stew, and brains and eggs would be tomorrow's breakfast. Everyone enjoyed the rewards of their efforts.

It was said that everything about a hog was utilized except the squeal. The farm hands would divide the internal organs, the stomach, the kidneys, the hearts and the ears, the feet and the tails. The intestines were slung and washed, and the small intestine linings were used for the casing for link sausage. Sometimes the hands would cook a pot of the cleaned linings, called chitterlings, and have a chitterling supper. Cooper said they were pretty good if you just boiled the shit out of them. He said he could eat one forty yards long if he didn't bite down on no corn.

Roller heard the crack of the .22 rifle and knew that the work was about to begin. He eased himself down out of the slippery tree and joined the throng of workers.

The fatted pigs that were ready to butcher had been penned in a little lean-to pen on the side of the main barn and flushed with cooked whole kernel corn for a few days before they were butchered.

The scalding vat was a big cast-iron syrup kettle that was also used to cook the corn and to evaporate cane syrup. After the pig was shot between the eyes, four men, one on each leg, hoisted him onto a mule-drawn travois with its head on the low end and its tail-end elevated. The jugular vein was cut immediately, and he was allowed to bleed as he rode the travois to the scalding vat. When the blood slowed its flow, the same four men, who had followed the travois to the vat, lifted the pig and eased him into the steaming water.

Roller remembered the first time he saw the men douse the whole pig into the water. "Dang," he said, "ya'll gonna cook the thing whole like that."

Someone explained to him that the pig would remain in the almost boiling water just long enough to steam the hair so that it could be scraped off more easily. The temperature had to be just right—too hot and it would "set" the hair, too cool and the hair wouldn't come out.

The rest of the butchering process was an assembly line operation. Each person had a particular job. The scalded pig was lifted from the water and placed on sheets of old tin that covered the ground. It was scraped of every hair. Everybody pitched in to shave the first pig, then each man had his own responsibilities during the continuous process.

Makeshift tables of old boards atop saw horses were set up, and the pig was laid on its side on the end of the table. Cooper was the "opener." He used an old hawk-bill knife to cut open the pig's belly from its throat to the rectum. He was careful not to cut into the linings of the stomach or the intestines, and when his cut was made he allowed the bowels and internal organs to spill off the table into an open zinc tub. Roller and Bruh brought buckets of water, and the pig was washed thoroughly before busy hands with razor-sharp knives could dismember and dissect the carcass piece by piece.

Roller and Bruh carried tub after tub of meat to the store

where Uncle George and Mr. Lawson and Mr. B trimmed and prepared it. The hams and shoulders were prepared for smoking by being heavily salted and stacked in wooden boxes. They then were buried in a layer of salt and allowed to cure for about a week before being hung in the smokehouse. The sides from the bigger, fatter pigs were salted and sold as salt meat. The sides from the smaller pigs were smoked and sold as smoked bacon.

The meat that was trimmed away from the better cuts was ground into sausage, and the fat was rendered into lard. Uncle George took great care to season the sausage to perfection. He had his own recipe; so did Mr. Lawson. Together they argued over every batch about whose recipe was the best. Uncle George always won and used his old family secret recipe of sage, black pepper, red pepper, a touch of nutmeg, and salt—the proportions he kept secret.

Some of the seasoned ground pork was sold as patty sausage, but the majority of it was stuffed into casings and made into link sausage.

The sausage mill had a horn-like attachment that mounted onto the exit orifice; it was actually a tube through which the ground meat was forced. The casing was laced over the tube so that, as the ground meat was squeezed out of the end of the tube, it was enclosed by the membrane casing.

The links of sausage were strung on poles and hung in the smokehouse for a few days in order for the hickory smoke to season and preserve them.

About mid-afternoon, Roller watched Cooper open the third and final kill of the day. The swirling breeze had laced the smoke from the scalding vat with an infusion of odors. The bloody fresh meat, burning hair, and the barnyard itself filled Roller's nostrils as Cooper made the critical cut to expose the steaming entrails of the gilt pig.

"Roller, you want to kill that ass rabbit?" Cooper asked.

"Well, yeah. What made you ask that?"

"I seen you up there in the tree a looking this morning, and I figured you was a planning something."

"Yeah, I'll get him one day. If you'll give me back my spear, I'll try him again."

129

"Naw, suh," Cooper looked around to be sure no one was listening. "You done enough damage with that spear. Why don't you shoot him with your flip?"

Roller thought a minute. Cooper had helped him make a slingshot—or flip—two years ago, and he had learned to shoot it with the same accuracy that he had developed with his other shooting skills. At one time he had thought about hunting the rabbit with the flip, but had decided that it would be too easy. Now, though, after several failed attempts to spear the rabbit—and the unfortunate boar pig incident—he thought it would be nice to kill the rabbit any way that he could. He had even thought about hunting him with his rifle.

Cooper had resumed talking, and Roller eventually returned his attention to what he was saying. "I done told you that you had to use what you got to get something what you don't got. Ain't that right?"

"Yeah."

"Well, that rabbit got all kinds a-ways to hide; he got fast feet, good ears, and eyes."

"Yeah."

"So, he be using what he got to get something he don't got."

"What is it that he don't have?" Roller quizzed.

"Same ass thang don't none of us have; the promise of to-morrow! He use what the good Lawd give him to live another day." Cooper finished the cut and motioned for Roller to hold the chest of the pig open.

"Yeah."

"But, you got something that rabbit ain't got." He nodded.

"Yeah?"

Cooper stepped to the side a little as the contents of the pig's body cavity emptied into the zinc tub below. He snipped at the still attached reproductive organs of the female pig and gestured to the others that she was ready to be washed and cut up as he stepped back. "Yeah, you got a head on your shoul-ders, you got the bility to cipher and reason. Lawd knows you do too much ass thinking sometime...but you got to out-think that rabbit.

"Yeah, well I'll think about it," Roller countered.

"I seen you bust a Coca-Cola bottle at thirty steps with that flip."

"Yeah."

"Well, my idea is to find a clear shot from a long way off. That way, maybe he won't see you so good, and it sho won't be all that easy."

"Yeah, I might try that one day. I'll need to practice up some with my flip. Been a long time since I shot it much. You'll need to help me find some of those steel balls to use as shot." He stepped back away from the table and pulled and aimed an imaginary flip.

"Yeah, okay," Cooper nodded.

"Hey Roller, catch!" shouted Bruh from across the table.

Roller turned just in time to see something coming directly at him. Instinctively he threw up both hands to catch the projectile, and did so just inches in front of his face. The inertia of the pig's bladder and the squeeze of Roller's grasping fingers sent warm, steamy urine spraying and peeing all over the place.

It took several seconds for Roller to shed the shock and dismay of what Bruh had done. By some incomprehensible good fortune the urine swashed by both ears but not a drop hit Roller in the face. It did splash on his hands and arms, but the long sleeves protected his arms.

Roller remained unbelievably calm. He just stood there thinking. What was Bruh doing? Had he had a momentary lapse of good sense, or had he gone completely and eternally insane? Had he done this without thinking just as Roller did things occasionally, or had he been thinking about it and planning it all day? Was this what he was grinning about at the dinner table when Roller had quizzed him about his subtle and unintentional facial first-quarter moon? Wasn't he aware that all of the good blood that they had somehow managed to share would suddenly and certainly spill out of their sibling veins and go bad right there on the ground between them? Didn't he remember what Roller had told him about his ass being grass and him being the lawnmower? Surely, he had forgotten that Roller had told him that if he ever messed with him again that he better give his heart to God because his ass belonged to him. What had come over this junior-high teenage jerk?

A thousand other questions rushed his brain as he stood there staring into Bruh's suddenly worried eyes. All of the busy hands that were involved in the butchering process stopped their slicing and trimming and stood still with black eyes darting from one of the white brothers to the other. No one uttered a sound.

To Cooper the silence was deafening. He knew that he should intervene, and yet he knew that somehow, someday this would be settled. Maybe it should be today. Maybe this was the time for this sibling rivalry to run its course. He wanted to interject some statement of reprimand to Bruh, some plea of refrain to Roller, some word of warning to the both of them, but he decided to say nothing, to do nothing, and like the rest of the hands to watch the outcome of this impending skirmish. He nodded.

The silent stare seemed to last for hours. They were like two coiled rattlesnakes, each awaiting the other to make a move and each a little apprehensive that the other would make a move.

Bruh knew the instant he released the pig's bladder that he had done something that he shouldn't have done. It had been one of those tempting impromptu actions that was done to a younger brother without thought of the outcome. He did not intend to initiate an altercation of any kind. He had been just funning, but it was too late. There was no way to magically reverse his toss of the bladder and undo what he had done, nor could he say anything that would diminish the severity of his action. He could not make a fast getaway because he could never run in a cowardly retreat. He would have to stand and face the charge that he knew would surely come.

Roller's mind continued to fill with questions about why Bruh had done this wretched act, and with an unexplainable restraint he actually took time to think out his strategy for revenge. A hundred Bible verses came to mind about "turning the other cheek," about "brotherly love," about the "patience of Job," but others like "an eye for an eye" and "getting the ox out of the ditch" seemed to justify his plan. Cooper's instructions about using something that you have to get something you don't have replayed in his mind, and he was able to repress the explosive anger that would have normally controlled his reaction.

It occurred to him that Bruh had been very lucky that none of the urine fell on the meat that was in process. It also occurred to him that if he made a direct across-the-table assault, he might tilt the tables over and spill the fresh meat onto the ground. He had become very cautious about "waste not, want not."

He realized that he would have to be on the same side of the table and much closer to Bruh in order to perfect an assault. He did not have that advantage, so he would have to get it. He would use something that he did have to get what he did not have. He broke his stare and flicked his eyes around the table and saw that most of the dark eyes of the workers were fixed on him and awaiting his retaliation. He relaxed his neck and shoulders and let his arms fall to his side. He managed to let a smile creep across his face and grunted a little throaty chuckle. The tension of the anticipatory onlookers subsided slightly, and their eyes quickened their darting stares. He tilted his head back and broke into laughter. He saw a few faces relax and halfheartedly grin as he bent at the waist and leaned into a full blown Woody Woodpecker cackle.

Everyone, including Bruh, reacted as he had guessed. They relaxed and assumed that Roller was going to laugh it off and wait for another time to start the mother of fights. He turned and tossed the bladder into the smoldering ashes of the scalding vat fire. He continued to laugh as he found a little water left in one of the zinc buckets and washed his hands.

Bruh slowly and cautiously relaxed his guard and eventually began to join in the chuckling that had transmitted to the gang of workers. Soon everyone was almost convulsing with laughter—everyone, that is, except Cooper. He knew what Roller was doing and secretly scolded himself for not trying to put a stop to what was about to take place. He knew that Muh had given her last dictate about fighting, and that the final word of this conflict would be hers.

Roller pounded his fist on the table as he laughed hysterically and pretended to have a stomach cramp as he stooped over below the level of the work table. Then in a flash he catapulted himself under the table, and the full thrust of his body buckled

Bruh's knees and tackled him, sprawling him backwards. His strike was swift and accurate, and he did not let up; he kept crabbing and crawling until he straddled Bruh's stomach. With a leg on each side of Bruh's torso, he squeezed with his knees and yanked on Bruh's shoulders and rolled to his left pulling Bruh up on top of his now straightened left leg. He locked his feet together and completed what everyone recognized as a scissors lock.

Roller had climbed trees, peddled his bike, walked in plowed fields, and waded in creeks, and his legs had become virtual stumps of muscles that were noticed by everyone when he wore short pants. He had long known that his superior strength to Bruh could be found in his legs, so he pulled hard on his calf and thigh muscles and squeezed Bruh's abdomen, forcing the air out of his lungs. With a loud moan, Bruh began to fight back as he managed to pull Roller's left hand away from his shoulders. With both hands he forced Roller's hand to bend downward at the wrist, and wrapped his fingers around Roller's thumb and lower arm and squeezed hard, forcing Roller's thumb to touch the inside of his arm.

His thumb joint and wrist wreaked with pain, but he ignored it and called on his legs to squeeze harder—and squeeze they did, so hard that a long, loud, buzzing fart replaced Bruh's moans. This time, Roller's laughter was real.

All of the hands, including Cooper, had encircled them to watch this brief battle with great interest and expectation, but also with much concern that Muh or Mr. B might somehow hold them responsible for allowing it to happen.

When Roller broke into laughter, everyone was relieved. His laughter was obviously real this time and indicated that he had no intention of continuing. He relaxed his grip and Bruh relaxed his as they helped each other up off the ground. They stood face to face, panting for breath but smiling as they grasped each other on the shoulders in a typical wrestlers closed stance.

When Muh parted her way through the circle, she saw the brothers locked together as if they were actively engaged in battle. Little did she know that the battle was over and that Bruh and Roller were actually embraced in a mutual truce. She assumed that the fight which Uncle George had seen out the back door of the store was still in progress.

"All right, boys, I've told you about this fighting for the last time," Muh almost shouted. She was shaking and trembling with anger.

Roller and Bruh were stunned to hear her. They relaxed their grips and turned to face her. They knew by her voice that this one was bad.

"But, Muh, we're not fighting," stammered Roller.

"Muh, we have already settled this," Bruh explained.

"Well, I'm going to settle it once and for all. Do you hear me?" She grabbed both boys by the nape of their shirts and led them toward the bighouse.

"I can't believe that ya'll did this after I've told you so many times not to be fighting. Ya'll have deliberately disobeyed me and now.... Well, get your fannies to the smokehouse. Do you hear me? Now get!"

It was much worse than they thought. The smokehouse was the place where all corporal punishment took place. Trips there had been few but memorable.

"Yes, ma'am," they obeyed in unison.

CHAPTER 12
THE FIGHT

Neither of the boys could believe their luck. There they were heading for, of all places, the smokehouse when, for the first time ever, they had settled their differences and had reconciled their sparring dispute without outside intervention. Neither had visited the smokehouse under these conditions in a long time. In fact Bruh had not had such punishment in years.

This was so unlike Muh. Her normal method of punishment was to let violations of her mandates pass with only a certain threat of a trip to the smokehouse until some straw broke the camel's back, and off she and the perpetrator marched to the dark refines of the little clapboard house.

Once inside the smokehouse the long dreaded lashing with a keen bridal-wreath spirea switch was much less damaging than the anticipation of it. It was the verbal lashing that hurt to the bone. Muh had a way of imposing great guilt and shame by recounting all the incidents that had prompted the punishment, and by explaining as to how each incident had "stricken her with unbearable mental anguish." When she finished her description of the abuse that she received from her very own progeny, the thrashing at hand was a welcome relief.

Both the brothers thought that they had outgrown the smokehouse punishment, especially Bruh. After all, he was in the ninth grade, and ninth graders didn't get switchings. Also, Roller had long considered that his most recent visit to the smokehouse would surely be the final one, for Muh had cried much louder and harder than he as she explained how she bore him from her womb with horrid pain, how she sacrificed daily for him so that he could have more than she and his daddy, how they both worked for a lifetime for the betterment of the family, how she prayed daily that he would turn out to be a good, decent boy, and how it hurt her far worse than it hurt him for her to have to punish him.

But to their dismay, here they were standing at the smokehouse door as Muh retreated to the bighouse. They looked at each other with disgusted sneers. They said nothing but somehow communicated to each other that their fighting days were over, that from this day forward they would resolve their differences without need of battle or intervention from Muh or anyone.

Their sneering quickly changed to puzzled glances as Muh returned carrying a cardboard box. She said nothing as she sat the box on the ground. Finding a limb that had fallen with the carpet of leaves from the pecan tree, she dragged the limb into the damp earth to form a shallow furrow in the shape of a square. She roughly paced the space at seven steps to each side. She mumbled something as she connected the lines at the last corner. When she returned to the box, she withdrew the little hand bell which normally informed everyone that a meal was about to be served, a wind-up alarm clock and—two pairs of boxing gloves!

"Now," she pitched a pair of gloves to each of them, "we're fixing to have the last fight that we'll ever have. Do you hear me?"

Roller and Bruh caught the gloves and stared at them in total bewilderment. They seemed to comprehend what Muh had said at the same instant and in unison lifted their eyes and puffed, "But, Muh...."

"Don't ya'll 'but Muh' me." Her eyes pierced through her wire-rimmed glasses with pointed determination. "I'm sick and tired of this fighting, and we're gonna get it over with once and for all. Do you hear me?"

They said nothing. They just stood there aghast.

"Now, get those gloves on, and get ready for round one. Let's see," she fiddled with the clock, "rounds last three minutes. Right? And, let's see, we'll say that this is a fight to the finish title match. Is that right? And, Roller, you can be Joe Lewis, okay? And Ben, you can be Marciano."

"But, Muh...."

"Now, let's get going." She helped the boys with the gloves and laced and tied the strings. "Ya'll been fighting since you were big enough to walk; now, today, you can fight all you want to whether you want to or not. Come on. I'm not playing. Do you hear me? This is a real fight, and if you don't fight, I mean really fight, I'm gonna be more than the referee. Ya'll shake hands, and Joe you go to that corner, and Rocky you take that corner," she pointed. "When I ring the bell, ya'll come out fighting, you hear." She took a place outside the imaginary ring.

Both the boys just stood there looking down at the gloves. They couldn't believe that Muh would do this. What had come over her? They didn't want to fight—not like this. They looked at each other sheepishly and shrugged their shoulders simultaneously. Roller made a step toward his corner just as the bell rang.

"All right, round one. Let's go. Come on fight!" Muh demanded. "What's wrong? Ya'll have always wanted to box, so come on now, box! Roller, I heard you say one day that you hated Bruh. Where is that hate now? Bruh, I heard you say, 'one of these days, I'll bust you good.' Well, it's one of these days right now. I want to get this over with once and for all. Ya'll want to bust one another, don't you? Well, get to busting! I've got work to do. Let's go!"

"But, Muh...."

Muh stepped into the ring, grabbing both boys by the nape of their shirts, and shoved them face to face. Her voice rang with authority, a tone they both recognized as the final word of warning. "Let me tell you young men one thing. There are two things that I can't tolerate, and ya'll know it—that's cussing and fighting. But today ya'll are gonna fight, and it's gonna be the last time that you're gonna fight, and if there's anything that's worse to me than cussing or fighting it's disobedience. Now, if ya'll know what's good for you, you'll obey me and get on with this fight. Do you hear me?"

She released them with a jerk, and they both knew that it was time to do some kind of a fight. They nodded and silently communicated to each other to pretend to engage in this unprovoked, unwanted skirmish.

Many times both boys had wished for this, but under different circumstances. They had longed for such an opportunity to see who would be victorious in a real boxing match, who could out-punch, out-last the other. But, this match was different— there was no cause, no heated tempers, no violent reaction to some provocation—there was just a command to fight. Somehow that was insufficient.

They sparred halfheartedly, flicking jabs and punches wildly and undeterminedly. They locked each others arms and pretended to be half wrestling as they counted the time down to the first bell.

The bell rang. "All right, now," Muh quipped, "that was a good start, but you both know that I know that you're just stalling. Ya'll are not fighting! I've seen ya'll fight better than that during the prayer at church. Now, I just know that round two will be better and that fighting will soon be a thing of the past. Do you hear me? Just think. Just a few more rounds, and there won't ever be any more fights. Isn't that great! But if we don't get it done with by then, we'll just fight five more rounds. Okay, let's go. Round two." She rang the bell.

The next two rounds were pretty much the same with Muh complaining between each round that the boys were acting—not fighting—and that she was ready for this to be the battle to end all battles. Finally, Bruh and Roller recognized the authoritative quiver in her voice at the end of round three, so the fourth round began with an increased vigor and earnestness.

Roller spent most of the round dodging and ducking and blocking Bruh's more serious punches. He tried to recall what Sidney had told him about boxing. Sidney was a great fan of the boxing game and knew quite a bit about the techniques and art of boxing. He remembered Sidney describing a great boxer who was one of the best to ever live. His name was Jack Johnson. He had knocked out every man that ever dared to get in the ring with him. He was a big, very black man, six feet, five inches tall weighing two hundred twenty-five pounds. He was fast but collected, and could take almost any punch that anyone could dish out, and was surely headed for a world championship match against somebody when he took up with, and eventually married, a white woman. So he was barred from boxing temporarily and missed his chance at a title fight. He had been a mas-

ter of the fundamentals that make champions out of men with
the talent and desire to box.

Johnson could shoot his right hand over a left jab with bullet speed. He could handle a right lead and counter with a left
hook with almost mechanical ease and precision. He could take
those inside short punches and step back with a right upper cut
that few men could survive. He was a natural boxer who needed
very little training, and his endurance was phenomenal and had
once sparred for twenty-five rounds with five alternating part-
ners, knocking two of them out, and was hardly winded when
the twenty-fifth bell sounded. He was Sidney's boxing idle as
Marciano was Roller's.

Roller began to test what Sidney had said by keeping his
hands high in front of his face in order to block Bruh's jabs and
by keeping his elbows close together to protect his stomach. He
crouched slightly, circling to his left, watching and anticipating
Bruh's punches. He began to see that a right hand thrown over
the left jab could land solidly on the side of Bruh's unprotected
face, and the more he studied the pattern of Bruh's punches and
counterpunches, the more openings he saw. He decided to flick
a quick left jab and was surprised at Bruh's quick reaction. Round
four ended just as Bruh countered with a swift right over the left
jab that caught Roller square on the nose. A bloody spray filled
the air, and for an instant Roller was blinded and dazed.

The ringing bell snapped Roller from his momentary state
of confusion, and his first conscious thought was that Sidney
had said that the best place to hit somebody was in the nose.
"The nose," he had said, "is the home of the stars. You hit a
man solid on the nose, and he'll see stars every time, and while
he's standing there thinking how pretty them stars are, you un-
screw on him and finish him off. But, you better be ready cause
if he can get past them stars filling his head, he'll be a mad cin-
namon bun!"

Roller glanced upward and silently thanked the sky above
for the bell. He knew that he had been very vulnerable for that
second or two following Bruh's right hand. Sidney was right—
the stinging pain in his nose, the ringing in his ears, and the
momentary loss of conscienceness had infuriated his inner be-

ing. He felt that certain rage building and spurting outward as torrent and violent eruptions of volcanic anger. *Saved by the bell.*

Round five was three minutes of boxing fury with both boxers scoring with a flurry of punches, but somehow Roller kept his nose protected, and just as the round ended he shot a strong left to Bruh's face and a right upper-cut busted Bruh's lip.

Both boys returned to their corners, staring at each other, panting for breath, bleeding, and angry. Muh was saying something as she had been all the while about the evils of fighting and the best medicine, but neither of the young gladiators heard a word.

The gang of colored men had left the cutting tables and moved around the corner of the millhouse and were silently huddled in awe of this unthinkable brotherly battle. They mumbled whispers to each other but showed no excitement or evidence of having a favorite as to who would be victorious.

Shoppers at the store tiptoed to the edge of the store porch and leaned on each other to see what was taking place. Cooper had shuffled down to the edge of the turkey pen to watch from behind one of the corner post. He, too, showed no emotion, but secretly pulled for Roller. He had known that this would happen one day, but he never dreamed that Muh would be involved, let alone be the instigator and referee. He grimaced each time Bruh connected with a solid punch, and without intention of doing so he imagined this to be some kind of title bout that would crown one of the boys as some kind of champion.

It had developed into a real match! Bruh's quick feet and hands and dexterity were surely taking their toll on Roller's younger but stockier body. But Roller's fledgling yet muscular legs and arms were in good shape, and he had managed to withstand all that Bruh could muster.

With glassy stares, they eagerly awaited the bell for the next round. Roller covered one of his nostrils with his thumb, then the other, and blew bloody phlegm spraying, then wiped the sweat that had beaded on his forehead and upper lip. Their steamy pants were in rapid unison. They both were ready to end this thing. They were both ready to win; they were ready to fight to the finish as they trembled with nervous fear and worry. A hundred curious ears heard the last bell ring.

141

CHAPTER 13
THE CLIPPINGS

On the first Thursday of each month, Mr. Camel came to the store. Mr. Camel was a salesman for Florida Hardware and Merchandise Co. He was a robust, jolly man with greying hair and jovial personality. Through the years he had become a real friend of the family, and he and Roller looked forward to seeing each other. Normally he had dinner with the family and always bragged on Annie Jenny's cooking.

His sales catalog was a gigantic wish book, leather bound with leather straps that snapped together to form handles; it was as big as a small suitcase and was filled with pictures of all sorts of tools, sporting goods, toys, and appliances. Mr. Camel always allowed Roller to thumb through the many fascinating pages while Mr. B quoted the order for the month, and quite often he would add some little trinket or small toy to the order especially for Roller at no extra charge.

Roller despised school for enough reasons, but he especially hated to have to miss Mr. Camel's visit. He profoundly hated to miss the December visit, for this would be when all of the Christmas stock of toys would be ordered.

He ran from the school bus into the store; Uncle George was standing by the big wood heater. "Don't slam that door!"

Roller had already released the door to make its full swinging return to the jamb.

"Please—well, don't slam that door when you leave," Uncle George begged loudly.

"Did you give Mr. Camel my letter?" Roller immediately quizzed.

"Yes, I did," Uncle George replied.

"Well?" Roller warmed by the heater.

"Well, what?"

"Well, what did he say?"

"He said that you must be up to something, said he'd see what he could do."

"Well, did he say that he would box it up where no one could see what it was?"

"He said he would see what he could do. That's all he said. What are you up to, Roller?"

"Nothing. I just ordered some Christmas presents, that's all, and I've got the money to pay for them when they come. I don't want anybody to open my box, okay?"

Uncle George grunted something as the front door opened. It was Uncle Sammy. Roller had not seen him in several days, and he wondered what tease he would have from him this time. They all greeted each other as Uncle Sammy joined them at the fire.

"Man, it's blustery out there today." Uncle Sammy proclaimed as he warmed his hands toward the heater.

"Yeah, windy too," said Roller.

Uncle Sammy chuckled. "Yeah, it is. Say, Roller, I hear we got a couple of prize fighters here bouts. That right?"

"Well, I don't know." The front door opened again. It was Cooper bringing in an arm load of firewood. He nodded to everybody as he shuffled his way toward the wood box.

"I want to know who won the fight," Uncle Sammy quizzed. "Cooper, I hear you watched the fight. Who do you think won?"

"Well, suh," Cooper explained as Roller helped him unload his arm load of wood, "I really think both of them lost." He nodded.

Uncle Sammy lifted his head back to look through his bifocal glasses and peeped at Cooper, then at Roller. "Both of them lost? What do you mean?"

Cooper started to shuffle out with Roller right behind. "You see, suh," Cooper nodded, "they was both a laying on the ground all fought out. I'd have to say that the referee won that fight. Ain't been no fighting since, so I say the referee won, yas, suh."

They made their way to the door and left Uncle Sammy still asking questions. Once outside as they headed for the barn,

Cooper explained, "I figured you'd need some ass help when I seen that Mr. Sammy come up."

"Yeah, thanks. Dang it! I bet I've had a hundred people ask me about that fight. Roller glanced back at the sitting place and continued. "It must really be the talk. I wonder who told him about it."

"Ain't no telling. Some of them niggers what was at the sto that day, I speck."

"Yeah, I speck so, too. Where we going?"

"Bruh wanted me to make him a bow and arrow for some play another he gone be in at school."

Roller had heard Bruh tell Muh that he had won the part of Robin Hood in the class play and that one of the props that he would need was an authentic looking bow and quill of arrows, and that he would ask Cooper to help him make them. As they passed the woodpile, Cooper asked Roller to fetch the ax as he went on to explain his plans.

"I seen a felled hickory down in the woods what had a shoot on it a growing long and lean. It will be just right for a bow if I can find it again. And that lemon bush down by the smoke house got some good straight shoots what'll make good arrows."

Roller pretended to be pulling a bow. "Yeah, that's good. Maybe I can borrow it and shoot that ole rabbit with it."

"Oh, hell, here I go getting in trouble again. Best you leave it alone, I speck. You'll be done kilt another hog."

"Now don't start that again. I'm trying to forget about it. I got to tell Daddy about it sometime, though. Maybe after Christmas."

They passed by the meal house and simultaneously looked back at the knothole. "Roller, how bout telling me bout Ole Ollie ass again while we be walking."

Roller clinched his lips and blew a heavy breath from his nose. "Not again!"

"Well, I'd be much obliged, but if you don't want to, it will be all right."

They walked on a few steps. "Well, all right. You see ole Ollie...." And again Roller recounted the episode and adorned it with a few exaggerations. Cooper's laughter echoed in the woods

144

as they walked.

They found the downed hickory, and sure enough a limb shoot had stretched long and straight toward the forest canopy and was of uniform diameter for most of its length. Cooper let Roller whack at it with the ax until it fell. Roller held it on top of the trunk of the horizontal tree while Cooper cut it clean at about six feet in length with one chop of the ax and used it as a walking staff as they talked and ambled back to the barn.

"Cooper?" Roller couldn't resist the chance to question him. "Yeah?"

"You say that old double-barrel shotgun like to have kicked you down when you were a little boy?"

"Yeah?"

"And you haven't shot a gun since?"

"That's right."

"Well, that makes me kinda scared to shoot a twelve gauge. Do you reckon it would kick me like that?"

"You see, Roller, what I did was, I pull both of them rabbit ear hammers back at the same time to shoot a squirrel out the top of a big ole poplar tree, and when I pulled the trigger to shoot the left barrel, I musta pull both triggers cause both barrels shot at the same time. You see I took a double ass whammy kick from that thang. Like to a ruined my shoulder!"

"Oh, I see."

"So, if you just pull one hammer at the time, you be all right."

"Well, uh...." He couldn't think of another question about the whereabouts of the shotgun without sounding suspicious and inquisitive about the involvement of Cooper's paw in the death of his grandfather. He paused. "Well, uh...," he stammered. "Uh, I guess your paw hid the gun from you after that. Huh?"

"He didn't have to hide it. I didn't want to see that ass gun no mo! Man, I been bout half ass scared of a gun ever since that day."

"Well, uh...." He decided to drop it. "Yeah, I guess so."

They crossed the paddock fence to approach the rear of the barn. "Roller, you don't remember when the barn burned do you?"

"Naw."

"Boy, it was a mess! Only time I ever seen Mr. B cry."

Yeah, you told me about it before."

"I did? Oh yeah."

Roller had noticed that Cooper repeated himself more and more lately. Cooper must be getting old, he thought. Old people tell the same stories over and over. Maybe it was the stroke. His foot seemed to be dragging a little worse than it had been before. Maybe he had suffered another small stroke as Dr. Harper had said he would.

They reached the little workshop room of the barn, and Roller watched as Cooper used a piece of rope to find the mid-point of the hickory limb. He held the end of a rope even with one end of the stick and pulled it along its length to the other end. He pinched the rope at the end of the stick, then folded the end of the rope and held it even with the pinch, and laid the doubled rope back on the stick with the rope end and the pinch at one end of the stick. He made a shallow notch in the stick at the loop of the rope with his hawk-billed knife. Then he laid his big, black, calloused hand on the notch so that the notch centered his palm and made a deeper notch on each side of his hand.

"Now," he said, "that'll mark the grip of this fine bow."

Cooper locked the grip of the bow in the old vise, and with a draw-knife he began to pull away the bark and layers of wood to flatten and taper the ends of the bow.

Roller saw that this was going to take much more time than he intended to spend, so he slipped away as Cooper pulled at the draw-knife and rambled on about the night the barn burned. He wanted to make the sitting place to watch the sun go down.

He slipped through the back door of the store and hustled a bright red apple out of the box that leaned against the meat counter. He gently eased the front door quietly to its jamb as he exited so as not to draw attention from Uncle George. Biting down hard on the apple, he held it tightly in his teeth as he made his familiar assault on the aging post oak. He squirmed and shifted his buttocks on the old limb butt and silently complained that his seat was getting smaller and smaller, almost to the point of discomfort.

Slowly he enjoyed the crisp red apple as he studied the familiar territory, the territory that served as the heart of his remote world, the central core around which all of his young life revolved. His eyes settled on the brilliant, orange-red sunset as he watched the tree line swallow the big ball of color that had swallowed the darkness as the day began, and as the sun sank away he sank into thought. He remembered a conversation that he and Cooper had had several months before.

"Roller," Cooper had said, "do you know what make the sun shine?"

"Yeah, the sun makes the sunshine."

"Naw, I mean, what makes the sun shine?"

"Oh, you mean what makes the sun shine—why is it so bright and all?"

"Yeah, that's it. What makes the sun do hits shining so bright?"

"Well, they say it's a big star, a big ball of fire."

"Yeah, I heard that too." Cooper paused for several minutes and then continued. "But you see, I believe every man got his own reason why the sun shines."

"What do you mean?"

"Well, you see, you got this farm and them animals and your family to make your sun shine. Mr. B got you chillen and Miss Muh and this farm and all to make his sun shine. You see what I'm talking bout. Your days be brighter if you got something to light up your life."

"Yeah," Roller answered in study of what Cooper had said. "It's the things you enjoy and care for that makes your day seem brighter, huh?"

Cooper nodded, but they didn't speak for some time. Finally Roller asked, "Cooper what makes your sun shine?"

Cooper thought a minute, nodded, and began one of his lengthy orals. "Hum," he rubbed his stubbled chin, "you know it don't take much for me to be as happy as a double-dick dog, and I ain't got no real family and my coon hunting days is bout over and my poon hunting days is bout over too; sho don't take much as it used to. Bout one or two times a month, bout all me and ole Annie Jenny can stand." He laughed out, and Roller

147

looked puzzled. "And most of my days ain't all that bright, and everybody's ball of fire gonna burn out one day. But, I tell you, I sho do enjoy fooling with them hogs and cows, and I miss ole White Hogan like if he'da been my child; and this farm, I do enjoy a walking this land and watching it change with the season, and your paw sho has been good to me, and I do love that man and Miss Muh and Mama and Bruh and Sis, I show do.... But, Roller, my sun shine cause a you."

"Me?"

"Yeah, I sho has enjoyed a piddling round with you. Me and you done had some good ass times, ain't we?"

Roller had often thought about how much Cooper meant to him, but he had never even thought that he could be the thing that made Cooper's sun shine. He never thought about being part of Cooper's only family, let alone the son he never had. He couldn't think of anything to say, but he had to say something. This conversation just couldn't end like this. He thought for several minutes as Cooper worked at the task at hand. He felt one of those strange feelings coming over him. He finally swallowed the knot in his throat and said, "Cooper, you're my real friend, and I'm glad."

Cooper blew his nose on an old flowery rag and nodded.

Only six more days of that hell-hole called school, then a fortnight of reprieve. He could hardly wait. Sis would be getting married a week from Sunday. He secretively hated that big Navy man who would be taking Sis away from him. He didn't want change to start. He was happy with the way things were, and he knew that his sun shined because of all of his family and friends—and that most of them were old and might leave his world anytime. *The bighouse without Sis.* His throat knotted again.

He thought of the wedding gift that he had ordered from Mr. Camel in hopes that she would like it. She would need a good fountain pen to write home. He had ordered her a Scripto ink pen with the little brass pump handle on the side.

Miss E was still a bitch. He hated her worse everyday, and he had told Mr. White again one day after lunch that school without recess was like the week without Sunday and that God meant for men to rest once in a while. Mr. White had laughed and told him that things would be better after Christmas. He certainly hoped so. The Christmas present that he had ordered for her would be perfect.

Bruh had made a great change since the fight. He had talked to him more and had even let him stay after school one day and go to basketball practice with him. They had hitchhiked home together, and they had actually enjoyed each other. Maybe they had both changed since the fight. The fight.... He would always remember how Muh had cried that last round and how the three of them had cried when she finally rang the bell to end it, how they had embraced each other and vowed never to fight again. The lesson had been well taught, and well learned.

The shadow of Queen Lizzie's tombstone had faded as he read the epitaph again. Cooper and the hands had started their walk home, and he knew that it was time for him to go to supper. The rabbit hopped from the thicket and nibbled at something next to one of the tombstones. Roller smiled as he climbed down and swung from the brace and threw the apple core in the general direction of the rabbit.

On Wednesday of the next week, Mama caught Roller while he was doing his homework and asked him to come do something for her when he got through. He was always ready for a break, so he obliged her promptly. She wanted to examine her hats to decide which one to wear to the wedding, and they were stored in a big hat box up on top of her armoire. She asked him to bring the hat box down for her.

He could stand on the foot of her bed and reach it, but there were two boxes there: an octagon-shaped cardboard box with a top and a smaller oval-shaped sewing box. Naturally, he retrieved the wrong box, and as he presented it to Mama, she emphatically told him that she needed the other box. He replaced it and got the other box, but he became curious about the contents of the oval box. After deciding on the hat, she asked Roller to return the box to the armoire and went into the kitchen to ask Muh's approval.

While she was gone, Roller secretly opened the sewing box. He had been reprimanded many times for meddling in other people's things so he hurriedly examined the contents. There were several old crocheted doilies, some old pictures of people he didn't know, and down on the bottom were several old newspaper clippings that seemed to be of no interest to him. Then suddenly, down in the stack of clipping,, he read a startling bold print head line:

The Valdosta Daily Times
February 20, 1907
LANIER SHOT DEAD BY A NEGRO
Well-known white man was killed at St. George yesterday.

When he heard Mama returning, he quickly replaced all the contents and quietly jumped from the bed. He would have to wait, but he would definitely come back to this later. Could it be that those clippings held information about his grandfather's death that could prove the innocence of Cooper's paw? Why hadn't Mama ever mentioned them? Why wouldn't she talk about it more? Why was she so secretive about it. He had to return when he had the house to himself.

The next few days the bighouse was a bustle of actively: cleaning, cooking, trying on and altering clothes, polishing shoes, and sweeping the yards, all in preparation for Sis's wedding. The terrible crop had mandated changes in the plans for a big fancy wedding, and a simple but pretty service was substituted. Sis was disappointed, but she, too, understood farm life. Mr. B was the most disappointed of all. He wanted so much to be able to give Sis the wedding of her dreams, but he also knew of all of his obligations at this time of the year and what each would cost even if just a minimum amount was dispersed for each. Christmas presents would be limited, and the year-end settlements with the hands would be proportionally reduced, but somehow he had to see to it that Santa Claus came to see not only his children, but all of the children of the farm. He strongly believed that Christmas should be a joyous time for all. This Christmas would be a trying time for him.

The rehearsal and party were on Saturday night, and Bruh and Roller were allowed to stay at home. They helped with the trade at the store and ate supper there, which consisted of sardines and saltines, cheese, and cold RC cola. After supper and after Uncle George closed the store, Roller ran, leaving Bruh behind, to the bighouse to investigate the newspaper clippings while no one was around.

He climbed up on Mama's bed and again retrieved the sewing box, sat down on his folded legs, and searched through the clippings to find the account of his grandfather's death. He found the clipping and read aloud:

The Valdosta Daily Times
February 20, 1907
LANIER SHOT DEAD BY A NEGRO
Well-known white man was killed at St. George yesterday. He was a partner of Mr. L.W. Shaw in the Naval Stores business and was highly esteemed, killed by a negro in a quarrel and robbed of $300—other negroes present.

Mr. L.W. Shaw was notified yesterday by wire from St. George of the tragic death of his partner in the navel stores business, Mr. R.W. Lanier.

The Times learned that he was killed on his way home from the station at St. George though the particulars could not be given by parties at St. George. Mr. Shaw went to the scene of the killing on the train last night.

Conductor Sergeant and other parties who came up on the train this morning from that section brought additional details of the killing. The facts as they learned them from parties at St. George were about as follows. Mr. Lanier went to the railroad station at St. George yesterday morning to meet Mr. Shaw who expected to go down there but did not go. The distance from the still is about three miles.

At the station, Mr. Lanier got $300 for his payroll and had it on him, going back to his home. There were four negroes on the wagon with him and he was paying some of them some money. The subject of a debt came up between him and another negro, the negro stating that he would pay it when he d—— pleased. The negro was impudent in his talk due to the fact that he had a gun. The gun however, did not prevent Mr. Lanier from resenting the negro's insult, striking him with his hand. The negro turned immediately and grabbed his gun and emptied it into Mr. Lanier's head killing him instantly. The other negroes fled from the scene while the murderer robbed the dead body and fled into the swamps. It is stated that he is still in that section. He is well known and he may be captured later though he has managed to evade arrest so far.

The killing occurred within a matter of a mile of Mr. Lanier's home. The other negroes who were with him ran to the house and gave news of the killing.

The deceased leaves a wife and three small children. He formerly lived in this county near Dasher and worked with Mr. E.H. Tomlinson. He also resided at Adel before that time. He is very well remembered in this section and is highly esteemed by all who knew him. Mr. Shaw said before leaving here yesterday that he was an excellent Naval Stores operator, a good man and citizen. Mr. Shaw was greatly shocked by the news of his death.

Bruh came looking for him, stopped at the bedroom door and listened as Roller read the last few sentences.

"Roller, what are you doing?" He demanded.

"Bruh, come here! This is about our granddaddy. Did you know this? Come here!"

Bruh joined him and read the article as Roller continued to search the clippings.

"Hey, Here's another one!" Roller began to read aloud the second article.

"Read it to yourself." Bruh ordered as he continued to read.

Roller read the article silently and then aloud as Bruh finished the first one and handed it back to him.

The Valdosta Daily Times
February 21, 1907
THE KILLING OF MR. LANIER
MR. L. W. SHAW RETURNS FROM ST. GEORGE ON
TRAIN LAST NIGHT.

He brought fuller details of the killing which was done by a negro named Will Small, the object being robbery. His wife found him by the road side.

Mr. L. W. Shaw returned last night from St. George where he was called by the tragic death of his partner in the navel stores business, Mr. R.W. Lanier.

Mr. Shaw states that a legal investigation of the killing would be made, probably today. He says that the evidence seems to indicate that Lanier was killed while he was making change for Frank Roberson who was paying him a small account in the commissary. There is nothing to show that he had quarrelled with the negroes or that there had been a dispute.

It is likely that there was a conspiracy between the negroes to kill and rob him, they believing that he had money. He had only a small amount according to Mr. Shaw's statement. He did not have the payroll of $300 as was stated. He had between fifteen and forty dollars on him, but the exact amount is not known.

The negroes worked for a tie camp near there and not for him, though they traded some at his commissary. They were expecting to leave that section and one of them, Frank Roberson, was paying him a small amount when he was shot dead by Will Small.

He was sitting in the buggy when the shot was fired and had driven from the road far enough for the wagons which the negroes were driving to go by. It is said that he remained in the buggy for some time and fell to the ground when he was robbed. He had several bills which the negro evidently took for a much larger sum than it really was.

His horse went on home and Mrs. Lanier, having heard the gun shot became fearful that something had happened. She called someone to put up the horse, while she ran down the road until she came to the body of her husband—cold in death by the road side. She sent a messenger to St. George to notify the people there of the tragedy, while she remained with the body until help from that place arrived.

The ordeal through which she passed under the circumstances can not be imagined. Left alone, with her murdered husband, three miles from the nearest neighbor and in a strange county, she must have suffered agonies worse than death for the time being.

The remains of the deceased were brought on from St. George on the train last night and were carried to a burying ground between Cecil and Nashville for interment, the funeral occurring today. Mr. Lanier was a native of North Carolina and had resided in this section for a number of years. He was married to Miss Shaw, a daughter of W. R. Shaw, who resided near Nashville about six years ago.

"We better put this stuff up and get out of here," Bruh pleaded. "You know not to meddle in Mama's stuff. Come on, put it up."

"I know, Bruh, but I had to. Did you know about this? Has Mama ever told you anything about this?" He asked other questions, but Bruh had gone, and Roller's questions echoed unheard in the bighouse.

He placed the two articles aside and returned the other papers to the box and the box back to its place on the armoire. Carefully he folded the old clippings, carried them to his bed, and hid them under the mattress until he could study them later.

Bruh had "Gang Busters" on the radio, but he just sat on the side of his bed reflecting on the articles, asking silent questions about what they had said and how terrible it must have been to Mama. No wonder that she didn't want to talk about it or even think about it. He felt a sudden compassion for her, and yet he had a long-standing compassion for the three innocent victims of the Klan hanging.

The articles had confused him. He wanted to sort out all of the events of the murder. He wanted to know more. He wanted Cooper's paw to be innocent.

The articles had named a Will Small as being the perpetrator and a Frank Roberson, so why were all four of the men hanged? Were the articles correct? It sounded like maybe there was a lot of hearsay in them. Why weren't the other two men named? What was Cooper's paw's name? What did impudent mean?

He raced into the living room to the built-in bookcase, found the old tattered dictionary that the family used, and searched it to find that impudent meant shamelessly bold.

Shamelessly bold, he thought. His granddaddy had hit a man for being shamelessly bold. Was that reason enough to hit somebody? He guessed it was back then. He had heard stories about white men beating colored people when they got out of hand.

He laid back down on his bed, fully clothed, and thought

about the events of his granddaddy's death and fell asleep, dreaming of two whole weeks of Christmas holidays.

CHAPTER 14
THE LIGHTER

The day of Sis' wedding had been exactly what Roller had expected—a busy day of eating, bathing and dressing, Sunday School and preaching service, dinner, and dressing again for the wedding. He wore a new hand-me-down charcoal wool suit, a white shirt, a grey bow tie, and brown lace-up shoes. Because the weather was cold, Mr. B had let Roller crank the car and run the heater to warm it for everyone to make the ride to the church. He sat there, pretending to be driving, thinking about all the things that he planned to do during the impending Christmas holidays, until Mr. B donned his felt fedora and walked briskly, as was his usual gate, to join Roller in the car. Roller slid across the nylon seat and gave way for him to take the wheel.

"Man, it's blustery, ain't it?" Roller initiated the conversation.

"Yes, it sure is." Mr. B responded, but otherwise sat waiting for the rest of the family in solitude as he stared at the front door of the bighouse. Roller studied his freshly shaved face, aware that Mr. B was not his usual self. His crisp facial lines and clear discerning eyes seemed to be straining, puzzled with concentration. Roller wanted to say something to him; he even thought briefly about telling him about his accidental killing of the prize boar pig, but he somehow knew that Mr. B was in no mood for conversation, especially conversation about the irresponsible and unnecessary death of the pig.

Finally, as Roller stared at Mr. B's profile, he saw something that he suddenly realized he had never seen before—a tear.

Roller promptly joined his stare at the front door and tried to think of something to say as he swallowed hard. "Are you sad about something, Daddy?"

Mr. B leaned left, pulled his handkerchief from his right hip pocket, blew his nose, and cleared his throat. "Roller, the only thing that doesn't change is that change is inevitable. But I don't like it. I just hate to see ya'll grow up. Seems like just last week that your mother and I went to adopt Sis. You know we couldn't have children, according to the doctors that is, so we decided to try to adopt a child, and we found this beautiful little two-month-old girl that needed a home, so we made her part of our family. She was a real spark of sunshine in our lives and still is, and I declare, here we are on the way to her wedding."

Roller thought about Cooper's explanation of the sunshine and answered, "Yes, sir."

"Then five years later your brother was born, then four years later you came along. It seems like we went so long without the company of children that we wanted so badly, and then seemingly overnight they start to leave. I hate change, but it's a part of life."

"Yes, sir, I do too. Why can't things just stay like they are?"

"Life goes on, Son. Time won't stand still for us. We have to learn to row with the flow."

"Yes, sir."

Roller decided to change the subject. He remembered again that he had to tell him about killing the boar pig, but this was surely not the time. No, he had to find something pleasant to talk about. He thought a minute, but couldn't think of anything all that pleasant. Then, impromptu, he asked, "Gonna be nice when they get the road paved, ain't it?"

"Yes," Mr. B answered after a pause. "They say they'll finish it at the first warm weather of the spring." He blew his nose again.

"Yes, sir. Maybe I can drive the car when they get through, huh?"

"We'll see."

They stared at the front door in silence until the rest of the family made their way to the car. They were all dressed in their finest Sunday attire.

Sis wore a white lacy dress and white veil. She had never looked more beautiful. Her dress took the whole back seat but Mama was able to slide in under the layers of white crinolines. The rest of the family crowded into the front seat. The drive to Wesley Chapel seemed to take a lot longer than usual with not a word spoken.

The wedding, by all standards, was a simple but pretty affair. The sanctuary was adequately decorated with sprays of red and white carnations and arbors of candles. Roller paid little attention to the exchange of vows. His mind drifted to White Hogan. He knew that the sale of White was helping to pay the expense of the wedding, but he couldn't help but think that he had rather be watching White sniff at a cow's butt than be watching this ceremony.

But he thought, too, about what Mr. B had said about change, and he secretly vowed, as the big sailor kissed the bride, that from this day forward he would face change head-on and strong. He would learn to "row with the flow" and take what life offered him and do the best he could. He would shed no more tears for things that he couldn't help, and, remembering what Cooper had said, he would use what he did have to acquire things that he did not have. He would enjoy the things that made his sun shine and tolerate the things that didn't. He would miss Sis, he would miss White Hogan, but he would no longer morn their leaving. Change was inevitable.

The drive home without Sis was quiet and solemn; only Bruh and Roller refused to sniff and blow their noses. When they arrived at the bighouse, a black 1949 Ford was parked out front. It was Mr. Saunders. He sat at the steering wheel waiting for them. When they all exited the car, he climbed out of the Ford and ambled down the freshly swept gravel yard to meet them. He tossed a cigarette aside and greeted the family.

"Ben, can I have a word with you?"

"Sure, Hal. What is it?" Mr. B allowed the rest of the family to go inside. Muh informed the boys in no uncertain terms to take off their Sunday suits and hang them immediately. "Do you hear me?"

Roller quickly undressed and hung his clothes. He snatched

on a pair of jeans, a flannel shirt, and his old shoes and hurriedly sought his bicycle. When he ran through the front door, Mr. B and Mr. Saunders were still talking, and as he rounded the corner of the house to retrieve his bike he froze in his tracks as he heard Mr. Saunders say something about Cooper.

"I just thought you oughta know about it, Ben. It could have been a real mess." Roller crept back toward them.

"Yeah, I sure do appreciate you telling me about it. I'll have a good talk with him. If he don't straighten up, that rotgut liquor is gonna kill him."

"Yes, sir, sho is." Mr. Saunders lit another cigarette and returned to his car.

"Well, I'll see you."

"Yeah, I'm much obliged to you. Say hello to your folks for me."

As Mr. Saunders drove away, Roller followed Mr. B inside and inquired about what had been said. Disgusted, Mr. B announced that Mr. Hal had found Cooper stone drunk, laying flat of his back right there in the middle of the road up there beyond Mr. Lawson's. "He was on his Sunday paper route before day this morning and almost ran over him. I tell you, he's headed for real trouble if he don't quit that drinking."

"Yes, sir. I'm gonna ride my bike up there and see about him."

"You better talk to him. He's gonna wake up dead one of these days."

"Yes, sir."

Roller ran from the house, straddled his bike, and peddled fast up the hard clay road to Cooper's house.

Annie Jenny sat gap-legged in a much too small wooden chair on the front porch, a dip of snuff filled her bottom lip to its capacity. She spat a stream of dark juice to the side of the porch.

"Hey, Roller, how'd the wedding go?"

Roller dropped his bike to the ground. "It was fine." It crossed his mind to say to her what Cooper had said that day about having it gapped open, but he knew better. "How's Cooper?"

"Aw, he's all right, just sleeping off a drunk. He was out

159

all night a drinking."

"Yeah, I heard he passed out in the middle of the road."

"Sho did. Right down there." She pointed down the road. "He didn't quiet make it home fore it got the best of em."

"Where had he been all night, dadgummit!"

"Lawd only knows. Sometimes he just cut up like that— ever once in a while."

The tenant house that they lived in was a typical weathered- wood, four-room, shotgun house. They shared the house with an old colored woman named Mag Azine Jones—Mag for short. Mag had a bedroom on the front and a small kitchen in the back. Cooper and Annie Jenny shared a bedroom on the front and a small kitchen in the back. A common front porch spanned the front of the house. They cooked on wood-fired stoves, and kero- sene lamps or open windows were their only sources of light. Each duplex had a fireplace on the end wall of the bedroom—no bathroom.

Roller could hear Cooper snoring as he eased up to the front door and peeped into the dark room. He noticed the familiar sooty, musty smell as he observed Cooper laying fully clothed atop some old quilts that covered the feather-mattress bed. He was obviously in a deep sleep.

Roller returned to the porch and sat down on the edge. His muscular legs swung freely as he stared at the ground and talked to Annie Jenny.

"That Cooper won't do. Dadgum stuff is gonna kill him if he don't leave it alone."

"Sho is, Roller." She spat again to the side of the porch. "You know that stroke still showing on him. Sometime first thang in the morning it take him a long time fore he can get that leg of his to working. He have to sit there on the bed and work with his leg afore he can put weight on it. Then he have to drag it around a while fore he can go. It's bad sometime."

"I wish there was something we could do for him." They sat there in silence for a while. Then Roller asked, "Jenny, has Cooper ever said anything to you about his pa?"

"You know, since you mention it, he been talking bout his paw a lot lately."

"Yeah, what did he say?"

"Well, you know like, all the stuff his paw taught em how to do and all."

"Yeah, and what else?"

"That's bout all, I reckon."

Roller had the feeling that Annie Jenny was not telling all that she had heard. "Aw, come on Jenny, what else has he said?" Roller anxiously stared into her black eyes.

"Well, he said a few things that he ought not a said."

"Like what?" He looked at her very sternly.

She spat again. "Said one time that if he could he'd shoot the white men what kilt his pa."

Roller hung his head again and thought for several minutes.

"Well, they say he killed a man. That's why they hanged him."

Annie Jenny shifted her weight around in the old ladder-back chair, sent another stream of tobacco juice to the edge of the porch, and grunted, "Uh huh.... Cooper say that the Klan hanged the whole crowd. Said they come to his house to burn it down if his paw didn't come out. Said they drug his paw off with a rope like he was a yelling calf going to the slaughter pen. Said his paw begged them that he didn't do nothing wrong, but they wouldn't pay no attention to em. Cooper was just a little boy, too. Musta been bad to see his paw done like that, huh?"

"Yeah, I hate it." He thought a minute. "What about his ma? Did he ever say anything about her?"

"Only thing is that she ran a begging and screaming after them Klan to leave her man lone, and that she won't never the same after that. Said she went tetched in the head, and the chillen had to look after her till she died."

"I'll swear!"

"Uh huh." She gathered another stream of spit and spurted it to the side of the porch.

They sat there in silence for several minutes, Roller deep in thought, Annie Jenny enjoying her dip of Macaboy snuff. Cooper's heavy breathing and sporadic snoring and the playful laughter of the colored children of the quarters were the only interruptions of the otherwise quiet and peaceful Sunday afternoon.

Roller retraced in his mind the events of the newspaper clippings, the conversations he had with Cooper and Mama, and what Annie Jenny had said. There were so many questions that had no answers.

His mental search for answers was interrupted. He missed part of what Annie Jenny was saying, but the last part of her utterance was profound.

"That boy ain't up to no good." She was talking about Grady, Jr., who came walking down the road from the next tenant house dressed in his Sunday finest suit and shoes. He always dressed much nicer than most of the colored men of the farm, and it was easy to question how he afforded such nice clothes. He was singing some indistinguishable Negro spiritual as he pranced down the hard clay road.

"He need to go on way from here! He got trouble for a middle name. Gone be a mess round here one of these days," she said softly.

Grady, Jr., nodded but barely acknowledged Roller and Annie Jenny as he passed. He clearly had some destination and wanted no waste of time.

"Where you reckon he's going so dressed up?" Roller quizzed after Grady, Jr., had walked past.

"Sho ain't going to no church, and you can bet on that! Prolly going over yonder to ole Mott's. Gonna be a mess over there one of these days, too. She's bout one sorry nigger."

Mott lived in a little two-room tenant shanty over in the field behind Miss Lucille's. Roller had heard talk of her selling moonshine whiskey and being real generous to the men who visited her. Roller knew enough about her to know why none of the colored women liked her. He had seen Cooper whistling his way home from her house on several occasions. Mr. B called her the "bitch in heat."

"Reckon that's where Cooper was last night?"

"Prolly was."

"She's bootlegging, ain't she?"

Even though Annie Jenny despised Mott and the things she did, she was cautious not to incriminate her. There was some

162

kind of unmentioned bond among colored people that made them protectors of each other when incrimination was the issue. They would lie for a dire enemy in lieu of giving information that might implicate that enemy in the eyes of the law.

"Not as I knows of."

"Aw, Annie Jenny, I hear men talking. I've heard them say that a man can get bout anything he wants over there. Fact is, Uncle Sammy calls her place the 'moon-poon saloon.' Says she sells moonshine and poon tang."

Annie Jenny's eyes opened wide as she shot a stream of chocolate-colored juice to the same spot on the ground at the edge of the porch, wiped her mouth, and chuckled, "Boy, you oughta go way from here. Go on now and find you something to do." She gestured with her hand as if shooing him toward the bighouse. Under her breath she chuckled again, "What you know bout poon tang?"

Roller vaulted from the porch, retrieved his bike, and, as he pushed the bike onto the road, he thought about Virginia Hart.

"Well, I don't know as much as I want to know but, I'm gonna. You can tell Cooper that I came and that he's in for a talking to. Tell him I'm gonna kick his ole black butt when he sobers up!"

"I'll tell him what you say. Ain't gone do no good, but I'll sho nuff tell him. Boy, your ma would whoop you good if she heard you talkin' like that!"

Roller stood and pushed down hard on the top pedal and made the rear wheel of the bike spin. "Yeah, well, I don't intend for her to hear me. I'll see you later Jenny." He kicked another wheel and pedaled toward home.

"Yeah, well, she can hear a lot better than you might think," Jenny shouted to his retreating backside.

He noticed as he coasted to approach Grady, Jr., making his determined stroll down the road, that he could hear a clicking noise. At first he thought that it was the clicking of taps on Grady's shoes, but he remembered that he didn't hear the clicking as he had passed him and Annie Jenny earlier.

He coasted up alongside Grady, Jr., and saw that he had a Zippo cigarette lighter in his right hand and was flicking the cap open and shut as he walked. He would occasionally flick the flint wheel and watch the lighter flame up, then snap the lid shut, then click the lid open and shut again.

Roller wondered where Grady, Jr., would have gotten a Zippo lighter. They cost about three dollars, and he had never seen a colored person with one.

"Hey, is that a Zippo?"

"Yeah," Grady, Jr., hardly acknowledged Roller.

"You gonna wear it out playing with it."

"Yeah, well, I like to hear it click, and I like to see it flame up like that."

"You going over to see Mott?"

"Maybe so." Grady looked at him as if he didn't want to be bothered. "You sho is meddlesome, Roller."

Grady, Jr., was the oldest boy of seven children born to Grady and Merlene. They lived in the last tenant house of the quarters. He had been to school some and always talked about leaving the farm and moving up north to Newark. Somewhat of a loner, he had a reputation of starting trouble, and Roller figured he must be about twenty years old.

He was always getting into fights, and Roller had heard that he carried one of those switch-blade knives in his pocket and that he had cut his own brother, Willie Joe, fighting over a piece of watermelon; that he got mean when he got to drinking.

Roller peddled around in little circles as he made his pace match that of Grady, Jr.

"What is it that ya'll do over there at Mott's all the time?"

Grady, Jr., said nothing. He clicked the Zippo with rhythm. Roller continued to quiz him.

"I see a lot of men a going and a coming from over there all the time. I hear a lot of loud talking over there at night sometimes."

"Ain't no white folks business what goes on over there, I reckon."

"Maybe not, but I hear Miss Lucile's done got a bait of it, and she's gonna call the sheriff one of these nights."

"That sheriff don't scare me none," Grady, Jr., smirked.

"Naw, he don't scare me none either long as he's up there

in Cuthbert, and I'm down here. He's a big man, and I'd hate for him to put that ax handle on me like I hear he does if you give him trouble."

"Well, I ain't gonna give him no trouble. Don't want him giving me none neither."

Roller pushed hard on the pedal and spun the back wheel of his bike. "I'll see you later."

"Yeah," Grady, Jr., acknowledged as if he was pleased Roller was leaving.

The leaves on the old oak were sparse and dull with not nearly enough foliage in which to hide, but Roller gave the tree another climb and sat at the sitting place for awhile.

He thought back on the wedding and wondered if the big sailor would keep Sis from visiting home. He hadn't seen Snow White since she got married, but had learned that she lived in a town called Waycross, Georgia, and that she was very happy there. He daydreamed about her beauty for a time and eventually resolved that when girls got married they left Vilulah and were seldom seen again.

Roller silently cursed the big sailor and secretly vowed that when he got married he would stay in Vilulah. This was his home, his world and he would live here and watch the seasons come and go and work to make it a better place for the people here that he loved so much. He knew little about what the world had to offer elsewhere, but the things that made his sun shine were here, and he could care less about searching for better.

Grady, Jr., sashayed by clicking his Zippo without acknowledging Roller. Roller squirmed and shifted his weight on the limb stump that was obviously getting smaller each time he sat there. He held onto the armrest branches and leaned forward to look at the end of the limb stump in order to investigate why it was getting smaller. It was obviously the same as it had always been except for some evidence of a woodpecker's damage to the softer core at the end of the old limb. *I'll kill the rascal if he continues to peck away at my sitting place.*

He shifted and relaxed his muscular buttocks and enjoyed the scenery. The wind had calmed and the air was cool and clear. Sunday afternoons were quiet.

Bruh's call interrupted his observance.

"What do you want?" he yelled in answer.

"Muh said to come get ready for BTU."

"Dang!" he whispered. "I'll be on dreckly," he yelled back.

BTU was Baptist Training Union at Vilulah. Night services at Wesley Chapel had been canceled because of the wedding, and it was mandatory to attend BTU when Wesley Chapel was not having services.

He studied the activity over at the "moon-poon saloon" and saw Grady, Jr., disappear inside and wondered what went on over there. Two colored men, he couldn't make out who they were, came outside and appeared to talk awhile. One of them was moving his arms around as if making strong gestures to aid his conversation. Roller wished to be able to hear what was being said. Finally the man pounded his open left palm with his right hand and returned inside. The lone colored man walked around the house and across the field beyond.

The rabbit made his predicable hop alongside the thicket as if he knew Roller was watching. He stopped and reared high on his hind legs as if looking toward the tree at Roller, almost taunting him. Roller thought back on the many skirmishes that they had engaged in, and again vowed that the day would come when he would have the advantage over the wily hare, and that his ass would be grass and he the lawnmower.

"Roller!" yelled Bruh.

"Okay," Roller yelled back. He took one last look at the rabbit and planned a hunt with the bow that Cooper had make for Bruh. He had shot it a few times and found it most difficult to get the pinpoint accuracy that would be needed to kill such a small and elusive target as the cunning rabbit that had escaped him time after time. Practice, lots of practice, would be necessary.

He slid off the sitting place and made his routine descent to the ground. His bike awaited him, and he pretended, as he arranged the bike for mounting, to put his foot into the silver-sequined stirrup of some shiny saddle atop some beautiful white stallion. Mounting the big white horse, erect and proud, he rode stately toward the bighouse.

After supper, which had consisted of little fancy sandwiches left over from the wedding reception, BTU seemed to drag for hours, but finally Roller lay in his bed, and in the privacy of a small lamp that hung just above his bed he read again the clippings of his grandfather's death.

It dawned on him that he did not know Cooper's paw's name. Cooper's full name was Emmett James Cooper. Maybe his paw had the same name and that Cooper was a junior like Bruh. He would find out. There was no mention of a Cooper in any of the clippings.

Sleep did not come easy. Roller's mind, so full of thoughts, resisted the rest that it needed. Once asleep, however, he slept so soundly that he missed the activity that had taken place.

Muh informed him at the breakfast table that the moon-poon saloon had burned during the night.

CHAPTER 15
THE REVELATION

In vain Roller had hoped that Miss E would give everyone a recess for Christmas. The last week of school before Christmas holidays was no different from all those previous, correcting countless mistakes hidden among millions of numbers.

Billy Chitwood had managed to evade the prison for one afternoon recess by having only one red check, by finding his error at first glance, and by being the first in line to have his paper reviewed. Roller was jealous, and Billy jeered him by describing how much fun he had and made sarcastic remarks about Roller having so many mistakes that he couldn't get outside. Billy's remarks were all in fun, though, as he and Roller had become best of friends. They got together at every opportunity.

Billy asked Roller to go home from school with him on Thursday before Christmas holidays and spend the night with him. Muh had called Mrs. Chitwood to confirm the invitation. Roller was excited; there would be lots of things to do in Fort Gaines.

Mama, of course, had given Roller several Bible verses and a short sermon about the evils of the city and the difference between right and wrong. She told him six times that if he had to question whether something was right or wrong, then it was probably wrong, to let his conscience be his guide.

Muh, too, gave him a verbal list of do's and don'ts, a reminder of his manners and to say his prayers, and a jar of mayhaw jelly to take to Mrs. Chitwood.

The class Christmas party would be on Friday afternoon. Each student had drawn the name of a classmate from a box. Roller had drawn Ellen Brady's, and he had gotten her a box of chocolate-covered cherries from the store. Muh had wrapped it and had also wrapped a cloth bag of marbles for Billy and a little fancy handkerchief for Miss E.

Roller had secretly wrapped his own Christmas present for Miss E in a shoebox with butcher paper and had stashed it at the store in one of several of his hiding places. He didn't want Muh to know about it, for she surely wouldn't let him give it to her.

He had packed his clothes for the next day, all of his presents except Miss E's, the mayhaw jelly, and his school books in a pasteboard box, and was hurriedly eating his breakfast when Cooper passed on his way to the barn. Roller went out to tell him that he wouldn't be back until the following afternoon.

When he opened the kitchen door, he immediately noticed that Cooper was not whistling and that something was different.

He yelled to him, "Cooper, wait a minute. How's your hammer hanging? I need to tell you something."

Cooper said nothing and acted as if he was in a hurry. He shuffled on without stopping.

Roller ran out to the road's edge. "Hey, wait a minute." As he approached him, he saw the reason for Cooper's lack of response.

"Hey, Cooper, what's wrong with your face?"

Cooper's mouth was drawn to the left and down. His lips were tight and his left cheek had several new wrinkles at the corner of his mouth.

"What's the matter? What happened to you? Did somebody hit you?"

Cooper spoke in a slurred speech with still lips.

"Don't know. Woke up like this this morning. Musta dreamed bout eating persimmons." He tried to smile, but the right corner of his mouth barely moved.

"Dang, Cooper," Roller said in anguish, "You need to go see Dr. Harper. I'm gonna tell Daddy."

"Naw, I be all right. Don't bother Mr. B." He stuttered and struggled a bit to finish. "Maybe it will loosen ass up on up in the day."

"Yeah, but maybe it won't. I'm gonna tell Daddy. Listen, I'm going to stay the night with Billy. I'll be home tomorrow

169

afternoon to check on you. You better take care of yourself. Do you hear me?"

Dang, he thought, *I sound like Muh.*

Cooper nodded and shuffled on.

Roller just stood there a minute watching him. One of those strange feelings came over him. His throat knotted, and sadness filled his heart and soul as he watched Cooper's dragging gait. He felt helpless, and he knew deep inside that Cooper would never be the same, that age and miles and a life of hard work and whiskey were together taking a slow but certain toll on him. Tears welled in his eyes as he remembered something from Ecclesiastes about "a time to reap and a time to sow, a time to laugh and a time to cry, and a time to live and a time to die," and he wondered if it was Cooper's time to die. Would he die before he came home from school? *Dang, I won't be home until tomorrow after school.* He thought briefly about canceling his plans to stay with Billy and coming home so that he could check on Cooper, but remembered the vow that he had made at Sis' wedding and promptly dried his tears on his shirt sleeve.

He ran inside and told Muh about Cooper.

"Muh, Cooper needs to go see Dr. Harper. His mouth is all drawn to one side, and he can't hardly talk."

"Can hardly talk," she corrected him.

"Yes, ma'am, and I think he's limping more too! Will you get Daddy to take him?"

"Roller," she paused to think of what to say, "Cooper has probably had another stroke. Dr. Harper said that he would, and he's gonna probably have some more till one of them takes his life. Now, you need to prepare for it cause there isn't anything that can be done about it. We'll all pray for Cooper, and I'll talk to your Daddy. Now, you get going; the bus will be here soon." She patted his hair with her fingers. "You need a hair cut. I don't want you gallivanting and traipsing all over town down there. You be a good boy. Do you hear me?"

"Yes, ma'am." Roller hesitantly gathered himself and his box and ambled, in deep thought, toward the store to catch the bus.

Mr. Lawson and Sidney were already at the store enjoying

the warmth of the old wood heater. Mr. Lawson's hyena laugh filled the store as Roller secretly retrieved his stashed present for Miss E.

Roller could tell that they were talking about the Moon-Poon Saloon. He overheard Sidney as he sort of whispered to Mr. Lawson, "Musta been a hot piece—to set fire to the place. I heard she was hot as fire, but I didn't know she threw sparks." They both laughed again.

He didn't have time to discuss it, but Roller knew in his mind that Grady, Jr., had started that fire. He knew it, but he had no proof. He had told Mr. B about Grady, Jr., going over there flicking his lighter as he walked, but Mr. B had explained that there was no proof about how the fire started, and the fact that Grady, Jr., carried a Zippo lighter was only circumstantial evidence.

Roller didn't quite understand circumstantial evidence, so he had later asked Uncle Sammy about it, and Uncle Sammy had explained,"Well, Roller the best example that I can think of is the story about the old farmer who went out to milk one morning, and just as he opened the gate to the stall where the milk cow was, he had a real bad pee pain. So he pulled out his tallywhacker to take a leak, and just as he was about to pee, the milk cow's heifer calf ran through the gate to get her breakfast. So the old farmer grabbed the calf by the tail with his free hand, and was trying to pull her out of the stall.

"Low and behold, the farmer's wife walked up. There he stood with his play-pretty in one hand and the heifer calf by the tail in the other hand. The farmer's wife demanded to know what he was doing. The old farmer insisted that he was just trying to keep that calf from getting the morning milk and that he was a victim of circumstantial evidence." Uncle Sammy had laughed hysterically. Roller had still been confused.

Mr. B came out of the back of the store just as the bus blew its horn. Roller ran to him and explained that he needed to check on Cooper. Mr. B leaned down and promised that he would as they hugged each other. "You be a sweet boy and don't forget who you are."

"Yes, sir." Roller ran out, but for some reason he remem-

171

bered the door and caught it and eased it back to its jamb.

The bus ride to school seemed unusually short. Roller sat quietly in thought with mixed emotions. He was excited about spending the night with Billy, elated that tomorrow would begin a two-week escape from the prison, yet sad and worried about Cooper.

As he made his way from the bus around the high school part of the building, he met Mr. White.

"Good morning Roller, looks like you've got quite a load there. Is one of those packages for me?"

Roller was flabbergasted. He hadn't even thought about buying Mr. White a present, and he felt that he should have. Mr. White had been so nice to him. He didn't know what to say as he stopped his burdensome pace, and a thousand things ran through his mind. He knew that Mr. White was just kidding him, but he really felt bad that he hadn't even thought about him when he was getting his Christmas order together.

Mr. White had stopped his stately stride and stood there waiting for a response from Roller. He rubbed his chin, and let a slight grin creep from the corner of his mouth as if he expected some profound rebuttal from Roller.

Finally, Roller exhaled a deep breath and spontaneously countered, "Well, if you'd get Miss E to let us out for recess every once in a while, you might get a bunch of Christmas presents."

Mr. White had held back a chuckle, but now he laughed out loud. He cut his laughter short and patted Roller's curly hair.

"Now Roller, you've got to give me some time on that. You know Miss E has been teaching for a long time, and she has her way of doing things. I can't just come in here in my first year and tell her she's got to change her ways now, can I?"

"Well," Roller returned, "you are the boss aren't you?"

Mr. White laughed again. "No, Roller, in this case, I'm not the boss. You just study hard and do your work and things will get better after Christmas. I'm sure of it. Now you run on. You'll be late for class."

"Yes, sir." Roller turned and continued his trek to his much-hated classroom. He thought about Mr. White as he walked. Mr.

172

White's caring and gentlemanly personality reminded him of Mr. B. He thought them both to be very good and kind men. *Next year, I'll get Mr. White a Christmas present.*

The bell rang signalling the start of the school day just as Roller laboriously entered the classroom with his cargo of books and clothes and packages.

He sat his box down on his desk and carried his presents to the Christmas tree as Miss E peered over her wire-rimmed glasses in observance of Roller's almost tardy arrival.

"Good morning, Mr. Hogan," she spat.

"Good morning," Roller replied.

"You were almost late to class, weren't you?"

"Yes, ma'am, but I wasn't." He stared into her wire-rimmed glasses.

The rest of the class was already sitting quietly at their desks. They could feel a tension in the air. They all knew that these two very strong-willed people were face to face here in a moment of confrontation. They all knew that everyday these adversaries met on this sacred battlefield, which was native soil to Miss E, and that every day the probability of conflict grew stronger and stronger. They had no doubt as to who would be the victor; they knew that Big Bertha was truly the mightiest of these foes and that her authority here dominated any and all intruders. They all sensed that, one day, one of these little encounters would spark a flash fire of battle which Miss E would surely extinguish as rapidly as it began, and that Roller would become a permanent inmate of her thraldom and would see the daylight of recess only when he entered the sixth grade next September.

"Well, take your seat, Mr. Hogan, and let's get to work."

"Yes, ma'am," Roller sighed with relief.

Roller managed to endure the rest of the day, hurriedly gathered his things, and followed Billy as the bell rang to end the school day.

They had to walk several blocks to Billy's house, which sat across town near the famous bluff that overlooked the mighty Chattahoochee River. They stopped off at Mill's Drug Store for a Coke and a candy bar with several of the kids that lived in town.

As they were walking on toward Billy's house, they met a distinguished looking old man who walked with a brisk bouncing gait. He was clean-shaven and proper, and his white starched shirt seemed to punctuate his pink baby-skin face and bald head.

He stopped as they approached and watched them for a step or two. He sucked the saliva from the corner of his mouth and spoke in a high, very refined, girlish pitch.

"Say, Billy, who's this young man walking with you today? I don't believe I've seen you, young fellow. What's your name? My, you're a fine-looking lad."

"Yes, sir, I'm Roller."

"Roller? Is that a nickname?"

"Yes, sir."

"Where do you live, Roller?"

"I live out at Vilulah."

"Oh yes, I bet Mr. B.B. Hogan's your Daddy. Is that right?"

"Yes, sir."

"Fine man, that B.B. Hogan. Yes, I know him. I know who you are now."

"Well, we got to get home," Billy quipped. "Come on Roller, let's go."

Roller gestured a farewell to the old man and hurried to catch up with Billy.

"Hey, who was that old man?"

"Mr. Freddie Willis."

"He seemed like a nice man."

"He's a queer!"

"He's a what?"

"A queer!"

"Oh yeah," Roller answered in puzzlement.

They walked on a while. "Billy, what's a queer?"

Billy stopped in his tracks. He looked at Roller. "You don't know what a queer is?"

"Well..., no, I don't, I don't reckon."

"A queer likes men instead of women. That's why I didn't want to stop and start any kind of talking with him. He likes boys, too."

"Oh," Roller answered assuredly.

174

They walked a bit further. "You mean he doesn't like women?"

"Roller," Billy insisted, "queers may like women, I guess, but they like to make sex with other men."

"Oh."

They walked several steps in silence. "Make sex? What do you mean, make sex?" Roller was totally confused. He knew that this had something to do with White Hogan and Virginia Hart and the Moon-Poon Saloon, but he just didn't know what it all meant. He couldn't make a connection of all the bits and pieces of conservation and information that he had absorbed over the last year or two. He knew just enough to want to know more.

They were approaching Billy's house. "I'll tell you all about it later," Billy bragged. In fact, we might hockey-sack ol' Freddie Willis tonight."

"What?"

They entered Billy's house, and Billy couldn't answer. Mrs. Chitwood met them at the door and greeted Roller with big and fat arms opened wide.

"Hey, here, Roller, honey. I'm so glad that you came to see us." She spoke with a very slow and Southern drawl. "We're just always so happy for Puddin's friends to come visit."

"Puddin'?"

"Now Mother," insisted Billy. He obviously didn't want to be called Puddin.

"Don't you 'Now Mother' me." She hugged him too. "You know you're my little Puddin', and you're gonna be my little Puddin' from now on. Just because you're getting to be such a big boy, don't mean I can't still call you Puddin'."

Mrs. Chitwood was a big, robust lady. Her jolly smile seemed to span her pink round face. Her clear blue eyes sparkled and seemed to smile in concert with her white-toothed grin. Billy had warned Roller that she loved children, especially his friends, and that she would "baby" him and "carry on" over him. Roller liked her immediately.

"I've got ya'll some cookies there on the table, Hon, and some good cold sweet milk in the fridge. Ya'll get yourselves a snack now cause it'll be awhile till supper, and, Lawd, honey," she held a puffy hand on each side of Roller's face, "we might even play 'cops and robbers' after supper."

"Yes, ma'am!" Roller replied, "and thank you for allowing me to come. I've been wanting to meet you. Muh sent you some mayhaw jelly."

"Well, you're sure welcome, sugar. Ain't that some pretty jelly? My, my, I might have to make some biscuits for supper! I'll bet that ol' Miss E gave ya'll some homework to do, didn't she? So ya'll will have to get that done before we can play. Won't you?"

The only redeeming thing that Miss E had done all year was to not give them homework on the day before Christmas holidays.

"No, ma'am," they answered in unison.

"You won't believe it, Mrs. Chitwood," Roller began but was interrupted by Mrs. Chitwood.

"Now listen, hon, all of the kiddies call me Mama Neva," she smiled again into Roller's eyes.

"Yes, ma'am. Well, you won't believe it, Mama Neva, we like to have fallen out of our desks when she didn't give us any homework. I think she felt bad about it when she saw all of those gifts under the tree for her."

Mama Neva laughed out. "Maybe she did; maybe she did."

"Come on, Roller," Billy insisted, "let's go play ball." He grabbed a handful of cookies and beckoned for Roller to have some.

Roller obliged. They carried their things into Billy's room, retrieved Billy's baseball and their gloves, and ran out. They jogged up and across the street to a little park. There were tennis courts there and plenty of open area to play ball. Other town kids were already gathering there to play. Some high school students played tennis; others sat on car hoods talking and smoking cigarettes.

Roller was not particularly interested in playing ball; he wanted to hear more of what Billy had been talking about. They found an area at the edge of the park and played pitch for a while. Then they played a game called Trimmer-Catch with some of the other kids where a batter would hit the ball, then run to first base, and return to home plate. The batter could stay at bat until he was thrown out at home plate or until a fly ball was caught. Whoever got the batter out then batted until he, too, made an out.

Finally, as the sun went down below the trees that lined the bluff of the river, Roller and Billy sat by one of the big sugarberry trees at the park boundary and began to talk. Roller insisted to know more about making sex. He couldn't believe that Billy knew so much; he couldn't believe that he knew so little. Billy boldly told him all that he knew and used four letter words that Roller had never heard. Roller asked questions, and Billy answered them as if he were an expert. They'd sit quietly while Roller thought over all of this new information; then more questions, more answers. Roller intently absorbed every bit and piece of Billy's profound knowledge of this most interesting subject.

It was a revelation to Roller. The thousand-piece puzzle that lay scattered there in his young virgin brain began to arrange and assemble itself. Form, shape, and purpose suddenly became obvious. There were still pieces of the puzzle that didn't quite fit the blank spaces, but the picture was clearer than Roller had ever imagined. He suddenly understood Uncle Sammy's version of circumstantial evidence. He understood about the Moon-Poon Saloon. He thought about Virginia Hart. He felt good!

He felt good until he thought about Cooper. He wondered how Cooper had been through the day; what Dr. Harper had been able to do for him; what would happen to Cooper next? Would one of those strokes kill Cooper before he got home tomorrow?

He sat there oblivious to all of the activity. His mind tumbled in thought. This newly acquired information from Billy, his regard for Cooper's well being, the prospective holidays, the mini-sermons of Mama and Muh, all somersaulted about there in his young head. He couldn't seem to finish a thought about one thing before another popped to the forefront of his mental attention. He couldn't focus on a thought for the interruption of another.

Finally, Billy's calling interrupted Roller's melee of thoughts.

"Come on, Roller. It's getting dark. We gotta get home."

Billy was already crossing the street when Roller scrambled to get to his feet.

"Hey, wait! Say, Billy, what is 'hockey sack'?"

Billy stopped for Roller to catch up. "You see, what you do is, you take a dump in a paper sack, then slip up on somebody's porch and set the sack on fire and then ring the doorbell or knock on the door. Then you haul-ass out in the bushes somewhere and watch them come out and stomp the fire out and get dooky all over their feet. It's fun. You wanta do ole Mr. Freddie Willis tonight?"

Roller hesitated. "I don't know Billy. I don't want to get in any kind of trouble." He remembered Mama's instructions about letting your conscience be your guide and about gallivanting and traipsing. "I uh, uh, just don't want to get in trouble."

"Ah, we won't get in no trouble. We'll be long gone before he can do anything. While he's cleaning his shoes, we'll be running to safety. Come on, I'm tired of that ol' man licking his lips at me."

Roller thought, "But what if he comes to the door barefooted and can't put the fire out?"

"Well, if he does, it ain't gonna hurt nothing. No little ol' paper sack's gonna start no house afire anyway."

"I don't know."

"Dang, Roller, don't you want to have some fun?"

"Yeah, but I...."

"But I, nothing. Let's give ole Freddie something to talk about. Whacha say?"

"We'll see."

Mama Neva had a nice supper prepared. But all during the meal Roller was engrossed in thought. He didn't want Billy to think that he was afraid of "hockey-sacking" the old man, but neither did he want to do anything that he might regret later. He thought about what Mr. B had said—"Don't forget who you are"—and figured that to mean not to forget what he had been taught about right and wrong; that who he was had something to do with about how he should act; that he should follow the example of his elders, and he certainly didn't think that any of his elders would use the bathroom in a sack and then set fire to it on somebody's porch.

Maybe, he thought, Mama Neva wouldn't let them out after dark. Maybe, it would start to rain or something. The Chitwood's had a TV. Maybe they would stay in and watch Lassie or something. Yeah, that's what he would suggest. After all, he didn't get to watch TV much.

****

Tommy Culpepper's store stayed open every night till midnight. Billy had asked Mama Neva if he and Roller could walk up town and get an ice cream cone.

"All right Puddin', but ya'll come straight back now. I don't want ya'll rambling all over town now, darling."

"Yes, ma'am."

****

In the darkness they watched for movement in the old man's house from a vacant lot across the street. A light was on inside, and a radio played the Arthur Godfrey Show, but there was no movement.

"I don't believe he's at home," Roller whispered. "Come on, let's go. I don't think we ought to do this."

"Oh, Roller, he's got to be in there. He doesn't go anywhere at night. Come on. See if you can crap in this sack."

Billy opened the brown paper bag and stood it upright behind a little clump of nandina bushes.

Roller was afraid. "Dadgummit, Billy, I can't crap in that sack. You do it."

"Shoot Roller, I don't have to go right now."

"Well, me neither, so let's go."

"Wait a minute. I feel a little something. I'll try."

Billy folded the top of the sack back about half way. He pulled down his pants and squatted down over the sack.

"Am I over it?" He looked between his legs to align himself. "Am I going to ring it?"

"Heck, I don't know. Just let it go, and see for yourself." Roller shivered in fear.

Billy strained out loud.

"Shhh, be quiet." Roller looked around nervously.

179

Billy began to giggle so hard that he lost his balance and fell backwards onto the sack, and with his pants down around his knees he couldn't get up. He sprawled around on the ground laughing hysterically, a whispering laugh. Roller joined his laughter and tried to help him stand up.

Billy regained his footing. They both muffled their uncontrolled laughter as Billy tried to brush the sand off his shiny white buttocks.

The episode had suddenly become fun to Roller. The humor and excitement had squelched his fear, and his mischievous nature had been awakened. They both giggled and laughed wildly as Billy tried in vain again to make a deposit in the bag.

Roller took his turn over the sack, but he too could not balance himself for laughing. He held on to the nandina shoots. "I can't with you watching," he strained.

By now Billy was literally rolling on the ground in laughter. He attempted to collect himself. "Here, let me try again. I feel one coming on. Some hockey-sacker you are! Move!"

Roller jerked up his jeans, but remained bent in laughter. Billy again strained over the sack, half laughing—half grunting. "Be quiet. I can't concentrate with you laughing like that. Don't watch me like that. Wait! Wait! Here it comes. Ummmp!"

Roller cupped his hands over his mouth to muffle his laughter just in time to hear three little thuds in the bottom of the sack. It sounded to him like Billy had dropped three marbles into the sack.

Billy, too, heard the tap-tap-tap in the sack, and fell forward head first on the ground in laughter. Roller fell to his knees on the ground holding his stomach in laughter. He crawled over to the bag and looked in at three little brown rabbit pill-like balls. He erupted in loud laughter and rolled there on the ground with Billy. There was no more controlling their volume. They could be heard for several blocks.

Roller broke the duet of laughter as he said gasping, "Billy, that ain't no hockey-sack; that's a pill-sack." Again they laughed in unison.

Then Billy, "Well, at least I scored. You shot a blank." They laughed.

"Yeah, I shot a blank, and you shot three buck-shot. I've been trying to kill an ol' rabbit that can do better than that."

Billy caught his breath, "All right, I got you beat. You better try again. The score is three to nothing."

"I'll try, but my stomach hurts from laughing. I don't think I can."

Roller tried over the bag once more, but Billy's hysterical laughing was too much of a distraction.

"Would you be quiet?" he strained.

Billy hushed his cackling just as the quiet stillness of the night was splintered by Roller's loud, buzzing fart. Their laughter again erupted, and Roller fell forward on his naked knees. Again, they rolled there on the ground in total hysteria.

Mr. Willis had turned off his radio and heard the commotion. He came to the front door, turned on the porch light, and yelled out, "Hey, what's going on out there?"

Instantly they stopped their laughter and froze there on the ground. They were well concealed behind the shrubbery and in the shadows of a distant streetlight.

"Shhh, don't move," whispered Billy. "He can't see us. He'll go back inside in a minute."

Roller's joviality quickly turned to fear. He lay motionless. How would he ever explain what they were doing should they be caught? How could he ever tell Muh that they were trying to do Number Two in a sack....so that they could set it on fire on a man's front porch....so that the man would have to stomp the fire out? No, definitely no! If they got caught, they would just have to lie. Lie? No! The only thing worse than cussing in the eyes of Muh and Mama and Daddy was lying. He remembered lessons from all of them. Thou shalt not bear false witness, a man's word is his bond, any man that will lie will steal.

He secretly prayed for the old man to go back inside so that they could escape. Instead, Mr. Willis turned off the front porch light and stood there looking out into the darkness. What kind of explanation could they make if they got caught, he wondered? He almost laughed out as he whispered to Billy, "We'll have to tell him, if we get caught that we were out here picking up rabbit pills." Billy choked back a snicker, "Yeah, but we only found three." They jerked in silent laughter.

Finally, Mr. Willis went inside. They saw a chance for escape and scampered to their feet, pulling up and snapping their jeans as they ran. Once in the clear, several blocks away, they slowed to a walk and laughed and joked about their attempted prank.

"It's a good thing ol' Mr. Willis couldn't see you with your britches down, Roller. He'd a probably wanted some of you."

"Dang Billy, don't even joke about that. I still find all that about queers hard to believe."

"It's the truth, I tell you. Ask somebody else if you don't believe me."

"I will. I'll ask Cooper when I get home."

Cooper. He thought about Cooper the rest of the night. He silently prayed for him as he drifted off to sleep.

****

Friday, the last day of school before Christmas holidays, was the best day of the year thus far. No, there was no recess for Roller, but the excitement of the little party, exchanging of gifts at the end of the school day, the return home to check on Cooper, and the long-awaited two-week vacation made his day very pleasant.

The Christmas tree party was an hour of fun, the best hour that Roller had seen in the confines of the fifth grade prison. Several of the mothers had made cookies and punch. They sang Christmas carols, and quiet talking was allowed. Roller and Billy talked about the night before at every opportunity. Once as Miss E walked over the imaginary hole in the floor and disappeared in an imaginary cloud of dust, they joked that Big Bertha could probably have filled the hockey-sack to the top. They laughed in muffled hysteria.

Miss E insisted that all of the gifts be handed out to their recipients before any of them were opened, and, as was customary, she would open her many gifts last while the class sat quietly and observed her. Then she would pass out to all the students a gift as they exited the room at the last bell.

Joanna Hamilton had drawn Roller's name and had given him a new Rawlings baseball. He loved it. He had wanted a new baseball for some time now. He thanked her. Billy gave Roller a pair of brown, cotton cowboy gloves with imitation leather-fringed cuffs. He immediately thought about the big cowboy that took White Hogan away as he opened the gift, but they fit good and he thanked Billy. He envisioned a ride on his trusty two-wheeled steed clad in cowboy garb now complete with gloves.

After a few minutes of bedlam as all of the students opened their gifts, Miss E called the class to order and proceeded to open her gifts. Roller's heart thumped hard and fast as she worked her way to his special present for her. He had put much thought into this gift. He had gotten Uncle George to label the package so that she would not be able to recognize the handwriting. He had left it in his box the morning that he brought it to school, had come back to the classroom ahead of the rest of the class after lunch, and had placed it under a mound of other gifts. Nobody had seen him. Muh had wrapped a handkerchief for her and labeled it as being from Roller. Maybe she wouldn't suspect anyone who would give her such a sweet little gift. He had not told anyone about the gift—not even Billy. Mr. Camel had mailed the invoice directly to him in order to keep his gift purchase confidential.

The gifts for Miss E, Cooper, Muh, and the rest of the family would remain a surprise. The moment he had discovered the gift in Mr. Camel's catalog, he knew that it was perfect. It only cost fifty cents, but it suited what needed to be said so well. It provided a subtle and very important message, yet it was practical. Surely she would see it as useful. Surely she would see its intended statement. Hopefully, she would see it every day!

Ironically, Miss E opened all of the other gifts, showing each of them to the class, and saved the special gift for last. She studied it for several seconds with a puzzled stare.

"This package," she said loud and plainly, "does not say who it's from." She glanced around the classroom and seemed to make eye contact with every pair of anxious eyes as she removed the twine and brown paper. "Apparently, I have a secret admirer."

Now Roller's heart pounded. He fought back any appearance of guilt as he fixed his eyes on the box and tried to look as inquisitive and innocent as all the rest of the class. She opened the box and removed a paper roll. She glanced around the classroom and unrolled the coil of paper and stared. "Oh," she sounded pleased, "it's a 1955 calendar. And it has a pretty Norman Rockwell print on the top." She turned it and held it up so the class could see. She turned it back, looked at it again, and described it to the class. "It's a young boy sitting at his desk doing his homework, and just outside at the window is his little dog looking in at him. The little dog is sitting on a table, and there on the table is a fishing pole and a can of worms. The boy looks so sad and miserable. The little dog looks as if he is anxious for the young boy to finish so that they can go to the fishing hole. Well, that's real cute. It appears that my secret admirer is trying to tell me something." She cast a stern stare around the classroom.

She glanced at her watch. It was about time for the bell. She lumbered her massive torso out of her chair and over to the corner of the room where she lifted a large box off a table. She walked slowly to the classroom door, sat the box down on the floor by the door, and ambled back to her desk and faced the class.

"Well, I'm sure that my secret admirer will be glad to hear that you won't have any homework over the holidays, but when we return we'll be getting into long division and we're way behind in geography and spelling, and we'll do three book reports before school is out. So I hope you all have a Merry Christmas, and will be ready to get down to work when we come back on January the third. Now, when the bell rings I want each of you to pick your present out of the box at the door. There is one in there for each of you."

Dang, she sounds like it's going to be worse after Christmas instead of better. She sounds like we haven't already gotten down to work! What does this slave driver expect of us? Why can't she let there be a little bit of fun in going to school? Boy, am I excited about her present! Everybody knew that she always gave her students a Rick-Rack paddle for Christmas. *Some present! Dang, why won't the bell ring? Let's get out of here! I've got better things to do. Enough is enough. I want to go home!*

Almost claustrophobic, he was oblivious of her yakking about the coming year and tensed in anticipation of the bell. He got ready. He had looked forward to this day since the first day of school. *Why won't the bell ring?*

Miss E was still spitting out her gloomy forecast for the coming year when the bell rang, though Roller had not heard anything that she was saying. He was like a sprinter at the starting blocks. He bolted straight up in the air at the sound of the bell and yelled at the top of his voice, "Amen!"

The rest of the class sat quietly awaiting this drill sergeant to dismiss her ranks. Only Roller had broke formation.

"Roller!" she shouted, "I'm not through!"

Her exploding command broke his stupor. He snapped to attention and realized that he was still on her sacred ground. He almost sat back down, but somehow he just couldn't. He couldn't stand even one more second of this dungeon; not one more order from this tyrant; not one more sound wave of her demanding voice. He decided, with abandon of any future consequences, that it was time to revolt against this suppression. The bell had rung. School was out. He was free. He would escape.

Roller picked up his box. Miss E's authoritative stare burned him as their eyes met. The entire class watched in disbelief as Roller responded.

"Well, I am." He walked out.

★★★★★★★★★★★★★★★

As the bus slowed to a stop to let Roller and Bruh off at the store, Roller searched the surroundings for Cooper. He was sitting out at the woodpile as if in anticipation of the bus. Roller was always amazed at how Cooper knew what time it was even though he didn't own a watch. He said he could tell time by the sun.

Roller dropped his box on the store porch and ran to the drink box for a Coca-Cola. Uncle George greeted him. Roller presumed that Uncle George might have carried Cooper to see Dr. Harper.

"Did you take Cooper to Dr. Harper?"

"No."

"Did Daddy or Punto take him?"

"No, Muh called Dr. Harper, and he said that there wasn't anything that he could do for him. Said for him to keep doing anything he feels like doing, but not to over-do it."

Roller sank in disgust. "Dang!" He opened another Coca-Cola for Cooper and hurried out to the wood pile.

Cooper's face was still drawn tight on the left side. The left side of his mouth frowned, but his speech was noticeably better.

"Hey, Roller, how's your hammer hanging?"

Roller handed him the cola. "I'm all right. How are you doing?"

Taking the cola, Cooper said, "Much obliged. Oh, I'm all right. I ain't learned how to shave my new face yet, but I be doing good. Be doing bout like a poon, I reckon."

"How's that?" Roller quizzed.

"Be looking bad, but feeling good." Cooper tried to laugh, but dropped his face in a muffled chuckle instead.

"You fool, you won't do. Say, you wanta go check some fences?"

"Yeah, but you need to take your rifle cause them squirrels are cutting that chinquapin tree over there cross the branch, and we need to get us a mess of em. Mr. B said he'd like to have some for breakfast in the morning."

"Okay, I'll be right back." Roller ran to the bighouse with his box and sloshing cola. He was excited that he would have a chance to do something that would please Mr. B, because he knew how he loved fried squirrel, grits, and gravy for breakfast. He was excited that Cooper was still able to work. He had been so afraid that he would come home and find Cooper laid up in bed, or even worse. He was excited that Sis would be home for the weekend. Thanks to Billy, he now knew why she and the big sailor had gone on a honeymoon.

He felt good.

CHAPTER 16
THE FAN

Roller squirmed on the sitting place. Again it seemed to him to be getting smaller each time he sat there. He leaned over to investigate the woodpecker damage and found that the soft core had been completely pecked away and that a round, dark cavity now extended inward to the hollow bowels of the old tree.

Silently he cursed the woodpecker, but somehow this invasion of his territory seemed to be a natural thing. It did not infuriate him as it would have a year ago. He did not have a vendetta toward the woodpecker and vow to kill him promptly. The woodpecker was just trying to prepare a nest site, and it might be nice to share the sitting place for a while with a nest of woodpeckers in the coming spring.

Again he inspected the familiar landscape from his observant perch. It was, as it always was on Sunday afternoon, very quiet and peaceful. A fresh cool breeze blew from the north, but the bitter cold that had gripped the Christmas holidays, at last, had subsided. The dull winter colors of the countryside were dominant and unchanging, the only exception being a splattering of blooming camellias in the cemetery and landscaping the church. He savored the cool quietness of his retreat.

The charred rubble of the Moon-Poon Saloon caught his eye as he sank into thoughts of the past two weeks.

Cooper was still doing about the same. Maybe not having that rot-gut liquor so convenient had been good for him. He had been a great companion to Roller during the Christmas holidays. They had checked just about all the fences. Roller had killed six cat squirrels, and Annie Jenny fried four of them for breakfast. Cooper had carried two home with him. Mr. B had been pleased, and Cooper was pleased. Uncle George had driven them up to Cemocheechobee Creek to Mama's favorite fishing hole so that they could bait it up for her—they sank two burlap bags of pelleted hog feed, and a few days later they returned with Mama to the hole for her to fish for suckers.

Suckers are a carp-like fish that run small streams during the cold months. Mama fished when the almanac said that the signs were right, and she was a superb fisherwoman. She would sit for hours on a nail keg with a cane pole, the hook baited with a small bit of earthworm and held just off the bottom near the sacks of feed. Cooper and Roller kept her a fire burning nearby to warm her. Some days she caught nothing; other days the strings of fish would be a heavy load for them to pull back up the steep path leading down to the hole.

Suckers had to be prepared just right; they were very bony. Roller and Cooper would scale and gut them, and Mama would filet the sides and gash the pink meat. With a sharp knife she would delicately cut a slit into the meat neatly down to the skin but not through the skin, then another slit about one-eighth of an inch from the first, and so on down the length of the filet. The gashing cut the tiny bones into many pieces that, when fried crisp, became undetectable in the delicious meat. They were Roller's favorite meal.

This time she had caught ten suckers weighing about two pounds each. They prepared the fish, and Annie Jenny deep-fried them for lunch on Saturday. The big sailor had never heard of suckers, but he acquired an immediate appetite for them and ate three whole sides plus sizable helpings of cole slaw, French fried potatoes, and hush puppies. Roller hated to see Sis leave, but was glad for the big sailor to leave on Sunday, Christmas Day. They had moved to Pensacola, Florida, where he would be stationed. It was another sad Sunday afternoon when they left. Everybody cried except Roller.

Christmas Eve had been a day worth all of its expectations: suckers for lunch, afternoon Christmas shoppers, fireworks, and Santa Claus that night. Everybody had worked real hard in the store that day, and late that afternoon, as Cooper brought in his last armload of firewood for the day, Roller followed him out to the woodpile and gave him his present.

Cooper sat on a block of wood and studied the square box

wrapped with butcher paper.

"Roller, you oughta not bought me no ass present."

"Well, I wanted to get you something and I.... Go ahead and open it."

Cooper held the box with his lame left hand and tore away the butcher paper with his right. He opened the box and pulled out a shining black General Electric nine-inch oscillating electric fan. He stared at it a moment, then at Roller.

"Boy, you won't do!" he finally whispered in a broken voice. "This sho is pretty.... But what I gonna do with it? Ain't got no lectricity to pull it with."

"Well, you member what you told me about using what you do have to get something that you don't have?"

"Yeah," Cooper pondered.

"Well, that's what we gonna do. By the time it gets hot enough to need that fan.... Just wait; you'll see."

"Now, Roller, don't you go bother Mr. B none about this. He got nuff to worry bout. After a year like last, prolly ain't no chance of getting no wire run no time soon."

"I'm not going to worry him, but I'm sho going to sow a few seeds."

Roller then remembered the conversation that he had with Mr. B. They had ridden up to Coleman to meet the train to pick up a load of Christmas fruit that had been ordered for the store. On the way back to the store, Mr. B began.

"Roller, I see you ordered an electric fan from Mr. Camel."

"Yes, sir, but I paid for it with my own money."

"Yeah, I know that, but I was just wondering about why you ordered it." Mr. B peeped over his glasses at Roller. He surmised that Roller was up to something.

"I ordered it for Cooper."

"For Cooper, huh?" He rubbed his chin as he drove the dusty clay road.

"Yes, sir."

"Well, son, you know that there's not any electricity in that house. Don't you?"

"There's not?" Roller acted surprised. "Uh...we...I knew that they didn't have running water but, I never thought about them not having lights. You mean.... To be honest, I did know that they didn't have electricity, but I was hoping that maybe by summertime that maybe we could run some wire.... I mean with the new paved road and all, seems like the hands oughta have electricity like everybody else. Don't you think?"

Mr. B quickly realized that Roller was on a campaign to get the tenant houses wired; he had seen a "Roller campaign" be-fore. He had seen how Roller could use cunning diligence to persuade his elders to see things his way, and most of the time he got his way—one way or another.

"Well, son, do you realize what it'd cost to wire a house?"

"No, sir."

"It's not cheap, and the thing is, we've got six tenant houses, and if you wire one of them, you have to wire them all. The hands wouldn't stand for some of the houses to be wired and some not."

"We've only got four houses along the new road though; maybe we could wire them and promise to wire the ones on the back road later. Maybe we could wire two of them this year and two next year and two the next."

"They wouldn't stand for that I tell you. How would we decide which two got wired first. How could you explain to them why we were wiring some but not all. It wouldn't work. It just wouldn't work."

They arrived at the store and backed up to the side door to unload the fruit, and as Mr. B started to exit the truck, Roller grabbed his arm, "What if," he pleaded, "what if I talked to all of them and worked it out that we wire two houses a year for the next three years? And if they are satisfied with that plan, could we do it?"

Mr. B breathed heavily from his nose almost in disgust. "Son, let's get through Christmas first, and we'll see about it. Now don't say anything about this to anyone, and maybe when they pave the road things will be better and we'll see. Okay?"

"Yes, sir." Roller was elated. Mr. B had not flatly refused his plan; this might work with time.

Roller figured that Santa Claus had been good to him in spite of the short crop. He and Bruh got new blue jeans and two new shirts, underwear, and socks. Bruh got a new pair of Converse basketball shoes, and Roller got a new J.C. Higgins baseball glove. Santa Claus left a note under the tree that promised a TV sometime during the new year. All in all, it had been a wonderful vacation with only the dread of going back to school encumbering an otherwise joyous fortnight.

Bruh.... He thought about Bruh. Somehow their relationship was changing much for the better. They had shared another project in searching for and cutting the Christmas tree. They had talked and joked with each other without incident, and they were closer than they had ever been.

Maybe they were growing up and realizing a need for each other; maybe the fight had taught them more than the uselessness of fighting. Maybe their Christian upbringing had touched their dispositions. But for whatever reason, they were finally brothers—not adversaries.

Bruh's basketball skills were greatly improving. He played point guard and was quick and smart. He had high hopes of starting for the varsity team next year. Roller played with him at every opportunity. They played a game called "4 Horses" and a game called "21." Bruh won every time, and Roller's restraint was tested by each loss. His competitive, winning spirit was strong and growing even stronger as he matured. He played to win—loosing was not his nature.

Roller's thoughts shifted to the future. He could hardly wait till spring and looked forward to the things that it would bring. A new crop would be planted, the garden, the road being paved, spring holidays from school, maybe a TV, maybe getting Cooper's house wired, maybe he and Billy could go camping.

Tomorrow was the first day of a new year, and, except for the dread of going back to school, the new year was welcome. Roller had heard all the farmers around say that they would be glad for this year to end. It had been a year worthy of forgetting, but a year that everyone would remember as long as they lived. It was called the year of the East wind, and it hardly ever rains in southwest Georgia when the wind is out of the east.

He wondered about the things to come in 1955. He would be released from Miss E's prison in late May, would be in the sixth grade in September, and would go to 4-H camp in June. He made a hundred plans for the new year which included more trips to swim with Virginia Hart.

"Our loss will be her gain, and with Christ she's gone to reign."

He wondered, too, as he read Queen Lizzy's tombstone, if any of the old people that populated his world would die in the coming year. He had come to expect that any one of several could die at anytime—they were all so old! Again he vowed to be prepared for it; death is a part of life. He refused to think about what the new year would hold for Cooper. Change is inevitable.

With one last scan of his landscape, he began his ascent, somehow knowing that the sitting place, like many other elements of his life, would soon be a thing of the past.

CHAPTER 17
THE NOTE

The spring rains had swelled and stained the normally crystal clear water of the upper swimming hole, and the minnows that Roller knew were there were not visible. As he leaned against the old oak tree, he stared at the pool, straining to pierce the cloudy water to see the carefree little fish darting back and forth.

The dogwood trees, the redbuds, and the grancy greybeards were in full bloom, and the sweet fragrance of blooming honeysuckle filled the air. Normally, this place of utmost beauty and sereneness would fill Roller with joy. Normally, the springtime melodies of the many mating and nesting birds would serenade him into peaceful oblivion. Normally, he would suck the fresh clean air into his lungs as if it were some kind of magic gas that would sustain him through the times that he couldn't be here. Normally, he would sit here quietly and savor this little piece of heaven, and dream of things that he wanted to do, or of things that he had done. Normally, Cooper would be here, he too, dreaming about days gone by, and occasionally breaking the silence with oral recollection of some of his favorite memories. Normally, the two of them would sit here as if the old oak tree acted as a conductor of some unspoken and indescribable current that bonded their spirits. Normally, here, only good thoughts filled Roller's head, and neither the demons of tribulation nor unpleasant memories were allowed to enter this sacred spot.

But today was not normal at all. Cooper had suffered another stroke several weeks back. Paralyzed from the waist down, he was totally confined to either his bed or, with help, to a wheelchair, and usually after school Roller rode his bike up to visit him. Usually Cooper could help him when he had a problem that had no answer.

But today was not usual. The sitting place had been claimed by a swarm of honey bees. The hole that the woodpecker had made had opened the hollow belly of the old tree and made a perfect natural hive. It had infuriated Roller that he had saved his tree from the road paving only to have it claimed by bees. But in time, he reconsidered that the sitting place was getting too small anyway, that the bees occupancy there was a natural thing, and that change was inevitable. Normally, he would have sought solitude there, but the bees were now in complete control of his lofty retreat.

Normally, the sitting place would offer some comfort, some resolve, when Roller faced a dilemma such as today.

But today was not normal. Today he sat at the old oak tree in search of some kind of miracle that not even the angels that guarded this heavenly place could provide. He was in trouble at school.

Today a very untimely event had occurred that turned his world positively upside down. Words could not describe how awful he felt. He would have to tell Muh about it, and he knew that it would just be terrible. He knew that she would cry. She wouldn't just cry; she would wail with disappointment in him. She would sob about how hard she and Mr. B were struggling to provide for the family, how they were struggling to raise their children in the right way, how badly they wanted them to turn out right. She would be crushed, for he had committed a crime that could not be excused by, "Well, he's just a boy," or, "He didn't know any better." No, there was no excuse for what he had done.

Roller glanced around to be sure he was alone, then started to talk to himself aloud as he stared at the pool.

"What am I gonna do? What am I gonna say to Muh? Dog, I think I'd rather die than to tell her, but Mr. White said that if I didn't tell her, that he would. I've got to tell her, but how?"

He thought awhile about how he might say to her what he had done in a way that could lighten the impact on her—but there was no way. When it all boiled down, she had to be told, and she would be devastated. She and Mama would pray long and hard that God please forgive and somehow gather him back under His wing and guide him out of this sinful life. Any thought of his impending confession made him sick, and those strange feelings that he felt occasionally would converge in full force upon him.

His thoughts returned to Mr. White. Mr. White had been so nice to him, and he felt ashamed that he had failed him, too. Roller was sure that Mr. White liked him. He always stopped to talk to him on campus and seemed genuinely interested in Roller's fifth grade progress and the recess situation.

Roller recalled his visit to Mr. White's office the first day of school after the Christmas break. Miss E had promptly sent him to the office before roll call that morning. After a wait for Mr. White to ring the bell for the first class to begin, he called Roller into his office.

"Well, Roller, what are you doing here?" Mr. White quizzed.

"Miss E sent me."

"Well," he chuckled, "she must not have liked what you gave her for Christmas."

It suddenly came to his mind that somehow she had found out that he was responsible for the print that so perfectly personified how he felt about school and her demands of perfection. He was careful not to admit anything until he knew for sure she knew.

"No, sir, I don't know, but she sent this note." He handed the note to Mr. White, but he had sneaked a peak at it and knew what the note said.

Mr. White read it aloud. "Mr. Hogan left class on the last day of school before he was dismissed. He also made a bold remark unacceptable in my class. Signed E.

Mr. White rubbed his chin and stared sternly at Roller. "I suspect you'd better tell me about this." He leaned back in his chair and peeped over his reading glasses at Roller.

Roller swallowed hard and tried to explain. "Mr. White, the bell rang, and I jumped up to leave, but Miss E was still going on and on about what all we had to do after Christmas." He dropped his head and looked down at his nervous hands, "And there I was—hadn't been out to recess but one time since school started, and school was out for two whole weeks, and there she was keeping us after the bell, telling us what we had waiting for us when we came back, and when...." He looked up at Mr. White and saw a twinkle of compassion in his eyes, "and I honestly couldn't stand it any more."

Mr. White rubbed his chin and stared out at the blue winter sky beyond his office window. After a few minutes of quiet thought, he began again. "So, what was this bold, unacceptable remark that you made?"

"Well, sir, she told me that she wasn't through when the bell rang, but I told her that I was through, and I walked out. And I know that I should have been more patient, but I just couldn't think of anything cept getting out of there, so I left."

Mr. White tightened his lips and squinted his eyes as if in deep thought about what to do. "Roller, you know that you can't leave a class till you're dismissed."

"Yes, sir."

"And you know that you can't make smart remarks to your teacher." He looked hard into Roller's eyes. "And you know that I've got to punish you for what you've done."

"Yes, sir."

Mr. White thought quietly a moment. "So? What do you think your punishment should be?"

Roller had been calmed by Mr. White's hint of compassion and concern. He immediately thought about using what he had to acquire something that he didn't have. He pondered briefly. "You know, I've seen other students who were being punished having to pick up trash on the school yard during recess, and I guess that I ought to have to do that."

Mr. White tried to hold back a grin as he realized what Roller was suggesting. "Hum...," he weighed the situation carefully. "Let's get this straight, Roller. I make you pick up trash during recess, which is hard work, because I don't allow even the smallest bit of trash on the grounds."

"Yes, sir."

"And you get to go outside during recess, which you claim that you haven't been able to do."

"Yes, sir."

"Not to play, you understand, but to pick up trash."

"Yes, sir."

"Kinda like Br'er Rabbit and the briar patch, huh?"

"Yes, sir."

"And for how many days do you think your punishment should last?"

"A lot."

"Well, in this case, the longer the sentence the lesser the punishment. Right?"

"Yes, sir. I guess so."

"Okay, three days."

"Yes, sir!"

"But, Roller I want you to promise me that you'll conduct yourself in a manner so that I don't see you in my office again. Is that understood? Do you promise?"

"Yes, sir."

****

But this visit to Mr. White's office had been quite different. This time Mr. White was very serious, very angry, and very disappointed as he read Miss E's note.

"Roller!" he said harshly as he snapped his eyes up from the note. "What in the world made you do a thing like this?"

Roller was so ashamed. He didn't answer; he just sank his head in shame and stared at the front of Mr. White's desk, fighting back tears of shame.

"Son, you promised not to be sent to my office again. Look at me! Answer me!"

Roller lifted his tear-drenched face and looked into Mr. White's authoritative stare.

"Yes, sir."

Mr. White grimaced in disgust and sat quietly for a while. He calmed himself. "All right, young man, as I recall you had one recess before Christmas. Is that right?"

"Yes, sir," Roller sniffed.

"And how many have you had since Christmas?"

"Well, not counting the three days that I picked up trash, four."

"Well, I'm afraid that you have had your last recess for this year. I want you to spend every minute that you're not doing homework or correcting papers or doing your chores at home copying the Webster's dictionary. I want you to start with 'A' and copy every letter, every word, every dot, every comma, and every period until you get to the word "promise," and after you write the definition of the word 'promise' you bring me everything you've copied. Do you understand?"

"Yes, sir."

"And when you get home this afternoon, I want you to tell your parents what you have done."

"Mr. White, please don't make me tell Muh. I'll write the whole dictionary all the way through 'Z' if you won't make me tell Muh. Please, sir."

"Either you tell her or I'll tell her, but I think she would think more kindly of this situation if you told her. I don't think you want for me to drive out to your home and tell your folks about this myself."

"Please, Mr. White!" Roller sobbed.

"Son, you have made a serious mistake, and I don't really know your parents all that good yet, but I understand that they are good Christian people, and I'm sure they'll be more lenient about this if you're grown-up enough to confess this and admit that you've made a mistake."

"No, sir, you don't know em! That's for sure."

****

Roller finally saw one of the minnows dart up and hover near the surface of the swimming hole. He longed to be as carefree and guiltless as the little fish, as happy as the mockingbird that sang his never-ending concerts, but this offered little comfort. And as the sun sank below the lush canopy of the tree-tops, Roller gathered himself to his feet, tossed a twig onto the surface of the pool, and walked up the dim path toward home, knowing that the fading light signaled the start of a long night and—since it was Friday—a long weekend. He stopped, looked back at the pool, and spoke loudly, "It may be a while, but I'll be back."

****

Roller could not hide his troubled mind, and Muh immediately asked him what was the matter. The lump in his throat would not allow him to speak. He shrugged his shoulders and ambled through the front bedroom into the living room thinking it would be more private there. He sat on the swivel-top piano stool and plunked a few notes waiting Muh to follow.

She followed him promptly, for she knew this look of despair, and she knew that it called for her immediate attention.

"Roller, Son, what on earth is the matter? You look like you've lost your last friend. What is it?"

Roller swallowed hard but, still could not speak. He just stared at the piano keys as tears welled up in his already sad eyes.

"What is it, Son? Is it Cooper?" Muh insisted.

Roller shook his head, still unable to speak.

"Did something happen at school?"

Roller nodded.

Muh knew all the right questions. She knew how to read Roller's expressions; she could tell that this was bad.

"Something happened at school? And you can't talk about it?"

Roller nodded.

"Roller, look at me. Do you hear me? What happened at school?"

Roller looked up and tried again to speak. He fought hard to relax his cramping throat, but the only word that he managed to utter was "Note."

"Note? You have a note from Miss E?"

He shook his head.

"Roller, Roller. Dry up, now, and talk to me. Do you hear me? What about a note?"

Roller gathered every ounce of fortitude remaining in his guilt-laden being, cleared his throat, sniffed, and wiped his cheeks on his shirt sleeve. "Billy passed a note to me that said something ugly, and I passed a note back to Billy. Only Miss E saw me and made me bring the note to her."

Muh's expression changed from being concerned and inquisitive to staunch bereavement. "Are you telling me that you wrote an ugly note? Are you telling me that you wrote a note that had a curse word? Look at me! Do you hear me?"

"Yes, ma'am."

"Yes, ma'am, what?" she demanded.

"Yes, ma'am. I wrote a cuss word," he whispered, still staring at the piano keys.

"Oh, my Lord, have mercy!" she gasped. She sat down on the edge of the sofa, held her head in her hands, and mumbled what Roller assumed to be a prayer under her breath. After several minutes of silence she calmly spoke again.

"And what did Miss E do?"

Roller sniffed. "She sent me to Mr. White."

"Oh, my Lord! How could you do this to me, Roller? I'm so embarrassed and ashamed of you. My Lord! And what did Mr. White do? Did he paddle you?"

"No, ma'am. He is making me copy the dictionary all the way to the word 'promise'."

Muh stood and busied around the room as if seeking relief from this dilemma. She wiped the dust from a porcelain figurine with her apron and sought another. After a few minutes of deafening quietness, Muh sniffed and finally, though she dreaded the answer, asked the necessary question.

"What was the word?"

Roller had also dreaded the question. He shuffled on the piano stool, stared at the floor, and tried to speak, but again his throat knotted in shame. Eventually he managed to softly respond to her demand as tears rolled down his cheeks.

"I can't say it to you, Muh."

She stared at him through watery eyes for several minutes that seemed like hours. Now her throat was knotted, and she, too, found it difficult to speak.

She managed to collect herself momentarily.

"Does it have four letters?"

Roller nodded.

She grimaced. "Does it start with a 'D'."

Roller secretly wished that it did, but he shook his head, "No, ma'am."

"Oh, my Lord! This is awful!" She paced again. She was very careful now. "Did it start with a...," but she decided not to finish the question. "No, you tell me. What does it start with?"

Roller drew forth every ounce of fortitude that he could muster.

"S."

"Oh, my Lord! Does it end in 't'."

Roller nodded.

"Oh, my Lord!" she cried. "Of all words that you could have said. Oh, my Lord, have mercy!"

"But, Muh, I didn't say it.... Nobody heard it. It's not like I made a bold statement of the word in front of a lot people," he sobbed.

"I declare, Roller, you have embarrassed me beyond words. It doesn't matter whether you said it out loud, or whether you wrote it, or how you expressed the word; what matters is that you could use the word period! Do you hear me?" She stormed out of the room.

Roller sat there drowning in shame and in dread of the certain trip to the smokehouse. He knew that there would be no delay of his thrashing this time as was Muh's usual method of punishment. No, this offense would mandate immediate attention and penalty. He hoped it would be soon.

Mama had been sitting quietly in her room just adjacent to the living room and had heard the whole episode. She was always very careful not to interfere in issues of argument with the family, but she couldn't help offering some kind of comfort to Roller, and after some time, she visited him.

"Roller, Son, I know that you're really feeling lousy about what you've done, but I think that you ought to remember that this is just one day of your life and that, unless the Lord decides to call you, you should have many, many days that will be better. It's not the end of the world, you know. And remember, too, that only Jesus Christ lived without sin; nobody's perfect. Just ask for forgiveness, and get on with your life." She put her gentle hand on the back of his curly head and sort of patted him with compassion. "Come on now, you better get your supper, and get busy with your copying, and you'll see, things will get better."

Roller was too ashamed to look at her. She was such a saintly lady, yet she seemed to understand that Roller was a bit mischievous and needed patience and guidance. He heeded her advice except for supper; he was not hungry and went straight to his room to begin the first of many pages of copying.

Bruh had a date with a girl named Peggy that night! He was double-dating with his older friend, Gene, who was able to get the family car on Friday nights. So, Roller had the room to himself, and, after everyone else had gone to bed, and being bored with all that writing, he sought the newspaper clippings that he had stashed away, and again read them over and over.

As always, he wondered about Cooper's paw being murdered. He wondered what his granddaddy was like. *Was he mean and hateful? Was that why he struck this Will Small? Had he struck him many times before? Were the news clippings right, or were they written in accord with what people wanted to read? Why was there no mention of Emmett James Cooper? And what about Cooper? Was Cooper being punished for the inequities of his father?*

Brother Edenfield had preached last Sunday about the first commandment, Exodus 20: 1-5, and he spent considerable time explaining verse five: "You shall not bow down to them or worship them; for I am a jealous God. I punish the children for the sins of the fathers to the third and fourth generations of those who hate me. But I keep faith with thousands with those who love me and keep my commandments."

Was Cooper being punished for the sins of his father? Were those strokes that he had suffered the wrath of a jealous God? It didn't make any sense to Roller. He was confused. Cooper never hurt a flea, and, besides, Mama said that only Jesus Christ lived without sin.

Sleep was slow to come that night, and when it did it was restless and interrupted with dreams of guilt.

CHAPTER 18
THE SCREECH OWL

Roller peddled hard up the newly paved road toward Cooper's house, knowing that Cooper would be waiting for him as he was every afternoon now that school was out. He had stayed at Miss Charlotte's pool longer than he had intended.

The hot June sun was settling below the trees beyond the field as he slid his bike up to the edge of the porch. The smell of smoked meat frying reminded him that it was supper time. Swimming always made him hungry.

Cooper was waiting just as he figured; sitting there in the old wicker wheelchair with a bowl of food in his lap.

"How's your hammer hanging?"

Cooper steadied the bowl with his lame left hand and gestured with his right hand while holding on to an old spoon. His voice was weak and barely audible, but Roller had learned his slurred speech and could understand everything he said.

"Well, it's sho nuff hanging; how you be?"

"I be fine. I've been over to the pool and almost stayed too long. What you got for supper?"

"Neckbones and rice. That woman swimming ass naked again?

"No, nothing like that. She did come down to the pool today, and we swam together for a while. She sure is pretty. She.... Never mind. Say, did you have a good day?"

"Yeah, pretty ass good."

"I see you shaved."

"Yeah, Mag helped me. I had to clean up cause Dr. Harper came out to check me."

Roller knew that he wouldn't get a straight answer. Cooper would have some cute response. "Good, what did he say?"

"Oh, he say I ain't young as I used to be. Said I had a good heart, but said my legs ain't worth a dog. Told me not to be chasing no young, high ass gals no more. Said if I caught one, I might hurt myself." He chuckled.

"You fool. Hey, that looks good. Reckon Jenny's got anymore of that stuff?"

"Don't know. Go see."

Roller hopped up on the porch and entered the familiar, dark, smelly room. Jenny was in her little kitchen. He called out to her, "Jenny, what you got to eat?"

"Come on! Got some fried side meat and some neckbones and rice and a hoecake of bread."

Annie Jenny had a small fire in the wood stove that added to the heat of the day. As always, she was sweating profusely. The light from a forty-watt bulb that hung down in the middle of the room cast a yellow glow on the black stove where she stood tending a cast iron frying pan. The G.E. nine-inch oscillating fan was plugged in a socket above the light bulb and sat on a small table in the middle of the floor. It rhythmically blew the hot smokey air around the room, but provided little relief from the stifling heat.

She ladled a bowl of rice steaming and heaping full and handed it to Roller. "Want some fried meat?"

"Naw, just a corner of that hoecake. Man, this looks good. Thanks Jenny. The little fan doesn't help much, does it?"

"Sho does help at night though. Makes sleeping a lot better."

"You know what you need now?"

"What's that?"

"A radio!"

She nodded. "Sho would be nice."

"I'll see what I can do. I'll go back out and talk to Cooper now. Thanks Jenny."

"You sho welcome; hope you enjoy it."

Roller went back out and sat down on the edge of the porch, his feet swinging, and slowly savored the rice and bread.

Cooper talked between mouthfuls. "Things is changing; you know it, Roller? Lawd, I done walked down that road there over forty years in the dust and mud, and now that it paved I can't walk no more. Yeah, I'm just like a lot a things that there ain't no use for no more. Like kerosene. Ain't no use for kerosene no more; now we got lectricity. And milk cows. Ain't no use for no milk cow when you can buy milk in the sto anytime you need it. And they tell me Mr. B thinking bout selling all the mules but one. Gonna keep one to work the garden with. Lawd, I hate to see them mules go. Ain't no need in keeping em when them tractors done took over all the work. I just hate to see em go. Them been some good ass mules, and they just gone make canned dog food out of em, they tell me. I reckon me and the mule business done petered out bout the same ass time."

Roller ate very slowly, listening closely to Cooper. He wanted to change the topic of conservation, but he also wanted to hear what he had to say. He nodded occasionally and let him talk.

"Naw, things is changing all right. Lawd, some of the times I done seen wouldn't do to talk about. And they tell me that ain't many more years, and they will be picking ass cotton with a machine. I sho hope I live to see it. I just can't believe no machine gonna pick cotton. Course, I never dreamed no machine would go down a row of peanuts and pick em and put em in a sack neither. Lawd, I done stacked a many a stack of peanuts, and then go back later and haul em stacks to the picker, and pour a tub full at the time on a wagon, and bale the hay and haul it to the barn. Yas suh, things done changed, and you gonna see bunch a changes in your life, Roller. Ain't no way to know what liable to come along."

Cooper rattled on, most of which Roller had heard many times before. "Lawd, I done picked a many a sack a cotton too. You know the crop sho does look good so far this year. Course I knowed it would; one extreme always follows another, you know. A good crop always follows a bad one. Wouldn't be surprised if the cotton make a bale and the peanuts make a ton to the acre. Mr. B sho do need to make a good crop with all these mouths to feed up and down this road, and he done spent all this money wiring these houses and all. He sho ass do.

"They tell me you been checking fences with that new boy

205

from down to Mr. Sammy's. His name is Willie, ain't that right?"

Roller didn't want Cooper to think that he had a new friend to take his place. "Oh, he's been looking after the hogs, but he's just a boy. He ain't even as old as I am. I think he's got a long row to hoe."

"Yeah, things sho is changing, all right. I sho do miss them hogs; never thought I'd miss the smell of hog shit, but I sho do. Lawd have mercy. But...." He thought in silence for several minutes. "But you know, I been real happy for the biggest part of my life.... been lucky to have a boss man like Mr. B; he sho nuff been good to me. So I reckon if the Lawd calls me on cross the river, I oughta be proud of the days he give me."

Roller had to change the subject now. "You know, I wish you hadn't said that word."

"What word?" Cooper looked up from the now bowl of bones.

"Shit."

"Yeah, that got you in a pile of trouble didn't it?"

"Sho did!"

"I forget now. Tell me how'd that ever come out."

"Well, I copied eighty-three pages of the dictionary word for word. But on Monday before school was out on Friday, I went to see Mr. White, and I told him that I thought I had learned my lesson, and that I sure would appreciate having the last week of school without worry of anything, and he sent Miss E a note saying that I was to pick up trash during recess for the rest of the year. Man, I coulda hugged his neck. So I got to go out for recess that last week. Man, I'm so glad to be finished with that big ol' ass woman, I don't know what to do. I sho do feel bad for those fourth graders going in there this fall.... They got a long row to hoe, too."

"Roller, you got a birthday coming up, ain't you?"

"Yep, be thirteen next week."

"You sho are coming along at a good time. Things were tough as rip when I was thirteen. You sho gonna see a lot of changes in your time."

"Well, Daddy said we got to row with the flow."

"Sho do."

206

"Say, I almost forgot to tell you about something. You know when I left here yesterday, it was bout the time that ol' cemetery rabbit been hopping out. So I got my bow and a good flying arrow, and I went for him."

"Did you get em?"

"Well, what I did was, I climbed up on top of one of those headstones back near the thicket. And it had one of those little cedar trees growing right by it that I could hide behind. It was just high enough that I could stand up and see over the top and get a good shot, and it was just thin enough that I could see through and tell if he hopped out. I figured he wouldn't look for me up high like that, and I'd been practicing at about that distance. Sure enough, the wind was in my face, and bout sundown he hopped out. He couldn't smell me, and he couldn't see me. And that rascal came tiptoeing right on up there where I wanted him. I stood up real easy-like, and got a good bead on him, and was just about to release the arrow, and you know what happened?"

"What?" Cooper quizzed anxiously.

"That dadgum little varmint had a little baby rabbit that came bouncing up there jumping around, playing and all, and I.... Well, I just couldn't shoot him. Or her! All this time I been calling him a him, and he turns out to be a she rabbit with a baby. So, anyway, even though she's done had me mad enough to kill her a hundred times, right then and there I just couldn't get mad enough. I let her go."

Cooper nodded and tried to smile, "Boy, I'm mighty proud. You see, you done learned that you can use what you got to get something you ain't got, but even more, you done learned that sometime the hunt is better than the kill. See, if you had a killed that rabbit, the game woulda been over, but as it is you done won the game cause you coulda killed her and yet the game can still go on. Lawd knows, I spect that rabbit done have hard enough time as it is. You done good!"

Cooper wiped his mouth with an old rag that he had spread over his lap and lit a readi-roll Winston filter cigarette. Jenny joined them on the porch, gap-legged in her old rocker, and filled her bottom lip with snuff. Mag leaned against the jamb of her

207

front door. The hands were making their way toward the barn as the daylight faded.

"Well, I got to be going; it's getting late." Roller hopped down from the porch and thanked Jenny again for the food.

Cooper nodded, "I don't suppose you got time to tell me again bout the time the cat got ole Ollie's ding-dong do you?"

"Not today; besides I just told you that story one day this week anyway."

"How bout tomorrow?"

"Yeah, I'll tell it to you tomorrow. Let's see, naw, tomorrow's Saturday. I got to help that new boy with the hogs and help in the store. If I have time—if not—I'll see you Sunday."

Jenny spat a stream of dark juice to the edge of the porch. "Say, Roller, me and Mag want to go up to Sand Bethel Sunday afternoon to the homecoming for the church. Gonna get Merlene," she gestured toward the next tenant house, "to check on Cooper all along. So maybe you can check on him, too. You know he can't hardly even get up and down outa the bed with out some help."

"Yeah, as far as I know I'll be around. Yeah, I'll check on him. Well, I gotta go; I'll see ya'll." He mounted his bike and peddled up to the edge of the grey-gravel, newly paved road.

Just as he was about to push hard and spin a wheel toward home, the eerie scream of a screech owl pierced the hot, dusky air. A chill came over all of them in spite of the summer heat as their eyes seemed to all meet at the same instant. Roller tried in vain to ignore it, but the expression on each of their faces had changed. A sign had come to them.

He knew without any reminder that colored people had signs for almost everything, and several of them instantly came to mind; a buzzard sailing just beneath an afternoon cloud was a sign of rain, fishing and hunting were bad if the wind blew from the east, crops had to be planted on the right phase of the moon, and Cooper even claimed that the signs had to be right for hog killing or the meat wouldn't cure properly.

He also knew that the screech of a screech owl heard before pitch black dark was a sign of death or bad news, that something bad would happen to you if you were alone, or that something bad would happen to you or somebody in your company if you were not alone.

Their eyes darted back and forth making contact with each other as an abrupt silence enveloped them. Even the crickets seemed to hush their chirping at the cry of the screech owl.

Finally, after several minutes of silence and as if to belittle the omen, Annie Jenny spat a stream of snuff juice to the edge of the porch and declared, "Roller, you better get home; Muh gonna be on your head dreckly if you ain't home by dark. Now get. Ain't nothing to that screech owl mess no how."

"Yeah, I'm late now. I'll see ya'll."

****

Jenny, in an unusual request, had asked to be off on Sunday. Mama cooked lunch: fried chicken, creamed potatoes, English peas, biscuits, and tomato gravy. Muh declared during lunch that they would be going to Arlington later to visit Aunt Nancy. Bruh asked for the pick-up to go visit Peggy. Roller pleaded to stay home to watch the new TV.

There was a round-table discussion about Ben driving carefully and the do's and don'ts for both him and Roller. Roller was to stay right there at the house. Ben was to be home by 5:00, and they both were to help Willie with the hogs late that afternoon and to be ready for Sunday night services at 7:00.

Roller enjoyed the solitude that afternoon. He watched a Western movie on Channel 3 and was again amazed that the family had finally gotten a TV, especially after the horrendous crop of '54. He didn't know how Mr. B had arranged to wire the tenant houses, buy a TV, and carry on as usual when the crop had been so short, but he was glad.

Being alone in the house gave him a chance to read again the clippings of his grandfather's death, and to return them to the sewing box where they belonged. He thought long and hard about the events described in them, and still wondered about the involvement of Cooper's paw. His imagination ran rampant as he envisioned different scenarios about what had happened that day so long ago. He finally settled on the theory that Cooper's paw was just in the wrong place at the wrong time, and was not actually the murderer, that Cooper's paw was one of the four men that Robert William encountered that day, and that when Will Small, who was a violent man, shot him point blank in the head, had panicked and fled into the swamp for fear of being accused of an ambush and robbery.

He wished for some piece of information, some thread of evidence, that would clear his mind about the innocence of Cooper's pa. He would never know for sure, he surmised, for all five of the people who were there and who knew the exact events had been killed. The clippings were only assumptions written by some white reporter who made his own account of the murder based on a few bits of information, but mainly on speculation.

His leisurely Sunday afternoon changed in an instant as a violent, rapid knock came at the screen door. A panicky voice startled Roller: "Help! Help! Anybody there?"

Roller jumped to his feet and ran to the porch. It was Punto, panting and awash with sweat. His eyes were wild with fear as he pointed up the highway. Gasping, he pleaded to Roller, "Hurry Roller, Mr. B home?"

"No! What is it, Punto?"

"Come quick! There's been a fire! Mr. Cooper's burnt real bad. Better call for Dr. Harper."

Roller's first urge was to run to his bike and peddle hard and fast to see about Cooper.

Punto stopped him, gasping for breath. "Roller," he grabbed his arm, "sho nuff better call the doctor fore you go!"

Roller ran back inside and looked hurriedly for Dr. Harper's phone number. He dialed two-one-seven nervously. There was no answer. He didn't know what to do. He felt that strange feeling come over him. He couldn't think. His only thought was to get to Cooper.

"Punto!" he shouted. "He don't answer! What should I do?" He shouted even louder, running back to the front door. Punto had managed to catch his breath a little. "Call George Washington Funeral Home and see if they can come get him and take him to the hospital in Cuthbert."

Roller frantically searched the phone book for the colored folks' funeral home phone number and hurriedly dialed it. A man answered in a low, deep, colored voice.

"George Washington Funeral Home."

"I need you to come pick up a man that's been burned," Roller yelled.

"Who's calling?"

"This is Roller Hogan—please hurry!"

"What's the man's name?"

"His name is Cooper. Emmett Cooper. Please, sir, hurry up."

"What's the address?"

"Dang," Roller thought a minute, "do you know where B.B. Hogan's Store is?"

The voice on the other end hummed in thought, "Naw, sir."

"Well, just come to Coleman and turn left on the new paved road, and come on till you see the house on the right."

"Is this man a colored man?" the voice inquired.

Roller was now irritated at the less than satisfactory concern of the man. "Look," he said sternly, "this is an emergency. This colored man has been burned. He needs to go to the doctor. Now come to Coleman and turn left on the new paved road, and come out bout four miles till you see the house; we'll be watching for you."

He hung up the phone and ran out to his bike. Punto was already in a full run back up the road, knowing that Roller would catch up quickly. As he approached the top of the hill, he passed Punto and could see the grey smoke bellowing from the front door of the tenant house. He peddled hard, not knowing what he could do when he got there, not knowing if Cooper would be alive.

Then, just as he slid his bike to a stop at the front steps and jumped up on the porch, Willie and Walter came lumbering through the dense, stifling smoke, coughing and gagging, dragging, one on each end of, what was left of a thin cotton mattress. They half stumbled into the fresh air and laid the still smoldering mattress on to the floor of the porch. They released their grasp of each corner and the sides slowly fell flat.

"My God," Roller gasp as he viewed the charred remains of Cooper. The sight was sickening; the smell was even worse.

There was no doubt that Cooper was dead. His eyes were opened wide, glazed, and fixed straight ahead. His eyelashes, eyebrows, and hair were singed. His right ear was mostly burned away, and large patches of pink, oozing flesh covered his right jaw and neck where the skin had blistered and ruptured. His feet and legs were deeply burned and still steaming from the water that Willie had doused on him in an attempt to extinguish the flaming death bed. His torso was a smelly, smoldering mass of blistered, bloody flesh.

His pajamas, which Roller recognized as being some that Mr. B had given him when he had his last stroke, were burned away except where he lay flat against the mattress, and a small patch covering his genitalia. Apparently Cooper's bladder had emptied, and the moisture from the urine had protected him there.

Willie and Walter had bolted to the edge of the porch for fresh air, and Roller suddenly realized that his lunch was coming up his throat. He rushed to the end of the porch and vomited. He wished, as he heaved, that he could as easily regurgitate from his mind the sight that he had just witnessed, that somehow he could vomit this whole tragedy away and that he would awake from this awful nightmare. But deep inside he knew that he would never escape the horror of Cooper's grotesque death-stare, and as the breeze pushed the smoky, putrid odor to the edge of the porch, he knew that he would never forget the smell of burning flesh, that he would never understand why such a gentle old man had to die such a painful and gruesome death.

****

He sat there on the edge of the porch, feet swinging nervously, and thought about a million things. He watched in a solemn daze as all of the women came and wailed loudly, floundering wildly on the ground in front of the little house. Like some streaking current of information through the hot afternoon air, the news of Cooper's death had spread through the quarters, and they all came, even the little children, and they all reacted the same. Loud screaming cries followed by a faint-like crumple to the ground, then boisterous wailing with violent pounding of the ground with clinched fist. Their cries were mixtures of loud moans and even louder weeping colored jargon that only they could understand. Only an occasional "Lawd, have mercy," came clear to Roller's ears. He watched helplessly as the Washington Funeral Home hearse carried Cooper away. He wanted so badly the company of someone that could comfort him. He wished for Muh.

He watched as Jenny and Mag returned from the church homecoming and received the news of Cooper's death, and he was surprised that Jenny remained so calm when she was told, as if it was expected of the other women for her to be in control and consoling to them. Several of the women joined Jenny and Mag and thoroughly cleaned the still smelly room.

Finally, as the sun began to fall, Roller straddled his bike and peddled slowly toward home.

****

Funeral plans were made for the following Saturday afternoon at Sand Bethel. After lunch on Wednesday and after everyone had left the table, Jenny asked Roller if he would come to her house later that afternoon, that she had something she wanted to show him.

****

Roller entered the familiar little dark room late that afternoon and immediately missed the presence of Cooper. Jenny, as it always seemed, was cooking something on her old wood stove.

"Jenny, it's me."

"Hey, Roller, come on in and have a seat. I'll be there dreckly. Just let me take this meat up."

He could feel the heat from the stove as he sat in an old straight-back chair and waited for Jenny to finish. He looked around the little room, and again thought how unfair it was that someone who was so loyal, so much a part of the family, had to live in this little crib of a house.

The wooden floor squeaked as she waddled from the kitchen wiping sweat from her face with an old rag. "Roller, there's some thangs I need to show you." She spat snuff juice in the open fireplace.

"You see, Cooper told me that if something happen to him, to give you this." She made her way to an old wardrobe that sat cramped in the corner by her bed.

Roller could feel his forehead wrinkle with curiosity as he watched her squeeze in between the wall and her bed and open the double doors to the cabinet. She pushed the right hand door against the wall and latched it there by twisting a well-placed nail in the wall that was bent at a ninety-degree angle. The left hand door, showing the unlevelness of the floor, rested heavily against the side of her bed.

She ambled back out of the little aisle between her bed and the wall, allowing Roller to access the wardrobe.

"Turn that light on so you can see better." She motioned toward the single light bulb hanging from the ceiling as she spat again in the fireplace. Roller pulled the chain, but the yellow light from the sixty-watt bulb made little improvement.

"Go on, look in there."

Roller approached the cabinet and strained to see its contents in the poor light. The left side of the cabinet was a stack of little drawers, but the right side was open with a rod across the top for hanging cloths. There were several hangers of old pants and shirts pressed against the right side of the cabinet, some of which Roller recognized as being previously worn by Mr. B. He gasped as his eyes adjusted to the poor light, for leaning there against the back corner stood the "spear."

"Dadgum, I wondered what he did with this thing." He pulled it out from its dark hiding place and grasped the corn cob throwing handle. He felt the familiar balance as he stepped back from the cabinet and drew the spear to its throwing position over his right shoulder. He fought back a tear as he cocked his arm back and forth and thought back on the unfortunate death of the prize boar. He swallowed hard and promised himself that he would go directly and tell Mr. B about what had happened to the pig.

"That ain't all what's there," Jenny insisted.

Roller laid the spear across the bed and returned to the cabinet and stared in. There, high on the left wall hanging from a nail, he found the "claw."

"How did he get this thing? I wondered what had happened to it. I must have laid it down somewhere, and he found it and kept it so I wouldn't get in trouble with it."

"Uh huh," Jenny responded. She spat again. "Look in there some more," she gestured toward the cabinet.

Roller couldn't see anything else. He tossed the claw on the bed and grasped the clothes by their hangers and slid them along the bar to the left, and there leaning against the far back corner was an old double-barrelled shotgun. He reached for it and pulled the heavy forearm toward him and lifted it out. He recognized it as an old twin-hammer, double-barrel, sometimes called a rabbit-ear shotgun. He held the gun carefully, pushed the breach latch, broke it open, checked the empty cylinders, and latched it back. He studied it curiously and wondered why Cooper never mentioned this gun. Then down near the cheek rest he saw carved in the stock the initials "E.J.C."

He thought about the initials aloud "E.J.C—Emmett James Cooper. Cooper told me that he hadn't shot a shotgun since he was nine years old. This must be his daddy's gun. E.J.C—Cooper must have had the same name as his daddy. He must have been a junior. Yeah, this was his daddy's gun.... So the gun that they found at my granddaddy's murder couldn't have been this gun because that one was burned in the forest fire."

Jenny just stood there with her normal lipfull of snuff letting Roller continue.

"Cooper's daddy was not the murderer! Damn those people! They hanged an innocent man! Well heck, they hanged three innocent men! But Cooper's paw was one of them." He thought back on the newspaper clippings. "It must have been that Will Small. I knew that Cooper couldn't be the son of a killer. I knew it all the time but.... I guess I had asked Cooper enough questions that he wanted to be sure that I saw this gun for my own satisfaction. He must have known a lot more about the death of my grandfather and the hanging of his paw than he ever talked about.

"Jenny? Did Cooper ever say anything about this gun to you?"

"Naw, he just told me to show it to you if anything ever happen to him. Said it was the only thing he had left of his old family. Roller, you know he sho did love you. Course he loved your whole family, but he use to talk in his sleep bout you."

Roller crimped the side of his mouth and breathed heavily from his nose. "Dang, dang, dang," he quipped, "all this time I thought Cooper might have been being punished for the sins of his father, but his father was innocent...at least of that sin. I don't understand.... I don't see why God would punish a kind man like Cooper with all those strokes and all...and let him die such an awful death.... I just don't understand.... I just don't."

Jenny spat strongly toward the fireplace and said something that Roller would never forget. She said, "Well, Son, life here on this earth can be a real bitch sometimes, and then you gotta die! You know, the good Lawd ain't promise us nothing on this earth, but he did promise us something in another world, and that's all we got."

Her words were more profound and more understandable that any sermon that he had ever heard at Wesley Chapel; they comforted him, and he was satisfied that Cooper's misfortunes were not the works of God but the works of life itself.

"There's something else I want to show you Roller. I ain't said nothing bout this cause you know how we is bout keeping our business to ourselves, but something ain't right bout Cooper burning hisself up smoking in bed."

Roller was still in deep thought about Jenny's enlightening little sermon and almost missed what she had said. He collected his thoughts. "What did you say?"

"Something ain't right here, Roller!"

"What do you mean?"

"Well, they say Cooper was smoking in bed and musta went to sleep, and his cigarette sot his bed on fire and burnt him to death."

"Yeah?"

"Well, when we was cleaning up the other day," she moved toward her little dresser, "I found this pack of cigarettes." She held up a pack of Winston Filter Cigarettes.

"Yeah?"

"Well, you see...this pack of cigarettes ain't got but one or two missing out of it."

"Yeah?"

"Well, I opened this very same pack of cigarettes for Cooper on Sunday morning fore I left to go to church."

"Yeah?"

"And I lit one for him and he smoke it fore I left, and I left the pack over here on the dresser, and Merlene say she didn't give him no smoke. And he couldn't get up to get no smoke for hisself, and even if he did he couldn't strike no match by hisself to smoke it with."

"Yeah?"

"And Roller, Cooper had a little tobacco sack in that same closet," she gestured toward the cabinet, "that he kept some money in that he had save up, and I got his money out and it wasn't but ninety-six dollars in there. And I know he had more than that. I mean I ain't never counted it, but I seen him counting it, and I just know he had more money than that, a lot more."

"Jenny, are you telling me that you think Cooper was burned by somebody and robbed of his money." He paced the floor slowly in deep thought.

"Well, it sho is mighty spicious to me."

"Hey, wait a minute," Roller injected as he stopped his pacing. "Cooper was burned worse on his legs and feet and lower body than his upper body.... At least, he looked that way to me. And if he had gone to sleep smoking, you would think that the fire would have started up around his upper body, and would have burned him worse where it started."

"Uh huh."

Roller paced again, this time out onto the porch and back inside. They said nothing for several minutes. Finally, Roller went to the edge of the porch and sat down, swinging his legs as he had done so many times. His mind ran wild with thoughts. Jenny joined him on the porch in her old chair but said nothing.

He replayed in his mind what might have happened to Cooper. If Cooper was smoking and set his own death fire, how did he get it lit. Somebody had to help him. Merlene checked on Cooper at about 1:00, and she said that she did not give him a smoke. Was she lying? Was it possible that Cooper had managed to get up and cross the room and light a cigarette without any help? Or did somebody come in while Cooper was sleeping

217

and pilfer for his money. Did Cooper wake up and catch the robber, and whoever it was set fire to Cooper to keep him quiet. Could Jenny be wrong about the money? Why wouldn't a robber get all the money? Was the person trying to relieve suspicion of robbery by leaving some of the money in the bag? Who could burn an old, helpless man for a few dollars? Dang, why didn't he call the sheriff or somebody to investigate it? What could be done about this at this late date? He would talk to Mr. B about this.

Roller was unaware of the passing traffic on the new paved road, deaf to all of the sounds of the quarters. He just sat there, feet dangling, head hung in deep thought. His mind raced.

Could somebody have come into the house after Merlene left on Sunday afternoon, robbed Cooper of his money, set fire to him upon being caught to give the appearance that Cooper went to sleep while smoking, and left the house without somebody in the quarters seeing him? Or would they say anything if they had seen somebody?

Roller remembered what Cooper said one time that "a man that'll set one fire would set another." He thought back to the Moon-Poon Saloon fire and the suspicious Grady, Jr. Yeah. Grady, Jr. It was a Sunday afternoon that Grady, Jr. had walked down this road clicking his lighter all dressed up like a rich man. And the Moon-Poon Saloon had burned that same night. And Cooper said that when the barn burned that there was one person that showed up to fight the fire with his fine clothes on. Could it be that Grady, Jr., had set fire to the barn, set fire to the Moon-Poon Saloon, and set fire to Cooper? Maybe Grady, Jr., got those fine clothes with money that he had stolen. Maybe he knew that Cooper had some money, and he knew that Merlene was to check on Cooper that afternoon because he was alone. Maybe he slipped in through the back door using the fence row for cover. Maybe he came in while Cooper was asleep, suffocated him with a pillow or something, searched for the hidden money, left some of the money to prevent the appearance of robbery, set fire to Cooper's bed to give the appearance of an accidental death, and went back home or across the field. Where was Grady, Jr., that afternoon? He had not been there like all of the others. Everyone in the quarters had come there that afternoon at some time or another except Grady, Jr. Why? Why didn't he come?

It eventually came to his mind, this was all just speculation, that there was no proof. He remembered Mr. B's and Uncle Sammy's explanation of circumstantial evidence. He knew deep inside that he would never know the truth.

Roller snapped back to reality as Annie Jenny handed him Cooper's old hawk-billed knife.

"He told me to give this to you, too, if anything ever happened to him."

Roller took the knife and stared at it almost in a stupor for several quiet moments. A thousand memories rushed to the forefront of his addled consciousness, and tears ran down his cheek as he choked on the only response that he could muster. "I'll swear, Cooper, you won't do."

****

There was no conversation as Bruh drove Roller to the funeral. It was a stifling, hot afternoon, and traffic dust along the old dirt road to Sand Bethel hung in the air like ivory clouds. Roller wore a hand-me-down, summer suit that Bruh had outgrown, a white shirt, a plaid bow-tie, and new, lace-up, brown shoes.

Sand Bethel sat atop a lonesome sandy ridge about five miles north of Coleman. It was a big, faded white, wooden-frame church that looked as if it had been abandoned. There was no landscaping, no trees, no grass. In spite of the heat, the old building looked cold and unwelcoming.

The hearse was backed up to the front door, and several men stood around outside fanning gnats and talking quietly. Cars were parked all along the little driveway and along the main road. Walter had driven the old pick-up loaded with residents of the quarters and had parked just beyond the church beside the road leading down a slight grade to the cemetery.

Bruh parked beyond the pick-up, and the two of them waited for the service which was on going in the church to dismiss and proceed to the gravesite.

They could hear Brother Major Page preaching hard and loud then soft and low. Then a congregational song, "Climbing

Jacob's Ladder," then more preaching from Right Reverend Romay Brown, then another song, "Amazing Grace," then a prayer that sounded like another preaching.

Finally the church got quiet, and a processional formed behind the two preachers. Walter, Willie, and Rupert carried one side of the wooden coffin. Punto, William, and Doc carried the other. They came around the corner of the church walking slowly and in stride, a slow march with a train of mourners arranging themselves in a four-abreast-parade behind them. Almost precisely as the last four fell into step, the whole throng began to sing, "Swing low, Sweet Chariot, Coming for to Carry me Home." They sang it as only colored people could sing it; they painted a picture with it. It was not just a melody of notes and words and many voices, it was an anthology of sad and happy, of earth and heaven, of today and tomorrow.

Roller fought hard the knot in his throat as the coffin passed by. He knew that Cooper wouldn't want him to cry, and he had promised himself long ago that he would not cry over things he could not help. But despite all his intentions and vows, tears trickled down his cheeks.

They were all in the train, all of the colored people that he knew and a lot that he didn't know were there—except Grady, Jr. They were all dressed nicely. The women all wore hats and held briskly swishing fans. They were all perspiring; they were all sad-eyed; they all sang; some were crying.

As the procession passed, Roller eased open the car door and fell into the march while Bruh remained in the car. He felt out of place, yet he felt he belonged there. He felt that he owed Cooper this last show of respect and love. He would help all the others put Cooper away for the last time, but in his mind he would keep alive a million memories. Yes, he belonged here.

The coffin was lowered down into the sandy earth with ropes, and the pallbearers stepped back and formed a line down the length of the grave. Roller had intended to stay back away from the service, to stand behind the crowd, but somehow as they circled around still singing he wound up opposite the line of pallbearers right next to the grave. He stood there with a mixture of sweat and tears dripping from his face staring down on top of the wooden box that held his friend.

The preachers began another lengthy eulogy sermon, but Roller heard very little. He thought about the swimming hole, about the sitting place, about checking fences. He cursed the screech owl as he remembered good times and bad times. He thought about Mr. B and Muh and how much he loved them. He thought about Billy Chitwood and Mr. White and White Hogan and Miss E and Grady, Jr., and last year and next year. A small grin curled his lips as he thought about what Cooper would have said to him: "Boy, you thinks too ass much, sometime." And then, there in the deep recesses of his reflections of days gone by, he thought he heard Cooper calling him down from the sitting place calling softly, "Roller, Roller." He was suddenly pulled back to reality as someone tugged on his coat sleeve and said softly, "Roller, Roller...the preacher ax if there's anything you wants to say."

Roller was startled. He glanced around at a thousand dark eyes all fixed on him. He didn't know what to say. He didn't know if he could speak with that knot there in his throat. But he had to say something; he wanted to say something. He cleared his throat and swallowed hard. He had not prepared for this, but he remembered what Cooper had taught him; to use what he had. He thought a second, then spoke strong and clear.

> "Our loss will be His gain
> and with Christ he has gone to reign"

And then, even stronger, he added,

> "He made our Sun Shine."

EPILOGUE

Robert William Lanier was buried at Pleasant Primitive Baptist Church near Nashville, Georgia, in 1907.

Mama passed away in 1964 and is buried at Wesley Chapel. They're together now.

Annie Jenny died in 1974 and is buried at Sand Bethel.

Roller told Mr. B about killing the pig in 1970. Mr. B died in 1976 and is buried at Wesley Chapel. A thousand angels sang at his funeral. He now sings with them.

The sitting place tree died very slowly and was removed in 1977. Muh's tree still stands just 9 ½ feet from county road #160.

Mr. White is retired and lives in Fitzgerald, Georgia. He should be in the Hall of Fame for Educators. So should Miss E.

Muh is ninety-two years old, still goes to Wesley Chapel every Sunday, and still will not tolerate cursing.

Sis divorced the big sailor, married again, and now lives with her family across the new paved road from the old store which was closed in 1973.

Bruh lives in Florida. A true friend, a loving brother.

Billy Chitwood is still a friend.

Virginia Hart married a rich man in Atlanta. She still lives there.

Grady, Jr. was killed in a night club brawl in Cocoa Beach, Florida, in 1992.

All of the hands are gone, the quarters are gone, those days are gone but the memories will never die.